In the Grip of Winter

and

The Siege of White Deer Park

by

Colin Dann

Illustrated by Terry Riley

RED FOX

In the Grip
of Winter

A Red Fox Book

This edition has been produced exclusively for W H Smith
by Random House Children's Books
20 Vauxhall Bridge Road, London SW1V 2SA

A division of Random House UK Ltd

London Melbourne Sydney Auckland
Johannesburg and agencies throughout the world

First printed in this edition 1991
Reissued 1994

3 5 7 9 10 8 6 4

Printed and bound in Great Britain by
Cox & Wyman Ltd, Reading, Berkshire

RANDOM HOUSE UK Limited Reg. No. 954009

ISBN 0 09 910311 7

Contents

For Kathy

—1—
First Signs

It was soon time for the animals and birds to face their first winter in White Deer Park. They had moved in a group from their old homes in Farthing Wood when it was destroyed by Man, and the strong links of friendship and the spirit of community forged during their long journey had caused them to build their new homes close to one another. So a certain corner of the White Deer Park Nature Reserve became almost a new Farthing Wood for them, and every creature found conditions exactly right for his particular requirements.

In the centre of this area lay the Hollow which, from their earliest arrival in the Park, had formed their meeting-place. In the autumn months they met less often and, eventually, as the evenings grew colder, both Adder

and Toad knew it was time for them to go underground
for the winter.

It was late October when Adder ceased to lie in wait
at the edge of the Edible Frogs' pond, a feat of patience
that had not brought him its hoped-for reward. 'This
cool weather makes me feel so sleepy,' he remarked to
Toad, whom he sometimes saw going for a swim.

'Me too,' replied Toad. 'I've been busy fattening up
while food is still available. I must confess that now I
really feel ready for a nice long snooze.'

'Where will you go?' Adder enquired.

'Oh, hereabouts. The earth is soft in this bank and
I've noticed quite a few holes remaining that must have
been dug in earlier years.'

'Mmm,' Adder mused. 'That would suit me admir-
ably. Those frogs would then have the benefit of my
presence in spirit throughout the winter.'

Toad chuckled. 'I'm sure they won't be aware of it,'
he said. 'They're digging themselves into the mud on
the pond bottom. Once they've settled, they'll be quite
oblivious of everything.'

'I shall, too,' admitted the snake. 'My only interest at
the moment is in sleep.'

'Er – have you made your farewells?' Toad asked him
hesitantly.

'Farewells? Stuff and nonsense!' Adder rasped. 'No-
one cares to seek me out when I'm around, so they'll
hardly miss me when I'm not.'

Toad felt embarrassed. 'Oh, I don't know,' he said
awkwardly. 'I think it's just that most of us feel you
prefer to be alone.'

'I *do*,' said Adder a little too quickly, as if trying to
dispel any doubts at all about the matter. 'However,
Toad, I've no objection to your company,' he added not
uncourteously.

'Thank you, Adder. Er – when do you plan to begin hibernation?'

'Straight away, of course. No point in hanging around above ground in these sort of temperatures.'

'If you can wait until tomorrow I'll join you,' Toad suggested. 'Just leave me time to call on Fox and Badger, and Owl, perhaps.'

'Oh, I can't sit here waiting for the frost to bite me while you go making social visits,' said Adder impatiently. 'I'm going underground tonight.'

'Very well,' said Toad. 'As you wish. But I really don't see what difference one more day would make.'

Adder made a gesture. 'I'll tell you what,' he offered. 'Let's choose a comfortable hole now, and then you'll know where to find me.'

Toad considered this was about the closest Adder was ever likely to come to being companionable, so he accepted readily.

Having chosen the best site, Adder promptly disappeared into the earth with a hastily lisped, 'Try not to wake me.' Toad wryly shook his head and set off to find his friends.

As he approached the Hollow, the sky was darkening fast, and a cold wind was whipping through the grass. Toad almost wished he had followed Adder into the shelter of the hole, but he felt he just could not have been so unfriendly. No movement could be discerned in or around the Hollow, so Toad sat down to wait, amusing himself by flicking up a stray beetle here and there. Presently a ghostly form could be seen lumbering towards him through the gloom. Toad made out Badger's grey outline.

'Hallo, my dear friend,' said Badger warmly. 'I'm surprised to see you out on a cold night like this.'

'It'll be the last time,' commented Toad. 'Before the Spring.'

'I see, I see,' Badger nodded. 'You've come to say goodbye. Well, it could be for quite some time, you know.' He paused and snuffled in the brisk air.

'Do you think it will be a hard winter?' Toad asked.

'Every winter is hard for some,' Badger answered. 'The weakest among us always suffer the most. The small creatures: the mice, the shrews, the voles and, particularly, the small birds – every winter takes its toll of them. But yes – I sense that this winter will be one to reckon with. There's something in that wind. . . .'

'I felt it, too,' Toad nodded. 'And Adder – he's already settled.'

'Just like him to disappear without trace,' Badger muttered. 'Well, at least it'll put an end to that nonsense of his with the Edible Frogs.'

'Yes, until next year,' Toad remarked drily. 'But, d'you know, Badger, he actually invited me to join him in his sleeping quarters – at least, in a roundabout sort of way.'

'Oh, he's all right really,' Badger granted. 'After all, you can't expect a great deal of warm feeling from a snake.'

While they were talking, they saw Fox and Vixen slip stealthily past in the moonlight, intent upon hunting. Toad was disappointed. 'They could have stopped for a word,' he complained, 'when I've made a point of coming to see you all. And in this wind, too.'

'Don't feel slighted, old friend,' Badger said earnestly. 'I'm sure they don't realize you're about to go underground. It wouldn't be like Fox.'

'No, I suppose not,' Toad assented. 'But he's not the close friend he used to be before Vixen came – at least not to me. Ah well, that's the feminine influence for you.'

Badger nodded his striped head, smiling gently. 'We old bachelors have little experience of such things, I'm afraid,' he said softly. 'We live out our solitary lives in rather a narrow way by comparison.'

Toad was touched by the note of wistfulness in Badger's voice. 'I – I never realized you felt that way about it, Badger,' he said in a low croak. 'But there are lady badgers in the park, surely?'

'Oh yes, it's different from Farthing Wood in that respect,' Badger agreed. 'But I've been living alone for too long now. I couldn't adjust.'

Toad was silent. He felt it was best not to add anything. There was a long pause and Toad shuffled a trifle uncomfortably. 'Hallo,' he said suddenly, 'here's another old bachelor,' as Tawny Owl fluttered to the ground beside them.

Owl nodded to them both, then said, 'I hope you weren't speaking derisively, Toad. I can't answer for you two, but I'm single from choice alone.'

'*Your* choice – or the choice of the lady owls?' Toad asked innocently. Badger muffled a laugh.

'Very amusing, I'm sure,' Owl snorted. 'I'd better go. I didn't come here to be insulted.'

Badger, so often the peacemaker, stepped in. 'Now, Owl, don't be so hasty. No offence was intended. Toad's come to see us because he's going into hibernation soon.'

'Humph!' Tawny Owl grunted, ruffling his feathers. But he did not go.

'Yes, tomorrow to be exact,' Toad informed him. 'And I shan't be sorry. I sympathize with you fellows who have to face whatever comes: ice, frost or snow. It's marvellous just to fall asleep and forget all about it – and then, simply wake up as soon as it's warm again.'

'There's certainly a lot to be said for it,' Badger remarked.

'But it takes months off your life,' Tawny Owl pointed out. 'You may as well be dead for six months of the year.'

'Not quite as long as that,' Toad corrected him. 'Anyway, it depends on the weather. In a mild winter, I might be out again in February.'

'Mark my words, Toad,' Tawny Owl said with emphasis. 'This is going to be a difficult one.'

'Then my heartfelt good wishes go with you,' Toad said sincerely. 'I hope you all come through.'

The three friends remained talking a while longer, while the cold wind continued to blow. Finally Tawny Owl declared he was hungry and flew off in search of prey. Something struck Toad at his departure and he fell to musing.

'You know, Badger,' he said presently, 'we shake our heads over old Adder and his designs on my cousins the frogs, but really he's not so much a threat to the denizens of White Deer Park as Fox or Owl, who go hunting here every night.'

'A thought that had also occurred to me,' Badger acknowledged. 'But there were foxes and owls – and other predators – in the park before we arrived. So in the same way the voles and fieldmice and rabbits of the Farthing Wood party run the same risk from the enemies already here.'

Toad nodded and sighed. 'My idea of the Nature Reserve as a new and safe home for all has not proved quite true,' he said ruefully.

'Nowhere is completely safe,' Badger assured him. 'But the Park is about as safe as anywhere could be for wild creatures, for there is no presence of Man. And in that respect it is a veritable haven compared with Farthing Wood.'

Toad grinned. 'You've soothed my mind as usual,' he

said. 'Well, Badger, I shall not delay you any longer. Farewell till Spring.' He turned to make his way back to the bank where Adder was already asleep. On his way he encountered Fox again. This time Fox stopped. Toad explained where he was going.

'You could perhaps give a message to Adder for me,' Fox requested. 'Tell him to go down deep. And you too, Toad,' he finished enigmatically.

'How deep?' queried Toad.

'As deep as it takes to escape the frost.' Fox shivered in the wind as if illustrating his warning.

'We shall take heed, Fox,' Toad answered. 'Have no fear.'

They parted and Toad crawled on towards his objective. Fox stood and watched him a long time. Then he shook himself vigorously and went to rejoin Vixen. Winter, he knew, was hovering just around the corner, waiting to pounce.

—2—
First Snow

During the next few weeks, as October passed into November and the leaves fell thick and fast in White Deer Park, the animals kept very much to themselves. Their main preoccupation was food.

Nature had provided an abundance of berries and nuts which, as all wild creatures know, is a sure sign of severe weather to come. So the squirrels and the voles and the fieldmice were able to feast themselves for a short period. There was a spell of heavy rain which brought out the slugs and worms, and Hedgehog and his friends fattened themselves up nicely before they made their winter homes under thick piles of leaves and brush in the undergrowth. As they disappeared to hibernate, the other animals knew that time was running out, and renewed their efforts. All ate well for a space.

The first heavy frost descended at the end of November and Mole, whose tremendous appetite was undimmed, found an abundance of earthworms deep underground. Their movements were restricted by the frozen ground near the surface and he amassed a large collection against emergencies. He was so proud of his efforts that he was bursting to tell someone about them. So he tunnelled his way through to Badger's set which was close by, and woke him from a late afternoon snooze.

'It's me! Mole!' he cried unnecessarily. 'Wake up, Badger. I want to tell you what I've been doing.'

Badger sat up slowly and sniffed at his small friend. 'You smell of worms,' he said abruptly.

'Of course I do,' Mole replied importantly. 'I've been harvesting them.'

'Harvesting them?'

'Yes, you know, collecting – er – gathering them. I've never known it to be so easy to catch so many. They're all securely stowed away in a nice big pile of earth where my nest is.'

'I didn't realize it was possible to stow away slippery things like worms,' Badger remarked. 'By the time you get back they'll all have wriggled away.'

'Oh no, they won't,' declared Mole. 'They can't,' he added mysteriously.

'Why, what have you done to them?'

'I've tied them up in knots!' cried Mole excitedly. 'And they can't undo themselves.' He began to giggle as he saw Badger's stupefied expression, and he was still giggling when Badger received another guest, in the shape of Fox.

'Have you been outside?' he asked, after greeting them.

They shook their heads.

'It's snowing,' he stated.

They followed him up Badger's exit tunnel to look. It was dusk, but the sloping ground in the little copse Badger had favoured as his new home was gleaming white. The trees themselves glowed mysteriously in their soft new clothing. They watched the large flat flakes drift silently downward. There was no wind. Everything seemed completely still save what was dropping steadily from the sky.

'It's already quite thick,' Fox told them. 'I can't see my tracks.'

'I've never seen snow falling before,' Mole said as he watched with fascination. His eyes, used to darkness, blinked rapidly in the brightness of the white carpet spread before them. 'Will it cover everything?'

'Not quite everything,' answered Badger. 'But it makes movement very difficult for small creatures. The birds don't have to worry, of course. Except in so far as feeding is concerned.'

'I can only remember one winter in Farthing Wood when it snowed,' said Fox. 'That was when I was very young. But there was only a light fall, and it didn't really hamper anyone's movements.'

'Oh yes,' nodded Badger. 'Of latter years there's not been a great deal of bad weather. But I recall the times when Winter meant Winter, and we had snow every year. Of course, my memory goes farther back than yours, Fox.'

Fox smiled slightly. He knew Badger loved to indulge in reminiscences, and he was aware of his proneness to exaggerate about 'life in the old days'.

'I remember one winter in particular,' Badger continued, delighted to have an audience. 'You hadn't appeared on the scene then, either of you, and I'm pretty certain Tawny Owl wasn't around at that time either.

Anyway, the snow lay on the ground for months, and I had to dig a regular track through it for foraging purposes. Everything was frozen hard – the pond, the stream, every small puddle. My father was still alive then and he taught us how to munch the snow for water. Otherwise we couldn't have drunk and we should have died.'

'What does it taste like? What does it taste like?' shrilled Mole.

'Oh, well – er – like water, I suppose,' replied Badger. 'Yes, and I shall never forget the number of birds and small creatures who perished from the cold.'

'Oh dear, oh dear!' Mole cried. 'I hope you don't mean moles?'

'Well, possibly not moles,' said Badger hurriedly. 'Mostly songbirds really. They couldn't find enough to eat and, naturally, their little bodies weren't able to withstand the bitter weather.'

'Poor things,' said Mole in a subdued tone. 'It's a pity they can't hibernate like Adder and Toad.'

The snow seemed to fall more thickly as they watched. Mole shivered.

'Go back inside,' the kindly Badger said at once. 'It's warm in my sleeping-chamber.'

'I'm not cold,' Mole told him, 'but thank you, Badger. No, it's just the eeriness that made me shiver. It's so quiet and still – it's uncanny.'

Through the ghostly trees they spotted a dark figure stepping through the snow. They all knew at once it was the Warden of the Nature Reserve on his rounds. They watched him stop periodically by a tree and tie something on to a low-hanging branch.

'What's he doing?' Mole asked, whose short-sightedness could only distinguish a tall blur of movement.

'I don't know for sure,' answered Badger. 'But it's my

guess he's leaving some sort of food for the birds.'

'Then that's bad news for us,' Fox said at once. 'Humans never do such things without a particular reason. It is well-known they can tell in advance what sort of weather is approaching. We must be in for some severe times.' He trotted over to look at the objects the Warden had left behind.

'You're right, Badger,' he called back. 'It *is* bird food. Nuts and fat and so on. I hope our feathered friends are up early,' he continued to himself, 'otherwise Squirrel and his pals will be having a feast at their expense.' He said as much to Badger on his return.

'Well, we must stop them,' said that thoughtful animal resolutely. 'The squirrels have buried enough acorns and beech-nuts to feed the whole of White Deer Park.'

'You'll be asleep when *they* get up,' Fox reminded him with a smile. 'You'd better leave it to me to have a word.'

'Will you and Vixen be warm enough in your den?' Badger asked suddenly. 'I've collected plenty of extra bedding for my set, and you're welcome to share it.'

'You're very kind,' replied Fox, 'but I think we're all right. We keep each other warm, you know,' he added.

Badger smiled. 'That must be a great comfort,' he remarked. He looked around. 'Well, I feel like a bit of a ramble. Coming, Fox?'

'With pleasure. Er – see you later, Mole?'

'No, I'll go back to my nest,' said the little animal. 'I'm sure to feel peckish again soon – you know what I'm like.'

'We do indeed,' laughed Fox. 'Shall we go, Badger?'

The two friends ambled off through the snowy wood. For some time neither spoke. Badger felt that Fox had something on his mind, so he remained quiet until his friend should be ready to talk. He watched the snowflakes settle on Fox's lithe chestnut body, grizzling his fur and making him appear prematurely aged.

At length Fox said, 'If we do have a long spell of snow, I shall have to start making plans for a food supply.'

'I don't think that will be necessary just yet,' Badger said calmly. 'We can see how things develop. The animals will make shift for themselves.'

'Of course they will,' said Fox hurriedly. 'They'll have to. But I have a feeling in my bones about this winter and – well, quite frankly, Badger, I'm more than a little concerned.'

Badger felt he should allay his companion's fears if he could. 'Don't go worrying yourself,' he told him. 'After all, to begin with Toad and Adder and the hedgehogs are not involved. I can look after myself and so can Weasel, Tawny Owl and Kestrel. Of the smaller creatures, the squirrels have only to dig up a fraction of their buried treasure to survive, and Mole has never been so well supplied. So who does that leave? Hare and his family, the rabbits, the voles and the fieldmice. All of *them* eat seeds and vegetation. You're a carnivore. You couldn't begin to be as proficient at finding stores of their food as they are themselves.'

'Yes, I suppose you're right,' Fox agreed. 'It's just that if any of them do get into difficulties I shall feel responsible for getting them out.'

'It's early days yet,' said Badger. 'You just think about Vixen for the time being. The others will manage, you'll see.'

'You're always a comforting chap,' Fox said warmly, 'and I'm truly grateful, Badger.'

They reached the Hollow together and Fox's next words made it clear that Badger had not succeeded in putting his mind at rest.

'This is where our new life began last summer,' he said, looking down at the familiar meeting-place of the Farthing Wood community. 'Let's hope the next few months won't see the end of it for some of us.'

—3—

First Losses

The first signs were not good for wild creatures as the old year drew to a close. December came in with a blizzard, and over the next few weeks a cruel, bitter frost held the Park in its grip night after night. During the daylight hours the sun gleamed fitfully but snow clouds blotted it out for most of the day, and so very little of the frost disappeared. The ground became as hard as iron, and ice coated the Edible Frogs' pond to a thickness of two inches.

A stream ran through most of the Reserve and, some distance from where the Farthing Wood animals had set up home, Whistler the heron could be found. He had chosen an area under some overhanging alder trees where fish abounded in the shallow reaches. Now each day he and his mate watched the slower-moving water by the stream's banks gather more ice. Soon only the centre of the stream, where it rippled swiftly over the tinkling pebbles, continued to flow. Whistler had to step on to the ice to be able to continue his hunting, but the fish were less plentiful further out in the water and the heron and his mate began to notice their diet suffering.

'It looks, my dear, as if we shall have to be rather less choosy in our fare,' Whistler observed in his slow, precise manner. 'From your greater knowledge of the Park, can you suggest any fresh avenues of approach?'

The female heron nodded. 'I told you long ago of a place upstream, where the water runs very fast, and which abounds in crayfish. But you told me you had no liking for shellfish.'

Whistler shrugged his great wings. 'Obviously I shall have to overcome my aversion, at least temporarily. Show me the way, if you please.'

The two water birds rose into the air together, their long, thin legs trailing beneath them like pairs of stilts. From the air, the Park was one vast expanse of rolling white, pierced by clumps of bare, snowclad trees. Whistler's damaged wing shrilled musically with its every beat, and his eyes began to water in the freezing temperature.

They landed after a brief flight, and Whistler's mate began to search the stream-bed. Here the water was completely free of ice. Suddenly her pointed beak stabbed downwards, and then re-emerged firmly clenching a feebly moving crayfish, which she swallowed at a gulp. Whistler joined the hunt and was soon successful. His mate watched for his reaction. 'Hm,' he murmured, swallowing hard. 'Not at all bad. It's surprising how an empty stomach may overcome the most rooted prejudice.'

As there were fish also to be had in this stretch of water, the two birds made an excellent meal. His satisfaction made Whistler call his friends from Farthing Wood to mind. He wondered what difficulties they might be experiencing.

'We mustn't be selfish,' he told his mate. 'This food source might well be of benefit to others. While you return to the roost, my clever one, I think I'll search out Fox and see if I can be of use to him.'

Accordingly he flew off in the direction of Fox's earth. As it was daylight he did not expect to find his friend above ground, and was surprised to see a very lean Vixen sitting by one of the entrance holes when he arrived. She appeared to be very disconsolate, but bravely tried to look cheerful as she greeted the heron.

'Is Fox below?' Whistler asked her.

'No,' she replied. 'Things have been getting rather hard, and he decided to go and see for himself how everyone else is coping.'

'The very reason I came to see you,' Whistler explained, and went on to describe his earlier success in the stream.

Despite her efforts at control, Vixen's mouth began to water freely as she heard of the fish Whistler and his mate had enjoyed.

'It would be more than a pleasure for me to help you catch some,' Whistler offered.

'I'm sure Fox would be most grateful,' Vixen said appreciatively. 'I think I should wait for him to return before we go. There might be one or two other animals who would like to join us.'

'I wonder how long he will be?' Whistler asked.

'I don't know exactly,' answered Vixen, 'but he's already been gone some hours.'

While they waited, she explained how their hunting

trips had become steadily less fruitful and how their diet had become one of carrion, insects and even snails when they had discovered a hibernating colony. 'But they tasted so good,' she added.

'Oh yes,' agreed the heron. 'I myself have made some adjustments in my eating pattern,' and he went on to tell her of the crayfish he had eaten.

Presently they saw the familiar figure of Fox approaching them, accompanied by a smaller one they could not at first distinguish. It turned out to be Weasel.

Whistler and the two animals greeted each other with pleasure. But Fox's expression returned to one of deep concern when Vixen questioned him on his discoveries.

'It's even worse than I'd expected,' he informed her miserably. 'The voles and fieldmice have already lost a considerable number of their party, and some of the older rabbits have died of the severe cold. If this weather continues for a long spell the mice, in particular, are going to be decimated.'

Whistler expressed his sympathy but, privately, was more alarmed at Fox's own appearance. Gone was the vigorous, supple body of the resourceful leader the animals had come to rely on during their long trek to the Nature Reserve. Gone was the bright-eyed, healthful expression of his face. And gone was the rich lustre of his coat, that had marked Fox as a creature in his prime. Now his eyes were downcast, his fur dull and staring, his movements slow and hesitant, while his body was not so much lean as distinctly bony. By comparison Weasel's much smaller form, always as slim as a sapling, looked in much better shape.

Whistler hurriedly told Fox about the proposed fishing. Without a great deal of interest, Fox agreed. Then he said, 'But of what use are fish to voles and fieldmice? They are hungry too.'

'Of course they are,' said Vixen. 'But you must keep your strength up if you wish to help them, even though that is going to be difficult.'

'Rabbits and fieldmice soon replace their numbers,' Whistler pointed out in an attempt to ease Fox's mind.

'Yes, but there may be no stock of fieldmice to replace numbers from,' Fox muttered. 'Their community has lost more in the last week than during the whole of our journey across the countryside. And the voles haven't fared much better.'

'Did you see Hare?' Vixen asked him.

'Yes. His family are all reasonably well though, like everyone else, they've taken on a lean look. The leverets are almost up to his size now, and quite independent.'

'How is Badger?' Whistler wanted to know.

'He wasn't at home,' replied Fox. 'But I've no fears on his account. He has more experience of life than any of us. He'll survive.'

'I'm sure we'll see a thaw soon,' said Weasel optimistically. 'The winter has a long way to go yet, and a cold spell like this rarely lasts for more than a few weeks.'

Fox did not reply, but they all knew he was wondering what could be done if it lasted through to the spring.

Whistler gave them directions to the fishing area and told them he would meet them there. When they arrived, they found he had wasted no time. Four reasonably sized fish and a couple of crayfish awaited them. The three animals fell to at once and made short work of the meal. Whistler enquired if they had had enough.

'Better to save some for another day,' remarked Vixen, 'than to feast now and starve tomorrow.'

Whistler acknowledged her wisdom. Then he said, 'I've seen nothing of the other birds. Has anyone encountered them recently?'

'Oh, Tawny Owl can always be found in his beech

coppice,' Weasel answered. 'He was dozing when we came past just now. He's found himself a snug hollow trunk out of this biting air. As to Kestrel, he flies so far afield you would be lucky to catch a glimpse of him.'

The animals enquired after the health of Whistler's mate. As she was the favourite topic of the heron's conversation, he answered enthusiastically. 'Oh, she is such a wonderful creature,' he told them. 'It was she, of course, who knew where to find the crayfish and showed me the spot. I'm sure I never shall be able to express sufficient gratitude to you all for allowing me to accompany you on your journey to the Park. Had I not met you, I should still be patrolling the waterside in that quarry, with no more company than a lot of raucous mallards and coots. Now I'm living in that perfect contentment of a paired wild creature which I'm sure you, Fox, also enjoy.'

Fox and Vixen smiled at each other and Weasel chuckled. 'Hold on,' he said. 'Some of us still opt for the single state, you know.'

'Ah, not for long, Weasel, if you are a wise beast,' Whistler admonished him. 'There is no comparison, I assure you.'

Weasel laughed again. 'Perhaps you're right,' he said. 'But, on the other hand, "better the devil you know" and so forth.'

This little exchange served to lighten their mood, and provided a welcome relief from their troubles. The animals thanked Whistler heartily for his generosity and, telling him to keep in touch, began to make their way back along the bank of the stream towards their homes. Dusk fell early at that time of year, and the cloud-covered sky hastened the darkness. Weasel left the fox couple for his den, and as Fox and Vixen approached the earth, they could see an agitated Mole waiting for them.

'Whatever is the matter?' Fox asked at once.

'Badger's disappeared,' said the distraught little creature, and broke into a sob.

'Now, now, calm down, Mole,' Fox said soothingly. 'He always leaves his set at this time in the evening. You know that.'

'Yes, but he hasn't been in it all day either,' wailed Mole. 'I've been along my connecting tunnel half a dozen times today to see him, and the set has been empty all along.'

Fox looked at Vixen. 'Hm,' he mused. 'That does seem strange.'

'I'm sure there's some simple explanation for his absence,' said Vixen. 'He may be on a visit or – '

'He wouldn't be likely to go visiting in this weather,' interrupted Mole. 'I'm so worried. Badger's habits never change. He sleeps during the day, and only wakes up in the evening.'

'When did you last see him?' Fox asked.

'Yesterday. We talked about the shortage of food, and I offered him some of my worms because he said *I* was looking plumper than usual. Then he started to talk about you, Fox, saying that it wasn't fair for you alone to feel responsible for all the animals' welfare, and that he was sure you were getting thinner and thinner because of it, and you needed some help.'

'That's Badger all over, the dear kind creature,' Vixen observed.

'Yes, and it makes the picture much clearer,' announced Fox. 'He's obviously gone off on some venture of his own with the idea of helping us in one way or another, though Heaven knows what he can possibly do. Don't be too alarmed, Mole. I think we shall see him back by the morning, and I'll ask Tawny Owl to keep an eye open for him tonight.'

'But what if he doesn't return?' persisted Mole. 'I know I shan't be comfortable until I know he's all right.'

'If he doesn't return,' replied Fox, 'I shall personally go out tomorrow to search for him, even if it means combing the entire Park.'

'Oh, thank you, Fox,' said Mole. 'I knew you would. I'll go home and stop bothering you now, and I'll look into Badger's set in the morning and let you know.'

Fox trotted off to speak to Tawny Owl, leaving Vixen and Mole to return to the comparative warmth of their underground shelters.

—4—

The Search for Badger

Mole went straight to Badger's set before he ate a single
worm the next day which, in his case, was the strongest
possible measure of his anxiety. The set was, again,
empty. He emerged from one of Badger's exit tunnels
and made his way as fast as his short legs would allow
him to Fox, cursing his slowness as he did so. But his
journey proved unnecessary for, when he reached the
earth, Vixen informed him that Fox had already set off
on his search. He had wasted no time on hearing from
Tawny Owl that Badger had not been seen returning
home, and all that they could do now was to wait for
news.

It was not long before Fox realized that, if he did not
find Badger within the area of the Reserve settled by the

Farthing Wood animals, or at least close by, he would never have the strength to travel the confines of the whole of White Deer Park. In addition to his own weaker state, there was the powdery snow, which in places had formed thick drifts, and was very tiring to walk through as he frequently sank in it as deep as his shoulders. Even as he trudged along it again began to snow heavily, so that visibility became very poor too.

Skirting the Hollow, he made a tour of the perimeter of their home area. The falling snow covered any tracks or scent that might have been useful, and Fox knew he was on an impossible task. He must recruit some assistance. A swifter and less heavy animal such as Hare would be able to cover a greater distance more easily, but most of all Fox wished for a sight of Kestrel. His piercing eyesight from high above the ground could locate the lumbering form of Badger faster than anyone's. For the moment, however, he must make do with Hare.

Luckily Hare was to be found sheltering with his mate in a scooped-out 'form' of snow behind a hawthorn tree. The leverets were elsewhere. Fox explained why he had come again so soon.

'That *is* surprising,' Hare said afterwards, 'old Badger going off like that. I wonder what he intended to do?'

'We've no way of knowing, at the moment,' answered Fox. 'The thing I'm afraid of is that he might have met with some accident. He doesn't normally wander far afield.'

'How can I help?' Hare asked.

'You're much fleeter of foot than me,' replied Fox, 'and can cover greater distances more easily. If I comb this side of the Park, could you investigate a bit further afield?'

Hare was silent for a time. Eventually he said cautiously, 'I *could*. But I don't relish the idea of going too far away from the home area. After all, there are other foxes in the Park beside yourself and Vixen, and I'm fair game for all of them.'

Fox nodded. 'I know,' he said. 'But I've never yet met a fox who could outrun a hare.'

Hare's mate had pricked up her ears at this latter turn in the conversation. 'Don't put his life too much at risk,' she begged Fox. 'He's the father of a family, you know. Badger is a loner and would leave behind no mate to mourn.'

'No, but the number of creatures who would mourn the loss of Badger would be far greater,' Fox pointed out.

Hare looked from one to the other, torn between conflicting loyalties.

'Well, I shan't press you,' Fox said finally. 'It may be that your duty to your family should come first, after all.' He started to move away, but Hare called him back.

'I *will* go,' he announced. 'I should never forgive myself if I turned down such a request for help.'

'Thank you,' said Fox simply. He described where he wanted Hare to go – the area beyond the Edible Frogs' pond. 'We'll confer later at the Hollow,' he added. 'I shall be there at dusk. Good luck.'

He left the two animals but did not fail to hear Hare being up-braided by his mate as he went – 'Why did you let him talk you into it like that?' and Hare's quiet reply, 'For the sake of Farthing Wood.' Now as Fox plodded on through the relentless snowfall, his spirits rose a little and some of the tiredness left him. He found some harder patches of snow, where it had begun to thaw and then frozen over, and he was able to increase his speed, all the time casting about for his old friend.

He came out into the open expanse of parkland where the White Deer herd usually roamed, and it was not long before he spotted a group of them feeding from bales of hay specially provided by the conscientious Warden. One of their number was the Great Stag himself, a huge figure who now did not look so imposing as before. The hard winter was taking its toll of all creatures, from the highest to the lowest. Against the dazzling snow carpet, the white hides of the deer looked duller than Fox had remembered. The Stag noticed him and stepped elegantly towards him.

'How do things go with you and yours?' he asked.

'Not well,' Fox answered. 'Food is hard to come by and the cold very cruel.'

'Yes, I don't recall many winters such as this,' said the Stag. 'For some reason this year *we* are not to be expected to fend entirely for ourselves. The humans, in their wisdom, have decided to buffer us against extreme hardship.'

'I understand your herd is unique,' said Fox, 'so it isn't surprising that your numbers are not allowed to become too depleted.'

The Stag nodded sagely. 'I'm only sorry you don't eat hay,' he said. 'We have more than enough.'

Fox thought of the rabbits and mice. 'There is something you could do,' he said, 'if you are so willing. My smaller, weaker friends are suffering particularly. If you didn't object, perhaps some stray stalks could be left aside for their use?'

'Of course. Certainly,' the Great Stag agreed readily. 'But you don't often come to these parts, do you? It would be a really difficult undertaking for creatures smaller than yourself.'

'That's true,' Fox answered. 'But if they are sufficiently hungry I'm sure they will come.'

The Great Stag pondered a moment. 'It is most unusual,' he observed, 'this mutual co-operation and concern your band of animals feels for each other. Normally, in the wild, each animal goes his own way and – well, the strongest survive. I find the idea of helping one another most interesting – even appealing. Perhaps we deer should also show a willingness to assist our brother creatures. Supposing I arrange it that each member of my herd carries a mouthful of hay and deposits it at a point more conveniently close to your friends?'

'That would indeed be kind,' Fox told him, and added that the best place to leave the food would be by the Hollow.

'It shall be done today,' the Stag said. 'But tell me, my friend, what brought you this way in the first place?'

'One of our party – Badger – has disappeared,' said Fox. 'I'm looking for him.'

'Hm, again this concern for others. Most interesting,' intoned the doyen of the deer herd. 'Well, if I hear of his whereabouts I shall most certainly come and tell you. I wish you all well.' He rejoined the rest of the herd and Fox continued on his way.

Presently he came within sight of the Warden's cottage and garden area beyond the fence and here he struck lucky again, for Kestrel was perched on top of one of the palings. The hawk called joyfully to him and flew over, wheeling playfully over Fox's head.

'Come down, Kestrel, I want your help,' shouted Fox.

The bird was at once all seriousness, and landed beside him. 'What is it?' he asked.

Fox told him.

'I'll go now – at once. Earlier today I was flying over the Park, but I had no sign of Badger.'

Fox told him of the rendezvous at dusk in the Hollow with Hare; then he said, 'Before you go, can I ask you to stay closer at hand for the next few days? You might be needed again.'

Kestrel agreed and swooped off to begin his exploration.

For the rest of the day, Fox methodically combed every part of the Reserve he could before he felt exhaustion to be imminent. With the last reserves of his strength he made his slow way back towards the meeting point. The snow had ceased by the time he reached the Hollow, where he discovered Vixen, Mole, Weasel and Tawny Owl waiting for news. He merely shook his head as he saw them.

Mole said nothing, almost as if he dare not speak.

'I asked Hare and Kestrel to help me,' Fox said wearily. 'I'm more hopeful of their news.'

Hare was the next to arrive, but he had no comfort for them. However they tried not to feel too disheartened until Kestrel had come.

'If anyone can find Badger that hawk can do it,' Weasel said encouragingly.

'Unfortunately that remark implies,' Tawny Owl pointed out, 'that if Kestrel can't find him the rest of us don't have a chance.'

They fell silent again, shifting their feet in the bitter cold. At last Kestrel arrived.

'I've searched every corner of the Reserve twice over,' he told them, 'and found not a trace of Badger anywhere. He seems to have disappeared into thin air.'

Mole broke down at this appalling news of his beloved Badger, and it was left to Vixen to try and console him.

'He can't just have vanished,' muttered Fox. 'There's something very odd about this.'

'Perhaps he's been adopted into another set,' suggested Hare.

'Never – not our Badger,' declared Weasel.

'Unless he were coerced?' Tawny Owl added.

'This is what is worrying me,' Fox admitted. 'It seems

the only solution: that Badger has somehow managed to get himself captured and taken underground, or at any rate carried off by something. But no, no . . . it's incredible.'

'Well, there's nothing any of us can do for the moment,' remarked Tawny Owl. 'I'm famished, and I need longer than usual to hunt up my supper these days. I'll bid you farewell till tomorrow.'

He had not been long gone, when the animals espied a group of deer coming towards them. Fox told of his talk with the Great White Stag, and they all watched as each deer dropped its mouthful of hay by the Hollow and quietly retreated. This put other thoughts into Fox's mind.

'Hare, on your way home, will you inform your cousins the rabbits about this?'

'I'll have a mouthful or two myself first,' he answered.

'I'll go and tell those poor mice,' Fox continued.

'No,' said Weasel. 'You're far too tired. You go and rest. *I'll* tell them.'

Fox was about to relate the Great Stag's comments on their mutual help for each other, but he was simply too worn out, and allowed Vixen to lead him back to their den.

Mole was the last to leave the Hollow. 'I won't believe it,' he kept muttering to himself. 'He *hasn't* disappeared. I'll find him. I'll find him.'

—5—
What had Happened to Badger

Badger had thought long and hard about the animals' difficulties, and it had occurred to him that none of them had any idea how the original inhabitants of the Reserve were coping with the winter. As they would know the resources of the Park far better than the recent arrivals from Farthing Wood, he decided there would be no harm done if he went to seek out advice where he could.

Saying nothing to any of his friends, he left his home at his usual time in the evening and set off on his quest. The night air was still and the moon glowed from a clear sky. It was intensely cold and Badger hurried along as quickly as he could with his rather shambling gait.

He had left the familiar region of the Park far behind before he encountered another creature. Under some shrubbery he surprised a stoat who was feeding from the carcase of a rabbit. The two strangers eyed each other warily.

'It's a bitter night,' Badger said at length.

'There's not enough for two,' the stoat replied, who obviously thought he had a competitor for his meal.

'I'm not after your food,' Badger told him. 'I can see you are very hungry.'

'Famished,' answered the stoat bluntly. 'Haven't eaten for three days.'

'Hunting difficult?' Badger asked unnecessarily.

'That's an understatement,' came the reply. 'There's nothing about. This rabbit died from the cold, I should say. Of course, it's frozen solid. But you have to eat what you can these days.' The animal wrenched off another mouthful and appeared to find it of great relish. 'What about you?' the stoat enquired. 'I don't think I've seen you around before.'

'No, you wouldn't have,' Badger told him. 'I don't usually wander as far as this. I'm one of the newcomers to the Park.'

'Oh, you're one of the great travellers, are you?' the stoat said with a touch of cynicism. 'Well, you've found no garden of abundance here, I'll bet.'

'Who could have expected weather like this?' Badger answered. 'In any case, the whole countryside must be affected.'

'Of course,' agreed the stoat. 'This winter will halve the population of this Reserve, though.'

'Do you think so? As bad as that?'

'Bound to,' the animal said shortly. 'Very little food means very few survive.'

Badger nodded. 'Yes, I suppose so.'

The stoat seemed to be waiting to be left alone again. Badger eventually noticed. 'Er – I'm sorry to have interrupted you,' he said. 'I'll leave you in peace.' He moved away and called back a hesitant, 'Good luck!' over his shoulder, but the stoat was too busy with his meal to respond.

However, the remarks he had made to Badger had made it pretty evident that none of the creatures in the Park was faring very well. He thought of the Great Stag, whose wisdom could perhaps serve the animals' interests in their hardship. But where was he to be found? Not in the woods, at any rate. He would be in open country. Badger continued on his way.

But he never reached the deer herd, though they were in his sights before the accident happened. He was descending a slight slope which was very slippery with ice. His feet skidded and he went hurtling down, unable to stop himself, just like a toboggan. At the bottom of the slope was a large rock. Badger was completely powerless to avoid it. One side of his body and one hind leg struck the rock heavily. Badly winded, he let out a cry of pain at the blow on his leg. When he could breathe freely again, he tried to hoist himself upright, but such a searing agony shot through the injured hind leg that he merely collapsed on his side once more.

There he lay for the rest of the night. He knew there was no possibility of walking, and the dreadful cold seemed to penetrate every inch of his fur. He wondered what would ever become of him. 'What hope have I got?' he asked himself. 'I'm a long way from my friends, I've no food, no shelter, and I can't move.' He fell into an uneasy doze.

When morning came, Badger awoke so cold and stiff he could barely even raise his head. But salvation was on the way, although he did not know it. The Warden

of the Park had been out distributing the bales of hay
for the White Deer herd, and was doing a general round
of the Reserve in his Land Rover. Stopping periodically
to view an area through his field-glasses, he spotted the
almost inert form of Badger and went to investigate. In
no time Badger found himself being lifted, taken to the
vehicle where he was laid gently down amongst some
old rugs, and transported back to the warmth and comfort of the Warden's cottage kitchen.

The Warden fetched an old dog basket, lined it with
sacking and old cloths and deposited the uncomplaining
Badger inside. Then he stood contemplating the animal
thoughtfully for a minute, before beginning to prepare
some food. Badger fell into another doze, induced by his
weakness and the warmth of the room.

When he next sleepily raised his eyelids, he found
some raw mince and warm milk placed in front of him.
He was able to move his body sufficiently to feed and he
ate greedily. His rescuer appeared to be delighted with
this, for Badger sensed eyes on him and looked up. The
man was smiling broadly, and Badger was astonished,
almost numbed by the brightness of the human face.
Never had he been so close to humankind before. There
was something mysterious – awe-inspiring – there: something quite beyond his own experience and
understanding.

But the Warden did not linger. Badger was left to
finish his meal and rest in peace. As he sank back on
the bed provided for him, he thought of his friends in
the Park that he had wanted to help. A lot of help *he*
had been to them. They were still suffering in the bleak
winter weather – battling against elements that soon
could overwhelm them entirely. He knew that his
absence would be noticed. The animals would be ignorant of his fate, and he as ignorant of theirs. Would he

be able to walk again? He realized the Warden wished to aid his recovery. But how long would he be kept here? He despised feeling so helpless.

Eventually his very helplessness overcame him, and in his weak state he fell asleep again. He did not know that, on several occasions while he slept, the Warden looked in, and was amused by his snoring. But there was a fresh supply of mince and water to drink when he woke at his usual hour in the evening.

When he had finished eating again, he became aware of a presence in the room, although he had heard nothing moving. In the gloom that he was so used to he soon noticed a pair of green eyes watching him unblinkingly from the doorway. They belonged to a large ginger cat, the Warden's pet.

'You're in a bad way,' the animal remarked, and walked on noiseless feet towards him in an elaborately unhurried way. By the basket the cat bent and sniffed curiously at Badger for a long time. 'You have the rank smell of a wild creature,' he announced.

The creature's coolness nonplussed Badger. He was not a mouse or a pigeon, but a large untamed animal whose normal strength must be totally unknown to the cat.

'Have you been eating my meat?' was the next question.

'Your master fed me,' Badger replied.

'I have no master,' the cat responded at once. 'I am my own master. I do as I choose.'

'Then why do you choose to eat meat provided by a human?' Badger asked subtly.

'Why ever not?' the cat wanted to know, flicking his tail slightly in irritation. 'It saves me the trouble of finding it for myself.'

Badger was silent.

'I've no objection to your eating it, anyway,' the cat said nonchalantly. 'There's plenty more where that came from, and all sorts of other things as well. Do you like fish?'

'I've eaten fish on occasion, yes,' Badger answered.

'Hm. What do you usually eat?'

'Grubs, roots, bulbs, small creatures. . . .'

'Rats?'

'Sometimes.'

'Good. Then we have something in common. My chief pleasure is hunting rats.'

'Are there many around here?' Badger asked, immediately thinking of their value to Fox and Vixen and Tawny Owl, too.

'Not since I arrived on the scene,' replied the cat boastfully, flexing his claws. 'The man brought me here as a kitten two winters ago.'

Their conversation was cut short by the sound of human steps. The Warden came into the room, and Badger was astounded to see a complete change of character come over the domestic animal. Running to its owner, it became at once the playful and affectionate pet, rubbing itself round his legs and purring noisily; then scampering off to a corner before returning to repeat the performance. The man spoke to his pet which increased the volume of purring instantly.

Badger soon understood it was the cat's mealtime now and the leg-rubbing ritual, together with stretching and mewing, continued until the food was ready. It then abruptly stopped while the more important task of eating was taken care of.

Badger came in for a word or two from the Warden also, though of course he understood nothing. Yet the sounds were very pleasing to him and comforting, too, and he was quite sure that had been the intention.

When the Warden left the kitchen again, the cat followed him. A short time afterwards he returned to put his ginger head round the door. 'I'm going to spend the rest of the evening in front of the fire,' he informed Badger. 'I feel very sleepy. But we'll talk again later. I hope you're comfortable for now?'

Badger assured him he was, and found himself alone again. He was soon musing over the strange mixture of his new acquaintance's personality: semi-domesticated and yet semi-independent. Despite himself, he felt drawn to the animal. He promised to be an interesting source of information.

Outside it was snowing again. In the warmth and security of the basket, Badger felt distinctly guilty as he thought again of his old companions. How he wished they could be sharing his new-found comfort with him now.

—6—

Conversations

The next day Badger felt a good deal stronger after plenty of rest and food. He particularly enjoyed a couple of apples the Warden thoughtfully gave him. With his returning strength, he began to look forward to being active again, and was pleased to receive another visit from the cat as a relief from the monotony.

The cat came running into the kitchen, his ginger fur glistening where the snowflakes were melting. 'It's really quite dreadfully cold out there,' he announced. 'Far too cold for me. I bet you'd sooner be in here too.'

'It's certainly warm here,' Badger admitted. 'But my set was always quite cosy, you know. There was plenty of dried bracken and leaves and grass and so on to pull round oneself.'

'But didn't the snow cover you?' asked the cat.

'No, no, my home's underground,' Badger explained. The cat looked surprised. 'Underground? How extraordinary,' he said.

'Not extraordinary at all,' Badger said a little defensively. 'A lot of wild creatures live underground. It's a lot safer and, as I said, very comfortable.'

'Who are your enemies?' whispered the cat.

'Humans principally,' Badger replied. 'And dogs.'

'Well, you've no fear from humans hereabouts,' the cat reassured him in a well-meaning way. 'There aren't any, except the man here, and he loves all wild creatures.'

'I know there's nothing to fear here,' Badger replied. 'That's why we all came to the Reserve in the first place. For safety.'

'Where did you come from, then?'

'Oh, a long, long way away. A place called Farthing Wood. We had to leave, because the humans were destroying the wood. Our homes were threatened, and if we had stayed we would have been killed.'

'How many other badgers were with you?' asked the cat.

'None. We were a motley party. Fox, Weasel, Tawny Owl, Mole, Toad, Kestrel, along with hedgehogs and rabbits and hares and squirrels and voles and fieldmice and even a snake.'

'This is most interesting,' declared the cat. 'It sounds as if half the countryside was on the march.'

'It wasn't really like that,' Badger smiled. 'We were only a small band and, naturally, we lost some of our number on the way. Considering the hazards we encountered, we were fortunate not to lose more.'

'I see,' said the cat, who did not at all. 'The mice were taken to provide food for you on the way.'

'No, no, no,' Badger cried in horror. 'They were companions on our journey. Before we set out, we all swore an oath to protect each other's safety – not to molest one another.'

'But surely,' persisted the cat, 'in the wild it is common for stronger animals to prey on the weak?'

Badger nodded. 'But we are no common group of animals,' he said with the greatest satisfaction.

'I'm beginning to understand that,' remarked the cat. 'Tell me about your adventures.'

'With pleasure,' said Badger. 'And the only way to do that is to begin at the beginning.'

So the cat sat perfectly still while he heard about the animals' escape from Farthing Wood and their journey across country, with all the dangers they had faced of the fire, the river crossing, the Hunt and the motorway. He also heard how the animals had seen the Warden before arriving at the Park. 'Well, well,' he said afterwards, 'quite a story. Makes my life seem very dull.'

'Each to his own,' Badger said sagely. 'I imagine you're content with your lot?'

'Oh yes, I have everything I want. Food, warmth – and I can come and go as I please. A cat can be happy with very little.'

'Have you never felt the desire to be completely free, completely in charge of your own life?' Badger enquired.

'But I am,' the cat protested. 'As I told you, I please myself.'

'It's not what we wild creatures would call really free,' Badger said provokingly. 'I rather think you're more attached to the man than you care to admit. I was interested to see the way you responded to him yesterday – you made quite a fuss of him.'

'Oh well,' the cat answered, beginning to lick his chest fur as a diversion, 'they expect something for their pains, don't they? The man likes to think I'm dependent on him.'

'Perhaps you are?'

'Not at all,' the cat said huffily. 'I can survive perfectly well on my own if I have to. You're just trying to rile me.'

'I certainly am not,' Badger said at once. 'But I'll tell you what. Once I can walk again I shall leave here. Why don't you come with me and prove to the human you don't really need him?'

The cat did not take up the challenge. 'How *is* your leg?' he asked. 'Still painful?'

Badger indicated that it was. The cat began to lick the wound sympathetically. But Badger had to call out to him to stop. 'Your tongue is so rough,' he explained. 'But you're very kind.'

There were human voices outside. The cat jumped up to the window-sill to look. 'Ah,' he said. 'The man who makes animals well is coming. He often comes here when a wild creature has been found in trouble. He will help you.'

The Warden came in with another human who was, indeed, a vet. Badger found himself quite unalarmed at being closely examined and tested, and then having his bad leg bound tightly with some materials. The two men then talked for a period, and the Warden seemed to be quite satisfied with what he was told. The vet made a fuss of the cat, calling him by his name, 'Ginger', and tickling his chin. Badger's new friend responded in the way expected, by purring very loudly and nuzzling the proffered finger. Then the animals were left alone again. Badger was amused, and decided to persist with his suggestion of the cat's adopting the wild way of life.

'Well, perhaps I may,' the cat said evasively, 'but I

think it will be quite a while yet before you're fit enough for the man to release you.'

'Release me?' said Badger sharply. 'I'm not to be kept here, am I?'

'Oh no,' said the cat. 'As soon as you are considered to be quite well enough to return to the wild, you'll be taken outside to run away freely.'

'I shouldn't have doubted really,' said Badger. 'I know that man really wants the best for wild creatures. If only all humans were of his type, there would be no need for any beast or bird to fear them. But I believe they are few and far between.'

'Oh, there's not many like him,' the cat averred. 'He's about the best you can hope for from their race.'

Badger noted the enthusiasm in the cat's voice, which certainly did suggest there was a bond of attachment between him and the Warden, despite the animal's claim to be independent. Then he thought of his own attachments. He wished he knew how his old friends were. By now they were sure to be concerned about his disappearance. He dared not think too much about how Mole might be feeling. He watched the cat washing himself meticulously, preparatory to curling up in his own bed. A thought struck him. He himself was unable to go to them, but he could send a messenger. The cat could be his legs.

'I wonder if I could ask you to do me quite a large favour?' Badger asked rather nervously, for he suspected the cat's reaction.

The cat paused in the middle of his toilet, the tip of his tongue protruding from his mouth and one hind leg raised into the air from his squatting position.

'I'm getting increasingly worried about my friends in the Reserve. They don't know where I am,' Badger went on. 'I know they'll be out looking for me, and they've more than enough to cope with just staying alive at the moment, without bothering about me.'

'I think I know what the request is to be,' the cat remarked, lying down.

'*Would* you be able to be so obliging as to carry a message of my safety to them?'

'To be perfectly honest,' the cat said, 'I don't think it is possible. Your friends are meat-eaters, or some of them are. They don't know me, and they're very hungry. Don't you think I would be exposing myself to more than a reasonable risk of attack by a fox or an owl?'

'I'm sure you would be too large a morsel for an owl,' Badger said reassuringly. 'As for Fox and Vixen they, like Tawny Owl, are mostly inactive in the daytime. You would be quite safe then, even if they might pose a threat after dark, which I personally don't believe. You are a reasonably large animal yourself, and sure to be beyond their scope. In any case, you showed no fear of *me* from the outset.'

'But I knew you were sick,' the cat pointed out, 'otherwise you wouldn't have been here. And, even if I am safe in daytime, I don't know the terrain. The Park is enormous, and completely covered by snow. I'd sink up to my neck at the first step.'

'No, you're too light-footed for that. You've been outside the cottage, anyway, in the snow.'

'Yes, but most of it has been cleared by the man where *we* want to walk. If I went into the depths of the Park where would I shelter? It would be a long trek to where your friends live, and then to come back again.'

'You could shelter in my set and be quite warm and safe,' Badger offered unrealistically. 'Any of them would show you where it is.'

'Impossible,' the cat declared roundly. 'I couldn't go

underground. No, I'm sorry, my friend, because I would like to help. But I really don't see that I can.'

Badger resorted to a final means of persuasion. Affecting a slightly malicious tone he said, 'So I was right. You couldn't survive alone, without human assistance.'

The cat looked at him angrily for a second. 'You seem to forget I wasn't born in the wild like you and your friends,' he snapped. 'I haven't the long experience of the lore of survival you have acquired from birth. You tell me you wild creatures are literally battling for life in what are, after all, exceptionally bad conditions. How well do you think I will manage, without the knowledge you are armed with?'

Badger felt this was an honest enough answer and that it would not be seemly to pursue the argument. But his friends *must* be informed. 'Then there's no alternative,' he told the cat quietly. 'I accept what you say as reasonable, and so it means I shall have to go myself.'

'Don't be so ridiculous!' cried the cat impatiently. 'I can understand you are fond of your friends, but you are taking unselfishness too far. They will just have to get along without you for a bit. You *can't* walk now, but it shouldn't be too long before you are able to return to them – perhaps a couple of weeks. I don't know how serious the damage is. Who knows? Perhaps the worst of the winter will be over by then.'

Badger shook his head. 'I couldn't possibly leave them in ignorance for a matter of weeks,' he persisted doggedly. 'You don't seem to understand. That oath we swore back in Farthing Wood – it hasn't lapsed. My friends won't just accept that I've vanished away. They will be risking their necks to find me.'

'Humph!' the cat snorted irritably. 'You seem to have a very high opinion of yourself.'

'Don't be absurd,' retorted Badger. 'Oh, you can say

what you like, but I've got to get word to them. If you won't go I mean what I say. I shall go myself even if it means crawling all the way.'

The cat realized he was in a corner. He could not possibly allow the crippled Badger to throw his life away, for that was what it would mean. So he had to relent.

'Very well, you've convinced me,' he said with reluctance. 'I'll start tomorrow if it isn't snowing. You'd better describe your friends to me in detail, so that I can recognize them.'

'I shall never forget this, Ginger Cat,' Badger said warmly. 'And, believe me, neither will the other animals. You've just made yourself a host of new friends.'

'Well, Badger' – the cat smiled – 'you're a very persuasive fellow.'

'You are now party to the Oath that binds all the creatures of Farthing Wood, Vixen and Whistler,' Badger reminded him. 'That means, if ever you yourself are in danger or difficulties – well, I think you understand me?'

'We understand each other,' said Ginger Cat.

—7—
A Meeting

No snow was falling in the morning and two very different animals, who were destined to meet that very day, were preparing to set out from opposite ends of the Park on behalf of Badger.

From the Warden's cottage Ginger Cat, having bade farewell to his new friend, was emerging. He jumped over the fence and looked with foreboding at the great white expanse before him over which he would have to travel. His first faltering steps found the snow surface reasonably firm, and his courage rose slightly. But he knew it was a long way in difficult conditions to Badger's companions.

Meanwhile in Badger's own set, Mole had determined to begin his search. He had formed the idea that Badger had somehow got lost or injured underground as he was not to be seen anywhere on the surface. So he had decided that, as he, Mole, was quite the kingpin among subterranean travellers, it should be he who must search this new area. He began by investigating all of Badger's tunnels in case he had had an accident while digging close to home. Of course he found no sign of any mishap. His next task was to surface and look for any other holes in the neighbourhood where Badger might have entered. This labour of love was as doomed to failure as it was devoted. But Mole kept trying, his stout little heart allowing him to emerge undismayed at every fresh disappointment. Each time he plunged down into the barren, frozen ground he thought that perhaps this time he was going to rescue his poor friend, and it was this idea which made his persevere.

Ginger Cat continued on his way, his silent footsteps taking him slowly, but steadily, towards his goal. He was beginning to feel very chilled and longed for the bright fireside of the cottage, where he basked content in the company of his human companion. As the morning wore on he got colder and colder and regretted his foolhardy mission. After all, what was an injured badger to him? For all the fine words about this wonderful Oath of theirs, he was an outsider, an individual. He was no member of a party. Why should he concern himself with whether Fox or Mole or Weasel or any of the rest of Badger's precious friends should lose their lives looking for him? They were all total strangers to Ginger Cat. Whatever he might have boasted to Badger, he was not a wild creature like they were, having to make shift through the seasons as best they could, come sun, wind, rain, snow and ice. He had an alternative – the alternative of keeping warm and comfortable all day if he felt like it; of sleeping by a blazing fire with a full stomach, ignorant of the raging elements of Nature. It had been his pride alone that had sent him on this absurd journey. Oh, how cold he felt!

All the time the cat was cursing his own misfortune, he was nearing Badger's home area. He passed by the Hollow without knowing its significance and then, suddenly, his senses were alert again as at last he saw movement ahead. He increased his speed and found a small black animal with a long snout crawling out of a hole. It was, of course, Mole.

Mole saw a large unknown animal approaching him and instantly ducked back underground.

'Don't go!' called Ginger Cat down the hole. 'You may be who I'm looking for. I have news of Badger.'

Mole reappeared at once. 'Badger? Where is he? Is he all right? Who are you?'

'He was injured,' Ginger Cat said. 'He's been rescued by the human you call the Naturalist, who is caring for him. Don't worry, he will soon be well.'

Mole did a little jig. 'Thank heaven he's still alive,' he said joyfully. 'But tell me who you are?'

Ginger Cat explained. Then, 'You must be Mole?' he enquired. 'Badger told me you lived underground.'

Mole confessed. 'We've all been so worried,' he said. 'No sign of him for three days. But you are our good friend. You've been very brave.'

'Badger told me about your long journey here from your old home,' said Ginger Cat.

'Will you come and meet the others?' Mole said enthusiastically. 'They'll be so grateful for your news.'

'No, I'm afraid I must decline. I want to be back before it gets dark, and it's a long way.'

'Of course. Tell me, when does Badger think he can come back to us?'

'Oh, Badger would come now if he could,' Ginger Cat

said with a smile. 'But he would be very wise, in my opinion, if he waits for the man to decide. Then he will be sure to be fully well again.'

Mole noticed this tribute to humankind, and realized the cat stood in a different relationship. 'Tell him we are all well,' Mole said. 'At least, tell him we are managing, and that we are missing him terribly.'

'I will, certainly. I hope I may see you again some time,' said Ginger Cat politely.

'Thank you again from all of Farthing Wood,' Mole answered importantly. 'There will always be a greeting for you here.'

Ginger Cat turned to make his way back. Mole watched him go. As the representative of the Farthing Wood community, he wondered if he had handled the meeting correctly. With a start, he remembered he had not offered the cat any refreshment. The animal had made a long journey, and now had the same distance to retrace. There were an abundance of worms in his larder. He called out.

The cat heard the noise and looked round. He could not make out Mole's words for he was a small creature and did not have a strong voice. Mole called again, but Ginger Cat still failed to understand and started to run back.

At that moment Kestrel, who had been patrolling the Park all day from the air for signs of Badger, spotted the two animals on the ground. He saw a large cat running towards his friend Mole, and naturally assumed it was an attack. Wheeling quickly, he dived earthwards and struck Ginger Cat like an arrow, his talons digging deep into the creature's flesh.

The cat howled and lashed out at the bird, but Kestrel was already ascending again for another plunge.

'Stop, Kestrel, stop!' called Mole frantically. 'He's a

friend!' But the hawk was too high to hear and was preparing to launch another strike. 'Quickly, into the hole,' Mole said desperately as the cat was instinctively flattening its body against the ground. Ginger Cat heard, but it was too late to move. Down swooped Kestrel again and Mole hurled himself against the ginger body, so that the hawk hesitated and lost the impetus of the descent. This time he heard Mole's pleas, 'No, no! Keep away, Kestrel! He's a friend – a friend!'

Kestrel landed and looked at Mole questioningly with his piercing eyes. Ginger Cat arched his wounded back and hissed aggressively.

'He came with news of Badger,' Mole explained lamely. 'All the way from the Naturalist's house. He wasn't pouncing on me.' He described the news the cat had brought.

Kestrel apologised inadequately for his actions, and told Mole what he had surmised from the air. He and Mole looked at Ginger Cat's back. The blood was flowing freely from the two large lacerations, dyeing the ginger fur and making it sticky.

'You and your confounded Oath,' muttered Ginger Cat weakly.

'We can't stay here,' said Mole. 'Kestrel, will you fetch Fox? I don't know what to do.'

Fox was not long in arriving on the scene, accompanied by Vixen. Without much difficulty, they persuaded Ginger Cat to go to shelter in their earth. He was too feeble now to argue. As they made their way along, Mole acquainted Fox with Badger's plight and of the cat's journey to see them.

'What a reward for such a good deed,' said Fox bitterly.

'I acted with the best intentions,' Kestrel hastened to

assure them. 'I thought only of Mole. How could I have known?'

'No-one's blaming you,' Fox replied. 'It's just a very unfortunate incident.'

Once inside the earth, Vixen took it upon herself to lick the wounds on the cat's back and to clean his fur. 'They are nasty cuts,' she observed, 'but they aren't bleeding any more. I hope you will share our meal later? When it is dark Fox and I will go out to see what we can find.'

Ginger Cat expressed his thanks and, himself convinced that his feebleness was more due to excessive tiredness than his wounds, fell gratefully asleep.

Mole stayed with him when the foxes went off on their foray and, before they returned, Ginger Cat awoke with a start in even pitcher blackness than before. 'It's all right,' said Mole. 'You're not alone.' The cat was amused at his tiny companion's effort at reassurance. He could have killed Mole with one paw, but of course had no desire to do so.

'You needn't stay, Mole,' he said smoothly. 'I'm a lot better for that nap. I'll be quite happy to wait on my own for my promised supper.'

'Just as you like,' said Mole readily. 'I'm as hungry as can be myself. I think I'll pay a visit to my own food store.' They exchanged farewells and Mole departed.

As soon as Ginger Cat was sure Mole had got right away, he himself stood up, stretched carefully, and shook his coat daintily. Despite himself, he winced at the pain that throbbed in his back. But he was ready to leave. He had no intention of waiting for Fox and Vixen to return. He would go hungry, but at least before morning he would be back in the warmth and cosiness of the cottage.

He emerged into the starlight, shivering in the bitter

cold, but was thankful to see no further snow had fallen. So his mission had been accomplished and he was gratified to have met Mole, Fox and Vixen. But he cherished a hope for revenge on the other of Badger's friends he had encountered. Was he, a cat, to allow himself to be bested by a bird – his natural prey? Hawk or no hawk, should the opportunity ever arise Kestrel would find he had made an error of judgement if he believed he could inflict any harm on an equally cunning hunter without redress.

— 8 —

Recovery

It was almost dawn when Ginger Cat limped back through his special flap into the Warden's lodge. Never before in his life had he felt so weary. He knew Badger would be agog for his news, but he was too tired to face his questions. So he lay down on the hall carpet where he was and dropped into an immediate sleep.

It was the noise of the Warden's rising that woke him. He stood up stiffly to greet the man's arrival. The Warden, of course, was overjoyed to see him but very concerned to find the wounds inflicted by Kestrel. These were attended to in no time and a large saucer of warm milk proffered while a well-deserved meal was prepared.

Badger could barely restrain his impatience for the man to leave the kitchen, but as soon as he did he started eagerly to demand to know all that had happened.

'I met your friends Mole and Fox and Vixen,' said Ginger Cat. 'They were relieved to hear of your safety. I also met Kestrel who is responsible for this,' he added in a hard voice, indicating his newly-bandaged back, and he went on to describe the incident.

'Oh dear, I really am so sorry,' Badger was most contrite. 'I can see exactly how it happened. He won't be able to forgive himself for injuring you.'

'Really?' hissed the cat sarcastically. 'I think he recovered his presence of mind fairly swiftly. It may be news to you that there is no love lost between cats and birds.'

'But I hope you won't hold this mistake against Kestrel,' Badger said worriedly.

Ginger Cat did not reply. Badger looked hard at him, but his bland expression was totally inscrutable.

'I will tell you one thing,' said the cat. 'You have lost your battle to persuade me to live wild. At the risk of appearing soft – and I don't care a jot – I would never leave this comfortable life to join you out there. I have had my taste now. I've experienced the worst weather I've known. I've been into one of your underground homes and pronounce it to be the most cheerless place I've ever seen or, rather, felt. I've seen the reality of what lack of food and poor shelter can do to an animal, and for that I had to look no further than the skinny, underfed bodies of your fox friends. But I'm going to turn the tables on you now. I say to you, Badger, that if you give up your cosy new home here to return to those appalling conditions amongst your friends you are absolutely mad.'

'But this isn't a home,' Badger pointed out. 'I'm merely being tended while I'm hurt. Once I'm on my feet again, whether I wish it or not, I shall be removed to the Park.'

Ginger Cat shrugged. 'You've seen how I behave and remarked on it,' he said. 'I'm quite sure a little feigned affection from you for your human benefactor would be very well received. That seems to be the only reward he expects for doing almost everything for us.'

'No, no,' Badger shook his head, smiling. 'I haven't the necessary technique. It's inbred in you cats to make yourself ingratiating. It's natural to you.'

'Well, I'm sure it wasn't always so,' Ginger Cat responded. 'It must have begun for a definite purpose. Why don't you decide to become the first domesticated badger?'

'No, it wouldn't be appropriate,' Badger replied. 'I'm too old to change my ways now. And, besides, I'm used to living underground, and tunnelling, and sleeping on beds of leaves and grass and moss and so on – not curled up in a basket like a lap dog.'

'Well, at least stay until the warmer weather,' Ginger Cat wheedled. He had become genuinely fond of Badger and was sincere in wishing him to be comfortable.

'Well, well,' nodded Badger, 'we'll see. But I hope you won't forget all about me if I do go. For my part, I can never repay your kindness in making that journey. And then you come back hurt! It's most distressing.'

'You may rest assured I should keep in touch,' declared Ginger Cat. 'But, tell me, is your home any better appointed than Fox's?'

'Oh yes,' Badger laughed. 'He and Vixen live very simply. But you went underground! I'm most impressed.' He chuckled as he thought of it.

Ginger Cat almost laughed. 'It's a topsy-turvy world,' he said. 'We'll have you curled up in front of the fire next.'

The days passed and Badger's leg grew stronger. He was able to limp a little way around the kitchen to begin with, and then the cat introduced him to the main room of the cottage and he practised walking backwards and forwards from one room to the other. After about a fortnight in the Warden's home Badger had become quite accustomed to his new life. Well-fed and well cared for, he looked sleeker and fitter than at any time since leaving Farthing Wood. He looked a new animal, and he began to dread the appearance of his longsuffering friends when he should return to them. He knew they would look haggard by comparison, and he felt they might look at him accusingly, envying his new-found health.

But he had to acknowledge that that was not all he was dubious about. There had been an element of truth in Ginger Cat's words. Perhaps he *had* grown too used to comfort now. He certainly did not relish the prospect of scraping a living again in the freezing desolation of the Park. He was worse equipped to do so now than before his accident. To adjust now to searching once more for his food, to learn again to live on less than he needed to eat and to adapt to those wicked temperatures from which there was no relief, was indeed a daunting thought.

He felt sure that the Warden would not simply turf him out into the cold once he was walking normally again, if there were still no sign of improvement in the weather. The change would be too sudden. So the temptation to stay on where he was, was constantly with him. Yet he knew he would feel guilty if he did stay unnecessarily long. How could he rest content in such luxury while all the time his old companions continued to suffer the worst sort of discomfort? But what if they were to join *him*? Was it possible?

Day after day the same thoughts went through his mind until the time finally arrived when he knew that his injured leg was completely well again. The strapping and bandages had been removed a week before, at the same time as those on Ginger Cat's back. Now he could shuffle around quite normally once more at his old pace. Now he must decide what he should do.

When he next saw Ginger Cat he told him he was completely recovered. The cat looked at him long and straight. 'Well?' he asked at length. 'What are your plans?'

Badger mentioned his idea of his friends joining them under the care of the Warden. 'Would the man take them in? Would he be able to, would he want to?' he kept asking.

'I don't know,' replied Ginger Cat. 'I don't know if he would have room for all. I *am* sure he would do his best for the animals who seemed most in need of help. But will they wish to come here?'

'Now it's my turn to say I don't know,' Badger confessed. 'But I could try persuading them.'

'You would have to exclude the birds,' Ginger Cat said pointedly.

Badger knew what was in his mind. 'I had already ruled them out,' he agreed.

'When will you leave?' the cat asked next.

'As soon as the man lets me go.'

'That will be when you make it apparent you are eager to return to the Park. You'd better make it obvious you want to follow him when he next goes outside.'

The opportunity eventually arose and, the Warden showing willingness, Badger stood once more on the borders of the Park, sniffing the air in all directions. The snow still lay packed on the ground, and the icy temperature cut at his pampered body like a knife. He half turned back, looking towards the open cottage door that symbolized the way through to comfort. Ginger Cat was sitting on the threshold. He stood up. 'I'll come with you part of the way,' he offered.

'Gladly,' replied Badger.

The Warden watched the two animals that had become fast friends walk slowly off. His job was done.

They skirted the Edible Frogs' pond and Badger remembered Toad and Adder were sleeping nearby, deep down in a bankside away from the weather. All they would know of the winter would be from the stories they would hear from their friends.

'I wonder how *they've* been?' Badger muttered to himself. Fox and Vixen, Mole, Weasel, Tawny Owl . . . his friends seemed as strangers. He had become more familiar of late with a human's pet than with his companions of old.

A little way further on Ginger Cat stopped. 'I'll turn back now,' he said. 'Go carefully. And my best wishes to Mole and the foxes.'

'Farewell,' said Badger. 'Your company has been delightful. I know we shall meet again.'

'Until then,' responded the cat.

Badger watched his sinewy form retrace its steps through the snow. The sky was leaden above the Park; the air still and threatening. A snowstorm was imminent. He must reach his set as quickly as possible. There would be plenty of time to see his friends tomorrow.

——9——

Old Friends, New Friends

The reticence Badger was feeling for re-adopting his old
life and friends he himself would never had admitted –
even if he had been conscious of it. But those same old
friends noticed the change in him at once from *their*
unchanged world. Mole, who had been haunting Badger's set regularly ever since the animals had heard of his
whereabouts, entered the set through his connecting tunnel. At first he thought a strange badger had comman-
deered the place, his old friend looked – and smelt – so
different.

'Oh! hallo, Mole,' Badger greeted him unenthusiast-
ically, as his little friend stood hesitantly. 'Yes, it *is* me.'

'I've been keeping a look-out for your return for days,'
Mole said. 'We've missed you so much. But it *was* kind

of the Warden's cat to come all this way to put our minds at rest. I'm only sorry about the accident that occurred.'

'He certainly deserved a better reception,' Badger remarked rather coldly, to Mole's consternation. 'He only made the journey at all because I forced him into it, really. However, he asked to be remembered to you.'

'Thank you,' said Mole in a small voice. He did not like this new, gruff individual.

There was a silence for some moments. Badger did not seem at all disposed to carry on a conversation, and Mole was becoming timid.

'You – you look d-different,' he stammered. 'Sort of fatter.'

'I probably am,' Badger agreed shortly. 'I was fed well.'

'I'm g-glad,' Mole whispered. 'I'll go and tell Fox you're here,' he added, and moved away in a confused way.

'Don't bother yourself,' said Badger. 'I suppose I ought to go. Er – I'll see you later, Mole.'

The crestfallen Mole watched his friend disappear up the exit tunnel without so much as a backward glance.

Outside it was dark and a fresh fall of snow had covered the Park. Badger's face became grim and he gritted his teeth. The contrast between the stark world of the wild and the comfort of human habitation was heightened still further in his mind. On his way to Fox's earth he was spied by Tawny Owl, who skimmed down from an oak branch.

'Welcome back, old friend,' the bird said, eyeing Badger openly. 'You seem to have prospered during your spell under the Warden's roof. You've got plump – and soft.'

Badger shrugged. 'It was a welcome relief from staring starvation in the face,' he said.

'I can see that,' Tawny Owl responded sarcastically. 'It must make it all the more difficult to adjust back again.'

'Why do I have to?' Badger asked bluntly.

Tawny Owl feigned ignorance. 'What *do* you mean, Badger?'

'Come along with me to see Fox,' Badger told him, 'and I'll put you both in the picture.'

'Hm,' Tawny Owl muttered. 'This should prove to be a most interesting meeting.'

Fox's earth was deserted when they arrived, and Badger said he would wait for Fox and Vixen's return. So he made himself as comfortable as he could underground while Tawny Owl perched in a nearby holly tree. He found his thoughts straying back to that warm kitchen in the Lodge. He imagined his friend Ginger Cat curled up in his basket, secure in the knowledge that he could depend on being fed without even stirring out of doors, and quite oblivious of the icy clutch of Winter that still held imprisoned every inhabitant of the Park.

Yes, the ways of the Wild could be dreadfully hard, and the arrival of Fox and Vixen at that juncture gave an emphasis to Badger's conclusion. Their emaciated frames, rimed with frost from the freezing air, slunk into the den and slumped, exhausted, on the hard ground. Badger, shocked beyond his expectation, was speechless. Presently the pair of foxes revived sufficiently to greet him. Of the two, Fox seemed thinnest and the most spent, which suggested that the best of the pickings of their nightly forays were going to Vixen. That would be Fox's way, Badger knew.

But Fox had lost none of his shrewdness. There was a look in his eyes that seemed to penetrate to Badger's most secret thoughts. His words, too, went straight to the heart of the matter. 'Well, are you back with us now for good?' he asked.

The question made Badger feel ashamed – ashamed of his well-fed appearance, his spotless coat. He felt as if he had betrayed Fox in a way, even if only in his thoughts. He did not know how to answer.

'The other way of life seems to agree with you,' Fox continued in a parallel of Tawny Owl's remark.

'Well, Fox, you know, I *was* injured,' Badger said defensively, almost apologetically.

'Of course you were,' Fox said. 'I'm sorry. How is your leg? Are you fully recovered?'

'Absolutely, thank you,' Badger replied a little more brightly. 'But, my dear Fox – and Vixen – you look as if you are suffering dreadfully.'

'Things are very, very hard,' Fox admitted, shaking his head slowly from side to side. 'Each day is harder. Only two of the voles are still alive, and scarcely more of the fieldmice. Rabbit and his friends have lost four of their number, too. And the squirrels find it almost impossible to dig through this never-ending snow to reach their buried nuts and berries so, they too, are dwindling. I really don't know what's to become of us all. We shall *all* die, Badger, if this weather doesn't lift soon, I'm sure of it.'

Badger felt that now was the time to play his trump card. 'There *is* an answer,' he said quietly.

'Well, let's have it. We're at our wits' end.'

'You don't *have* to live in the Park,' Badger explained. 'Come back with me to the Warden's cottage.'

Fox and Vixen looked at him in amazement.

'You can't mean it, Badger?' Vixen spoke for the first time.

'Of course I mean it,' Badger insisted. 'Why are you looking at me in that way? I was looked after, fed properly, and restored to health – and now I'm fitter than I've been for ages.'

'But you were injured and found by the Warden,' Fox repeated to himself uncomprehendingly. 'The welfare of the creatures of the Park is his concern so, naturally, he nursed you until you were better.'

'Exactly!' cried Badger. 'You've said it yourself. So isn't *your* welfare, and the rabbits' welfare, and the voles' welfare, and everyone else's welfare also of interest to him?'

At this point Tawny Owl poked his head down the hole. He felt he was missing an interesting discussion and wanted to hear. Fox's voice was audible next.

'Are you suggesting, then,' he was saying in an incredulous tone, 'that all of us band together and follow you to the Warden's Lodge?'

'Yes, I am.'

'And then what would we do? All rush inside the next time he appears at the door?'

'I don't know exactly what plan we could make,' Badger allowed. 'But we could work something out. Ginger Cat might help us think of something. Don't you see, Fox, your worries about food would be over? You would have no need even to think about it. It would be provided for you automatically.'

Tawny Owl stepped into the den. He could not resist participating any longer. 'I think our friend Badger has spent a little too much time amongst domestic creatures like cats,' he said drily. 'He's beginning to talk like one of them.'

'I can't believe it's our Badger talking,' Vixen said. 'Whatever has happened to him?'

'Oh, why can't you understand?' Badger wailed. 'I'm thinking of your good. Look at you – you're half-starved. A few more weeks and there may not be any trace left of the animals of Farthing Wood. Is that what you want?'

'Badger, your wits have become softened by your dependence on human aid,' Tawny Owl told him. 'I believe you've forgotten how to think for yourself. How could all the creatures from Farthing Wood be accommodated in your precious Warden's house? Squirrels, rabbits, hares, foxes . . . he isn't running a zoo.'

'He would find a way, I'm sure,' Badger replied vaguely. 'He would *have* to, once he sees the pitiful state of you all. It's his job, isn't it?'

'You're not making sense, Badger. You seem to have forgotten all the *original* inhabitants of White Deer Park,' Fox reminded him. 'We're just a small part of the fauna here. What if they all decided to come too?'

'The whole idea is the most absurd thing I've ever heard,' Tawny Owl said bluntly. 'I'm sorry you were injured, Badger, but I'm more sorry you were ever taken into captivity. It seems to have turned your brain.'

'I didn't say anything about *you* coming,' Badger snapped irritably. 'You and Kestrel wouldn't be welcome. Ginger Cat will vouch for that.'

Fox and Tawny Owl exchanged glances. It really did seem as if Badger had undergone a change of character. Vixen tried to smooth things over. 'You'll feel differently when you've got used to your old life again, Badger,' she said soothingly. 'I can see you're finding it difficult to pick up the threads again, and that's understandable. We'll win through yet, if we all pull together. Think what you Farthing Wood animals have survived before. If any creatures can see it through, you can.'

Badger was furious at the rejection of his idea. He rounded on his old friends angrily. 'You don't understand,' he fumed. 'I don't want my old life anymore. I didn't have to come back, but I did – for you. If you won't join me, I'll go back alone.'

'Back to your new friend the cat, no doubt,' Tawny Owl said. 'He's really got to work on you, hasn't he?'

'The Warden is my friend, too,' Badger barked.

'Well, it's quite obviously a clear case of preference,' Tawny Owl told him. 'You must go where your inclinations direct you.'

'Sssh, Owl,' Fox warned him. 'This is getting out of hand.' He turned to Badger. 'My dear friend, you can't mean what you say. We've been inseparable. You can't turn your back on us now?'

'*You* turned your back on *me*,' Badger insisted with a glare. 'My suggestion was made in good faith. I can't force you to come. It's your choice. As far as I'm concerned, *I* have no intention of starving to death. If you all want to die together, I must leave you to it.' With that he turned and left the earth.

His three prior companions were stunned. None of them ventured a word. Fox went to the exit and peered out at the retreating figure. He wanted to call out, to bring him back, but he could think of nothing more to say. A cold shiver ran along his body. It had begun to snow again.

—10—

A Question of Loyalties

In the morning Mole arrived at the foxes' earth in a very piteous state. He had remained in the set where Badger had left him, hoping to see him again. But after the talk with Fox, Vixen and Tawny Owl, Badger had returned to his set in an unpleasant mood and had been very unkind to Mole.

'He told me I was a confounded nuisance and a sni-veller, and that I must leave him in peace or suffer the consequences,' he sobbed to Fox.

Vixen intervened. 'You must accept that Badger's simply not himself at the moment, Mole,' she counselled. 'None of us understands exactly what's happened. But if he's still our Badger, sooner or later his real feelings will show through. I know they will.'

'Oh, do you think so, Vixen?' Mole wept. 'Oh, I hope so, I hope so . . . .'

'Has Badger gone back?' Fox asked Mole.

'Gone back where?' queried Mole who, of course, was unaware of the scene of the previous night.

Fox was obliged to explain. 'He wants to go back to the Warden. He can't face his old life any more.' He described the meeting with Badger in his earth.

'What ever can we do?' Mole shrilled. 'We can't just let him go.'

'Perhaps it's the best thing for us to do, at present,' Vixen said. 'Then he can get this new way of life out of his system. If I know Badger, very soon he will begin to feel very guilty indeed, and then he'll come to his senses.'

'I think we should inform everyone of this business,' said Fox, 'and the best way to do it is for us all to meet – everyone – in Badger's empty set. I'll get Tawny Owl and Kestrel to round all the animals up. It's too cold to meet in the Hollow.'

'When do we meet?' Mole wanted to know.

'This very day,' said Fox. 'You go·to the set now, Mole. I'll contact Kestrel. Vixen, will you speak to Owl? There must be no delay.'

While preparations were being made, Badger was well on his way across the Park to his destination. Already a slight sense of shame hung over him as he turned his back on the Farthing Wood animals' home area. But he also felt resentment of his treatment by Fox and Tawny Owl, and looked forward to Ginger Cat's com- miserations.

He had not bothered to hunt for any food, because he knew the Warden could be relied on to look after his stomach. He saw Kestrel flying over the Park and hoped he would not notice him. In the case of Kestrel this was a vain hope, for the hawk did not miss much that moved on the ground. Badger watched him swoop down.

'Well, what do you want?' Badger grunted ungraciously. 'I suppose you've come to insult me as well?'

'Not at all, not at all,' Kestrel declared indignantly. 'Fox has sent me to round up all our friends. I'm still looking for Weasel.'

'What for? A meeting?' Badger asked uninterestedly.

'Yes. No need to guess what it's about.'

'Me, I suppose? Well, I'm not surprised. But listen, Kestrel, tell Fox from me not to interfere. I can live where I choose. You must know as well as I do *they'll* all be dead inside a month the way things are going.'

'Not if I can help it,' Kestrel replied quickly. 'I hunt outside the Park every day and bring back what I can for them. And I know Whistler does too. Of course, at night Tawny Owl does what he can. *We* haven't forgotten the Oath.'

Badger looked away, a little shamefaced, at this pointed rejoinder. But he would not turn back. 'I wish you all well,' he said, 'but when the solution to your problems was offered it was refused. *I* can't be blamed.'

Kestrel directed one of his piercing glares at Badger and flew away resignedly. But later that day, he and Badger were due to meet again in very different circumstances.

Ginger Cat was sitting by the Warden's fence, blinking dozily in a few brief moments of sunlight that had managed to penetrate the clouds. Badger called him as he saw him. He expected the cat to come towards him, but he did not move. He called again. 'Hallo – it's me – Badger!'

Ginger Cat looked at him enigmatically. 'So I see,' he said coolly.

Badger stopped in his tracks, completely taken aback by this most unexpected lack of enthusiasm. 'Whatever's the matter?' he asked. 'I thought you would be pleased to see me.'

'I'm surprised to see you again at all so soon,' murmured Ginger Cat, yawning widely.

'But I've come back,' Badger explained. 'You know – for good.'

The cat looked at him long and steadily. 'What do you mean – for good?'

'I've made my decision, and I'm going to live with you.'

'What *are* you talking about? You live underground, you told me.'

'No, no, not any more. I'm finished with all that. I don't want that sort of existence. I've left my old friends because they wouldn't come with me.'

'Of course they wouldn't,' Ginger Cat said. 'I never expected them to. I thought all those pie-in-the-sky ideas of yours would be forgotten once you'd got back to your real home.'

These last words really jarred on Badger's sensibility. 'But I have a new home now . . . or I thought I had,' he faltered. 'Don't you remember, we talked about the Warden looking after Fox and Mole and everyone?'

'Indeed I do,' the cat answered. 'But I would have been astonished in the extreme if your wild friends chose of their own accord to leave their homes. Would *you* have come here if you hadn't been brought?'

'Er – no, I suppose not,' Badger admitted. 'But that doesn't matter. *I've* chosen this way of life.'

'How convenient for you,' Ginger Cat observed bitingly.

'*Aren't* you pleased to see me?' the bewildered Badger cried. 'I thought we were friends.'

'Oh yes,' the cat shrugged. 'But we were forced into each other's company, after all. One makes the most of a situation.'

'Well – er – aren't you going to invite me in?' Badger asked hesitantly.

'You're too bulky to go through my cat flap,' Ginger Cat pointed out. 'You'll have to wait for the man to find you. But I don't think you'll get the reaction you want from him. He looked after you until you were well again and, in his view, you should now be living in your natural state.'

'We'll see about that,' Badger answered hotly, but he was beginning to feel he had made a fool of himself. He went and sat by the front door and, as luck would have it, the Warden appeared soon after. A cry of amazement escaped him as he saw his old charge looking hopefully up at him. He bent down, examined the healed leg, patted Badger, and looked at him in a puzzled way for a moment. Then he seemed to think of something and turned back inside. Badger immediately tried to follow him, but the Warden kindly, but firmly, pushed him back and shut the door. Badger was heart-broken.

'You see,' Ginger Cat's soft voice purred at him. 'He doesn't want you any more. Oh, he'll probably bring you a bowl of·food in a minute or two. He imagines you've come for that. But your home is not his cottage any more.'

The realization of his stupidity flashed into Badger's mind in a blinding flood of light. What a miscalculation he had made! *He* was not a domestic animal. How could he have thought he understood human ways? Both the cat and the human were on another plane of existence, in a world he could never comprehend. He had humiliated himself, and in the process he had lost the respect of the cat and, what was worse – far worse! – spurned his real friends.

The bowl of food predicted by Ginger Cat was brought
out, and a dish of warm milk with it. More to save the
Warden a disappointment than because of any feeling
of appetite, Badger ate and drank. Then, with a wry
look at the cat, he turned back without a further word
– back to his waiting set.

A short distance from the cottage he looked behind
him. The Warden was not to be seen, but Ginger Cat
was still sitting, watching his retreat. Badger heard a
flutter of wings above and Kestrel alighted beside him.

'Keep going, Badger,' he told him. 'You're going in
the right direction this time.'

Badger knew the hawk had guessed what had happened and smiled sadly at him. 'Yes, Kestrel,' he whispered, 'I have indeed been a foolish creature.'

Behind them, unknown to them, Ginger Cat had spotted his enemy. Now, belly flat to the icy ground, he was
creeping stealthily forward on his noiseless feet. With a
tremendous spurt, he leapt on the unsuspecting hawk,
teeth and claws as sharp as razors finding their mark.
But Kestrel was no sparrow or blackbird. He was a
hunter, a killer himself, and his powerful wings flailed,
beating against his assailant, while his lethal beak darted
in all directions in an attempt to strike.

Badger looked round in horror. The bird, taken unawares, was struggling desperately against the attack.
Badger was hopelessly torn between his affection for the
cat, albeit recently somewhat battered, and his loyalty
to an old friend. He could see Kestrel's struggles weak-
ening and, in a trice, it was as if a veil had been lifted
from his eyes. The Oath!

Badger rushed into the fray. Bringing all his considerable weight and power into the attack he fell on Ginger
Cat, lunging with bared teeth at his throat. The cat let

out a scream and spat at him in fury. But the grip was loosened and Kestrel was able to free himself, flying up into the air instantly.

Now the fight was left to the two animals, and soon Badger's superior strength began to tell. He knew the cat was at his mercy and that one snap of his jaws could kill him. His instinct told him to do it, but he held back. Although he had made the cat party to the Oath, the animal had forfeited his right to protection by attacking another of its adherents. But Badger recalled the good turn Ginger Cat had done him and now he must repay it. He stepped away, his sides heaving, and, like an arrow, the cat sped away, back to safety.

The significance of Badger's rescue was not lost on Kestrel. 'Welcome back to the fold,' he screeched from the air.

'It's quite safe for you now,' Badger called back. 'Come down and let me see if you're injured.'

Kestrel did so and Badger noticed the marks of the cat's claws. He began to lick at his friend's body.

'Most obliged,' said the hawk. 'Thanks for your help. For just a moment I wondered if you were going to.'

'I know,' said Badger. 'Oh, what a supreme idiot I've been. I've entered unknown waters and found myself out of my depth. It's so absurd. I'd rather die *with* you all than live without you.'

'We *won't* die,' Kestrel insisted. 'It's going to be tough, but we are tough creatures.'

'They're not deep scratches,' Badger was saying. 'They'll soon heal.'

'Er – Badger – why did you let the cat go?'

Badger explained.

'I thought as much. That means I still have him after my blood.'

'Just stay in the air in this vicinity,' Badger told him. 'But the cat will know why I didn't kill him and that my debt is repaid. He has a fair nature. I don't think he will be out for revenge any more.'

'I hope you're right,' said Kestrel. 'Well, if you hurry, you will surprise the rest of them holding forth about you in your set.'

'I'll see you there,' Badger replied.

—11—

An Expedition

The meeting of the animals of Farthing Wood to discuss
Badger's strange behaviour and what should be done
about it had not long begun when Kestrel arrived. He
saw Whistler standing at the entrance to the set.

'Are you on guard?' he asked the heron.

'No. My legs are too long for me to go in there.' He
pointed with his long bill to the entrance tunnel.

'In that case,' said Kestrel, 'you'll be the first to know
that Badger is himself again.' He went on to describe
his rescue from Ginger Cat.

'That *will* delight everyone,' Whistler said. 'You go in
and tell them before Tawny Owl runs him down too
much.' He winked elaborately.

Kestrel walked into the set. As he joined the meeting,

it was evident that Tawny Owl was replying to a suggestion from someone that they should bring Badger back by force.

'What for?' he hooted. 'Leave him to his own devices. He turned his back on us. Why should we bother any longer?'

'You're beginning to talk just like Adder,' said Mole. 'It would be wrong of us to desert him.'

'That's just what he's done to us,' snorted Owl.

'Two wrongs don't make a right,' Mole replied, rather weakly.

'You can all save your breath,' Kestrel informed them. 'Badger's on his way back.'

They looked at him dumbfounded. Then he explained again about Badger's change of heart and his rescue.

'You see, Mole,' Vixen said kindly, 'I knew his real character would win through.'

'Oh, *I* never lost faith in him,' Mole declared proudly, while Tawny Owl looked rather abashed. 'Dear Badger! So he came to help you, Kestrel?'

'He saved my life,' Kestrel said honestly. 'No question about it.'

'I'm very happy,' said Fox. 'I feel that this heralds an improvement in our affairs. Well, Kestrel, should we stay for him?'

'Oh yes!' answered Kestrel emphatically. 'Now we're all together. He's depending on seeing us.'

'So be it,' said Fox and the animals settled down to wait patiently.

Late in the afternoon Badger greeted Whistler outside his home. He paused at the set entrance nervously, unsure of his other friends' reception.

'Oh, you're a hero again,' Whistler reassured him. 'Kestrel has told them all about it.'

Badger smiled and, taking a deep breath, went to meet his fate.

He need not have worried. Most of the animals had not seen him since his accident and received him like a long-lost friend. Mole was in raptures, Fox and Vixen relieved, and even Tawny Owl gave him a gruff, 'Glad to see you, Badger.'

A tacit understanding seemed to exist on both sides not to mention Badger's recent aberration, and all was forgotten. But Badger gloomily noticed the depletion in numbers of the little band that had set out the previous spring to look for their new home. Leaving aside the absence of the hibernating hedgehogs, Toad and Adder, there were gaps in the ranks of the squirrels and the rabbits, while Vole was accompanied only by his own mate and Fieldmouse by just two others of his family. Of the rest, lean bodies and hungry eyes told their tale. Only Mole, apart from himself, seemed unchanged.

Fox followed Badger's gaze. 'The winter has not left us unscathed,' he summarised.

'No.' Badger shook his head sadly. 'But perhaps we should turn the meeting towards a more positive course. Unscathed we are not, but we should now plan how we can emerge from the season undefeated.'

'For many of us that call is too late,' Vole said bitterly.

'Then let us resolve to lose no more,' Badger responded.

'There's not a lot that can be done,' Fox said with untypical pessimism. The winter had taken its toll of spirit, too.

'Fox has done everything possible for him to do,' Hare added loyally. 'But none of us can control the weather conditions. When the entire Park lies buried under two feet of snow, it needs more than animal ingenuity to cope with the situation.'

'Let me tell you,' said Badger quietly, 'I think we really do need help from another source.'

'Are you thinking again along the same lines we all think you are thinking?' asked Weasel cryptically.

'No.' Badger replied at once. 'Not the Warden. But I *am* thinking about human help.' He looked round at his companions whose faces had, for the most part, dropped.

'Only it would be help,' he intoned slowly to emphasize his words, 'that the humans wouldn't know they were giving.'

'Whatever can you mean, Badger?' Rabbit asked.

'Well, listen. Now it's well-known that humans waste as much of their food as they eat. Why, then, shouldn't we make use of what they don't want?'

'I could never bring myself to resort to scavenging,' Tawny Owl said, rustling his wings importantly.

'Don't be pompous, Owl,' Badger said. 'When the other choice is starvation you should be ready to resort to anything.'

'Badger's quite right,' agreed Fox. 'We must consider any plan that will keep us alive. Please explain further, Badger.'

'You'll remember that Toad told us the story of his travels. Well, on the other side of the Park, not far from the boundary fence, there are human habitations and gardens. It was from one of those very gardens that he actually began his long journey back to Farthing Wood. And somewhere in those gardens, you can count on it, we will come across some of those tall things they put their unwanted food in.'

'You've certainly hit on something,' Fox conceded. 'But it will be a great way, and few of us are now strong enough to travel great distances. For the smaller animals it is completely out of the question.'

'I'll go,' said Badger. 'I'm the fittest of all at present. And the birds can go with me. Then they can carry back anything of use I find. Of course, if anyone else feels able to join me, I'd be delighted.'

'I shall accompany you, naturally,' said Fox.

Badger looked at his wasted form with misgiving. He knew Fox felt that in any such venture it was his duty to attend. 'Well, Fox, you know,' Badger said awkwardly, 'are you sure that – '

'That I'm strong enough?' Fox anticipated him. 'Of course I am. I should never forgive myself if I stayed behind.'

'There is never any doubt about your being brave enough anyway,' Vixen said lovingly and nuzzled him.

So it was arranged that Fox, Badger, Tawny Owl, Kestrel and Whistler would form the expedition. It would be essential to travel in the dark, so they decided they must go at the very first opportunity, which was that very night.

'How I wish Toad was around to direct us,' Fox said.

'Couldn't we dig him up?' Mole suggested. 'I bet I could reach him.'

Badger laughed. 'Impossible, I'm afraid, Mole,' he told him. 'You'd get no sense out of him. He's in his winter sleep and nothing will wake him up except a rise in temperature. In fact, to expose him suddenly to these temperatures would probably kill him.'

'Oh dear, I hadn't thought of that,' said Mole.

'I remember he mentioned a ditch on the other side of the fence,' Fox mused. 'If we can find that, and then that first road he travelled down from his captor's garden, we should make it all right.'

'Leave it to me,' offered Tawny Owl. 'I'll find you your ditch – and the road.'

'How long will it take you to cross the Park?' asked Fieldmouse. 'It must be miles.'

'It would be no problem at all if it weren't for the fact that we are so hampered by snow,' said Fox. 'But we must reach the houses while it's still dark. It should be dusk now. I suggest we start straight away.'

The others agreed and, without further ado, Fox and Badger with Tawny Owl and Kestrel, made their way out of the chamber to assorted cries of 'Good luck!' Outside the set they acquainted Whistler with their idea, and he was delighted to be of use.

Fox and Badger went, shoulder to shoulder, across the snowy waste in the direction of the Reserve's far fence. Kestrel and Whistler fluttered slowly in the unaccustomed darkness for short distances while they waited for the two animals to catch them up. Tawny Owl the night bird flew on ahead on silent wings to locate the ditch that was their marker.

'What do you expect to find?' Fox asked Badger.

Badger found it strange to be in the role of leader, which at present he clearly was. 'Oh, I don't know. Meat and vegetable scraps – there could be all sorts of things,' he answered vaguely. Then he wished he had not spoken, for he saw the eager look in the famished Fox's eyes and his mouth begin to water.

'It really has hit you hard, hasn't it, old friend?' he whispered to him. For a time Fox did not answer, and Badger wondered if he had heard. Then Fox spoke.

'It's been the hardest trial I've ever faced,' he said wearily. 'Harder than anything we faced on our journey here, including the Hunt.'

'It is so sad that, after the triumph of overcoming

every hazard en route to reach our new home, so many of our friends have perished before they really had a chance to enjoy their new life.'

'It *is* sad,' agreed Fox, 'but there is no doubt that old age has played its part. The life span of a mouse is very short.'

'But the rabbits? The squirrels?'

'I know, I know. It's not the start to our new life I had envisaged,' Fox muttered. 'But then, how many would have survived staying behind in Farthing Wood? If we get through the rest of the winter without losing any more of our numbers, there will be a breeding stock, at any rate, of all the animals to ensure a permanent representation of the Farthing Wood party in the Park.'

'Except in one or two cases,' Badger said, smiling sadly.

'I'm sorry, Badger,' Fox said awkwardly. 'I really put my foot in it. I wasn't thinking.'

'Don't worry. I know what you meant. And it seems our priority must be to save Vole and Fieldmouse at all costs.'

'That is so,' said Fox. 'And that's where the difficulty lies. The White Deer herd have, on occasion, brought some of their hay for our vegetarians to eat. The problem is, the mice don't really like stalks. It's the seeds they want. And berries and insects. Of course, they're virtually unobtainable.'

'Well,' said Badger, 'perhaps we'll find something for them.'

When they next caught up with the birds, Tawny Owl was waiting as well. He told them he had found the ditch and the road down which they must go.

'Did you find the houses, too?' asked Badger.

'Er – yes,' he replied uncertainly.

'What's wrong?' asked Fox.

'Well, we shall all have to be cautious,' he explained. 'It seems there are others around on the same errand.'

—12—
A Raid

'Foxes?'

'Yes, a pair.'

'Where?'

'Along the road.'

'Well, we aren't the only creatures in the Park who are suffering. We sometimes tend to forget that.'

'How do we know they're from the Park?' Kestrel mentioned.

'True,' admitted Fox. 'But it's most likely.'

Before they reached the boundary of the Park, he asked to have a brief rest. Badger's concerned expression was unconcealed. 'I'll be all right,' Fox assured them all. 'I've lost a little of my strength, I'm afraid.'

Eventually they reached the fence and found a spot

where previous animals had scooped away the ground underneath in order to come and go as they pleased. Badger and Fox scrambled underneath and crossed the ditch. Tawny Owl led them to the road.

The surface was like glass where motor traffic had beaten down the falls of snow into a tight mass. But it was quiet now and empty. The animals padded slowly along it until the first of the human dwellings was reached.

'Wait here,' said Tawny Owl. 'I'll investigate.' Badger and Fox hid themselves in the darkest spot against the garden wall, while Whistler and Kestrel perched high up on a chimney pot.

'This one's no good,' Tawny Owl later informed them. 'The wall is too high for you and so are the gates.' They moved on to the next house to find the same problem. Fox looked at Badger significantly.

'Owl!' Badger called in a low voice. 'See if you can find the other foxes again. Perhaps they know something we don't.'

Tawny Owl returned with astonishing news. He had located the strange foxes in the grounds of a large house some distance away from the others. They had simply jumped the comparatively low fence and were nosing around a number of sheds and hutches. From sounds he had heard, Owl had discovered that one of these was a chicken coop, and this was obviously the foxes' target.

'Chickens!' exclaimed Fox.

'The same,' said Tawny Owl.

'But the racket! They'll wake the entire neighbourhood.' Despite his protestations, Fox was having the utmost difficulty in preventing himself from drooling. The thought of food had an overwhelming effect on him.

'There might be enough for all of us,' Badger hinted.

'What? You can't mean it, Badger. You wouldn't condone such – ' Fox broke off. He knew he was blustering; playing a part – and so did Badger. For it had been the first thought to cross his mind, too. After all, in straitened circumstances, one has to consider any opening.

'I wonder how they get them out?' Badger muttered.

'Come and see,' Tawny Owl said.

They followed him further along the road, the other birds accompanying. Owl perched on the fence he had told them about.

'There's certainly a strong scent of fox,' said Badger.

'And also of chickens,' Fox whispered.

'Carefully now,' Tawny Owl warned the two animals as he, Kestrel and Whistler fluttered into the grounds.

Fox and Badger looked at the fence. 'Can you jump it?' Badger asked.

'If I were fully fit – nothing easier. But a lot of my stamina's gone. However, I'll have a jolly good try. What about you?'

'*I'm* no jumper,' answered Badger. 'You go ahead, and I'll scout round the outside of the fence and see if there's another way in. I'll join you inside.'

He watched Fox backing away from the fence in order to give himself a good run up to it. Then he saw him leap upwards, just scraping the fence-top, before he landed the other side. Badger was now alone on the road side of the fence. He shuffled along its length, looking for a suitable opening. But there seemed to be no way through. There was a gate halfway along one side which, of course, was closed. He paused, wondering whether he should call out. Just then there broke out the most appalling din. There was a loud crash, immediately followed by the most frenzied squawks and a clattering of wings. Badger correctly surmised that one of the foxes was attempting to break in to the coop. The noise grew absolutely deafening, and then he heard a barking and human shouts.

Cowering against the fence, not knowing if he should stay or run, Badger saw two foxes leap the fence into the road, a hen dangling from each of their pairs of jaws. Then they were off, racing down the road as fast as their burdens would allow them. Suddenly he heard three or four gunshots in quick succession and a very scared third fox – his own friend – leapt the fence almost on top of him.

'Quick!' Fox shouted hoarsely. 'This way!' And he raced away in the opposite direction to that taken by the two raiders. Badger sloped after him as fast as he could go – and in the nick of time. Out of the gate in the fence came a huge, ferocious and furious dog followed by two men – one young, one elderly – each with shotguns. The dog instantly set off after the foxes carrying the chickens. These animals were badly hampered by their heavy loads and the dog gained on them quickly. But the two men were taking aim with their guns. One called the dog, which checked its headlong rush, and then two more shots rang out. The two foxes dropped like stones and rolled over in the snow, the maimed chickens flapping helplessly in the gutter.

The men went to examine the fox carcasses, and seemed satisfied with their work. The younger one put the injured chickens out of their misery, and picked them up by their feet. The dog pranced around him, tongue lolling and tail wagging.

From their hiding-place under a parked car, Badger and Fox watched the men and their dog trudge back to the garden, their hearts beating wildly. Only when the gate in the fence had once again been fastened after them did they dare to move.

'Phew!' gasped Fox who really had felt in fear of his life. 'That was a little *too* close for my liking.'

'Yes,' Badger agreed. 'It's certainly a good thing we hadn't reached that garden first.'

'But I don't know if I should have tried what those poor devils did anyway,' Fox confessed. 'I've never been one for taking such prey.'

'Maybe they were desperate like us,' Badger suggested pointedly.'

Fox ignored him. 'Where are the birds?' he asked.

Tawny Owl was the first to find them. 'So much for your ideas of invading gardens,' he said to Badger crossly. 'Could have had us all killed.'

'*You* were the one to tell us about the chickens,' said Badger. 'We still haven't investigated my suggestion.'

'I don't think I could go back in there again,' Fox said. 'Is the coast clear now, Owl?'

'No,' he replied. 'Those foxes turned the coop over and the stupid hens are running all over the place. The men will have their work cut out collecting them together again.'

'Give them time,' said Badger. 'After coming all this way we can't go back with nothing.'

'Will you keep us informed please, Owl?' Fox asked. 'Badger and I will wait here.'

'Can't see the point,' muttered Tawny Owl. 'Badger can't get into the garden anyway.'

Badger looked at Fox. 'This garden is our only chance,' he said. 'It's the only one with a fence. Are you sure you couldn't make just one more jump?'

Fox wavered. It seemed as if he was fated always to be the one on whom everyone else depended.

'You know I would gladly go if I could get in,' Badger added. 'But I've looked all round for a hole and there's just nothing.'

Fox smiled a little smile of resignation. 'It looks as if I have no choice really, doesn't it?' he said.

So Tawny Owl flew back to watch the proceedings, and Fox and Badger huddled together under the car again to wait. Some time passed and they heard nothing. Badger was restless. 'I think I'll just wander a little further along this road just in case there's anything of interest,' he told his companion.

He had not been gone long when Fox heard a familiar whistle in the air, and then saw the long thin legs of Whistler standing by the car. He emerged from his hideaway.

'Ah, there you are,' said the heron. 'I've some excellent news for you. The men have hung the dead chickens up in a shed and I think, if you really make yourself as flat as possible you could get under the door. There's a gap just about wide enough for you.'

Fox's ears pricked up. 'Things are looking up,' he replied. 'Is all quiet again?'

'The men have set all to rights and returned inside,' Whistler answered.

'And the dog?'

'Er – chained to a kennel,' said Whistler. 'But I'm sure you can handle him.'

'What are you saying?' cried Fox in exasperation. 'Am I, in my state, a match for a dog of that size?'

'Not physically, of course,' said the heron calmly. 'But we all know of your powers of persuasion.'

'I'm afraid you must have too high an opinion of me,' Fox returned, shaking his head. 'You may have heard of a previous exploit of mine, regarding a bull-mastiff – a stupid dog. But this situation is altogether different. This dog, whatever it is, is twice the size with twice the strength whereas I – well, you have only to look at me.'

'You are indeed underweight,' Whistler acknowledged. 'But that is to be expected. Are you saying your mental faculties have been affected by the winter?'

'It's a question of spirit and courage – and the will to do something,' Fox said wearily. 'I'm simply not the same animal any more. On the journey from Farthing Wood I had plenty of spirit. Determination, too. I had a *purpose*. It's different now.

'But, my dear Fox,' Whistler said with a worried look. 'I can't bear to hear you talk like this. You, above all my friends, have always been an example of tenacity and resourcefulness and resolution to look up to. You inspired the others – you still do. And surely you *still* have a purpose. To survive. Think of Vixen if not of yourself.'

For a moment something of the old look returned to Fox's poor haggard face. He was thinking of what he had been like when Vixen had first encountered him. The pitiful shadow of himself that he now was would never have won her regard and admiration as he had then. Then his eyes glazed over again.

'No, it's no use, Whistler,' he said lamely. 'I'm sorry if I'm letting you down but I'm beaten before I start. I'll simply wilt in front of that monster.'

Whistler was really alarmed at Fox's lack of motivation. Even his mention of Vixen had not done the trick. He flew back to Tawny Owl and Kestrel for advice.

'Yes, he's taken things very hard,' Kestrel said when the heron had related his conversation.

'Humph!' snorted Tawny Owl. 'I believe in calling things by their proper name. His spirit is completely broken, and he's no longer the brave leader we once knew.'

'How can we help him?' asked Whistler. 'It's awful to see him cowering in the road under that car.'

'Only a full stomach and the arrival of Spring can help him now,' said Tawny Owl. 'He's a beaten animal.'

Unbeknown to the three birds, the subject of their discussion had crept up to the garden fence and could overhear every word. If the scene had been pre-arranged it could not have had a better result. Fox's pride, battered as it was, refused to accept the verdict of Tawny Owl, and his body visibly stiffened. He thought again of Vixen and what it would mean to her if he failed. He could not bear to sink in her estimation. He pulled himself more erect and backed away from the fence.

The birds were still talking when they saw him leap the fence for the third time, but with an added grace that made them fall silent. He went warily across the centre of the grounds of the house, giving the re-established chicken coop a wide berth. He saw the dog, half in and half out of the kennel, with its head on its paws, and he approached cautiously step by step. Having convinced himself that it was dozing, Fox looked around for the shed Whistler had described to him. He soon found it.

In his emaciated state it was no problem for him to crawl under the door. The chickens were hanging by the feet from nails in the side of the shed. Fox pulled one free and backed under the gap again. Here he met with a difficulty for the chicken got caught. However, with a backward tug, he wrenched it free and ran back to the fence.

The birds fully expected him to jump the fence and be satisfied with his good luck. But Fox had evidently decided to do things in style. He dropped the chicken, then loped back to the shed and scrambled under the door again. All this time the dog had not stirred a muscle. Fox found the second hen to be much larger and needed two pulls to bring it to the ground. Back he came

under the shed door and then the larger hen became
firmly wedged. Fox tugged it this way and that, but its
plump body would not shift. Whistler was on the point
of flying over to tell Fox that perhaps it would be best
to be content with one and to get away while the going
was good, when Badger's voice was heard calling beyond
the fence.

'Fox! Owl! Are you there?' he was saying.

'We're here,' hissed Tawny Owl from his branch. 'Be
quiet. The dog's asleep.'

'I've found a regular dump of food,' he called back
excitedly, regardless of the warning. 'At the end of the
road. Come and look.'

Kestrel flew over to the fence and perched on the top.
'Wait a moment, Badger,' he whispered. 'Fox is in the
grounds collecting chickens.'

Badger's jaw dropped. He could not comprehend that
Kestrel was referring to the two dead ones. 'He must be
mad!' he cried. 'Does he want to commit suicide?'

Kestrel calmed him down. 'It's not what you think,'
he said. 'We'll explain later.'

Fox had given the second chicken a particularly vicious wrench and it was almost free. But at that moment
the dog awoke and yawned widely. It stood up, shaking
its body vigorously. Fox heard the sound and froze. How
far did that chain stretch? He peered round the side of
the shed. The dog was some twenty feet away, but Fox
had no idea if it could reach him if it made a lunge. He
waited. The dog began to sniff the snow all round its
kennel. It found something of interest and sniffed harder,
running in looping patterns through the snow, its nose
always on the ground. Fox watched it go to the full
length of its chain in the direction opposite to where he
was standing and gulped as he saw how far it stretched.
If it came his way it could easily reach him. He waited

no longer. He heaved the chicken free and ran almost in front of the dog as it was returning on the axis of the chain's length. It saw him and immediately started to bark again.

Fox raced for the fence and cleared it easily. 'Take this!' he cried as he dropped the chicken on the road side of the fence by Badger. Then, incredibly, in the teeth of danger he backed away for yet another jump. The dog was barking incessantly as Fox leapt the fence again to snap up the chicken he had left behind. Lights were appearing once more in the house. But Fox was up and over the fence for the last time with the second chicken in his jaws. Without hesitation he took the opposite direction to that taken by the first two foxes, leaving poor Badger to struggle after him with the heavier hen. Tawny Owl, Kestrel and Whistler swooped over the fence behind them.

'The Park's that way!' called Tawny Owl. 'You're going in the wrong direction!' But Fox did not seem to hear.

Badger had no idea what Fox had in mind, but he gamely followed him as quickly as he could, expecting every minute to find the huge dog bearing down on him from behind. But though the deafening barking continued, no dog – nor men – appeared. Then suddenly the noise ceased. It seemed as if this is what Fox had been expecting, for he immediately stopped running and dropped the chicken, the better to take some deep breaths while he waited for Badger to catch him up.

'Not a bad haul, eh?' he said coolly to his friends as they bunched together. He seemed his old self.

'I don't understand,' said Badger.

'Understand what?'

'Why we weren't chased,' Badger panted.

'It's obvious,' Fox confided. 'When the men came out

of the house the second time they expected to see their chicken coop overturned again. As soon as they saw it intact, with no more chickens missing, they assumed the dog's barking had driven off any further prowlers. How could they know I knew about the dead hens in the shed?'

'Bravo, Fox. You're to be congratulated,' said Whistler. 'And you've proved you're still a shade sharper than most of us.'

Tawny Owl disliked anyone to be overpraised when he considered he had exceptional abilities himself. 'Oh well,' he said huffily, 'when you're down as low as you can be, you can only go upwards.'

The others glared at him but Fox, in his new-found confidence, only chuckled.

'Yet a little cunning can go a long way,' he said.

—13—
Live and Let Live

Badger was delighted at Fox's reinstatement as the animals' resourceful leader, and Whistler politely failed to mention that the idea of stealing the dead chickens had been his.

'I also have found something of interest,' Badger then announced.

'Ah yes – your discovery,' murmured Kestrel. 'What is it?'

'I hope it's something of value to our smaller friends,' said Fox. 'We mustn't forget that we still have nothing for *them*, and that is why I didn't turn back for the Park.'

'Well, come and see,' said Badger excitedly. 'There's everything we need.'

'How far is it?' Fox wanted to know. 'I feel quite worn out.'

'Of course you are, jumping backwards and forwards over that fence all those times – without mentioning the journey here. But it's not far along the road. We've run most of the way already.'

'You take the others with you, and show them what you want them to carry back,' Fox suggested. 'I'll wait here and take a breather and look after the chickens.'

So Badger, accompanied by the three birds, proceeded to the end of the road, where in fact a small general store that served the neighbourhood was situated. To the rear of the shop was a yard where discarded cartons, packets and unwanted stocks abounded. Amongst this was enough greenstuff to feed all the rabbits and hares comfortably, wasted bags of mixed nuts left over from Christmas and even quantities of pet food such as millet sprays for cage birds. Badger seemed to think the voles and fieldmice might like the latter, while the squirrels would be delighted by the nuts.

What would have been the astonishment of any human awake at that hour and looking on, to see a small aerial procession of a hawk, an owl and a heron on their way back to the Nature Reserve carrying their assorted gifts? Kestrel led the way with a collection of millet sprays in his pointed beak, then came Tawny Owl, a little self-consciously, laden with string bags of nuts – one in his beak and one clutched in his talons – and finally Whistler, his huge bill stuffed with cabbage leaves and a selection of greenery.

Badger watched them on their way and then rejoined Fox. 'I thought you might have indulged in a mouthful or two while you were waiting,' he said, referring to the chickens, 'just to keep your strength up.'

'No,' said Fox. 'We shall all feast together when we

get back to the Park. You and I and Vixen and Weasel. And, of course, Owl and Kestrel, though I know Whistler prefers fish. But first we have a journey ahead of us.'

Dawn was threatening to break as they went back along the road, Fox now carrying the larger chicken. They passed the scene of the raid and then the two dead foxes. Now they were just stiff corpses in the snow, lying where they had dropped and staining its whiteness with their blood.

'These hens should have been theirs by rights,' Fox muttered as he paused briefly at the sight. 'It could have been Vixen and me.' Then they went on, crossed the ditch, and re-entered the Park at the same point.

It was well on into the morning when the two animals, after frequent stops to rest from their loads, arrived back at Badger's set.

'Will you eat with me?' Badger asked, 'or shall I come and join you and Vixen?'

'Just as you like,' Fox said wearily.

'May I suggest the set then?' said Badger, aware that it offered considerably more comfort than the sparseness of the foxes' earth.

'I must have a nap first,' Fox said decidedly. 'I'll help you take our quarry underground, and then I'll be back when it's dark, with Vixen.'

'I'm tired too,' agreed Badger as they deposited the chickens in a safe place. 'But it was well worth the effort, wasn't it?'

'Without a doubt,' replied Fox.

Later that day Fox, Badger, Vixen, Weasel, Tawny Owl and Kestrel were together in Badger's set. There was plenty to eat for all, and each of them felt it was the first good meal they had had in a long while. Kestrel informed Fox and Badger that he, Owl and Whistler had made several trips back and forth to the food dump and that all the animals had eaten well and were feeling a lot more cheerful.

'I really believe that Badger's brainwave will prove to be our salvation,' Fox said optimistically. Vixen looked at her mate lovingly. She had heard the tale of Fox's courage and cunning from Kestrel and was prouder of him than ever.

'It certainly seems that Badger's stay with humankind has produced some useful thinking,' remarked Tawny Owl.

'Owl and I and the heron can make regular flights to pick up more supplies,' said Kestrel. 'With just a little luck our depleted party should be around to welcome the spring.'

'But what of all of *us*?' Weasel demanded. 'Where do the supplies for the meat-eaters come from? Those small birds killed by the cold we sometimes pick up don't make a proper meal.'

All were silent, faced with a problem none of them had really considered. Badger thought of Ginger Cat's rats but diplomatically decided to say nothing.

'There can be no more raids on chicken coops,' said Fox. 'That would be suicidal.'

'Was there no meat amongst the wasted food?' Vixen asked.

'I have to admit we didn't really look,' said Kestrel. 'But that is easily remedied.'

'Perhaps, Owl, you could investigate tomorrow night?' Fox suggested.

'Perhaps I could, perhaps I couldn't,' he answered grumpily. 'I may have other plans.'

'Don't worry – I'll go,' said Kestrel in disgust. 'I can fly there in the daytime. No-one will notice a hovering hawk.'

'I didn't say I *wouldn't* go,' Tawny Owl rejoined. 'If you had waited, I no doubt would have offered.'

'Can't bear to be *asked* to do anything,' Kestrel muttered. 'Pompous old – '

He was interrupted by an unearthly scream outside the set.

'Whatever's that?' he cried.

'Have you never heard the scream of a captured hare?' Weasel asked.

'HARE!' they all shouted and Fox and Badger went racing for the exit. The others followed. Outside they smelt blood and Fox snuffled the crisp, icy air. 'This way!' he called. A little further off there was a patch of blood on the snow, and a trail of drops leading away from it. They followed and, eventually, found what they were looking for. Under a holly bush a stoat was devouring the limp body of a young hare. It looked up in alarm at the approaching group and quickly snatched up its prey, preparatory to flight.

'You needn't run,' said Fox. 'If that is one of our friends you have killed, we are too late. And, if not, we don't need the food.'

'I'm afraid it's one of the leverets, Hare's offspring,' Weasel announced.

'I have to eat, too, you know,' the stoat said defensively in a voice unnaturally shrill. 'I hunt what I can. N-no offence meant.'

'It's the law of the Wild,' said Badger. 'We mean you no harm.' He turned to the others. 'I met this fellow once before,' he said. 'Like us, he's finding it difficult to survive.'

'Of course,' said Fox. 'Who are we to complain?'

'What a strange world it is,' murmured Vixen. 'That poor little friend of ours came here, believing he had found safety, only to end up like this.'

The stoat was looking from one to the other, still unsure of its best action and half inclined to run.

'What's the difference?' Tawny Owl shrugged. 'He could as easily have been killed by the winter.'

'For most of us no home is without its dangers,' Fox observed. 'It's something we have to accept without question. However, my friend,' he continued, looking at the stoat, 'I wish you had hunted in another corner of the Park.'

The stoat seemed to sense it was safe now and increased in boldness. 'And you foxes – you hunt too. Where do you go in the Park to find food?'

'Yes, yes. We take the point,' answered Fox. 'Wherever we can find it – the same as you.'

'Never have I known such a winter,' the stoat went on. 'My mate has already died. I can see by your leanness you have suffered as well. But the badger seems very sleek.'

Badger shifted his stance a little uncomfortably.

'Yes, I saw you on another occasion,' the stoat said. 'You weren't so stout then. You must have been luckier than the rest of us.'

'If injuring myself severely can be called lucky, I have been,' Badger said enigmatically.

The stoat, of course, looked puzzled.

'He was discovered by the Warden and taken into care,' Weasel explained.

'A sort of fattening up process,' said Tawny Owl mischievously.

'All right, all right,' said Badger. 'Am I never to be allowed to forget it? Would you rather I hadn't been found and frozen to death?'

'Don't be absurd, Badger,' replied Tawny Owl. 'Nobody was more pleased than I at your recovery.'

'Well then, how much longer do I have to endure these carping comments?' Badger said irritably.

'Oh dear,' said the stoat grinning. 'The incident appears to be a bit of a bone of contention between you.'

'Let's drop the subject,' suggested Fox, 'and leave our friend here to eat in peace. And I sincerely hope Hare is nowhere at hand to overhear my remarks. He'd never forgive me.'

'I promise I'll endeavour to keep away from this area,' the stoat said agreeably. 'You've been more than polite.'

'Live and let live,' answered Fox. 'The Park belongs to all of us.'

He led the others away and they gradually dispersed to their own homes.

'H'm, quite a philosophical evening,' remarked Tawny Owl as he fluttered silently to his roost.

—14—
A New Danger

The winter wore relentlessly on, the old year fading into the new with no sign of change. The birds continued their trips to the food dump and were able to find a kind of meat – perhaps unwanted sausages or bacon or the like – to supplement what the meat-eaters were able to find in the Reserve. Now that the threat of imminent starvation had been lessened, the animals gritted their teeth, confident that it was now just a case of lasting out until the better weather came.

In other ways they were no more comfortable than before. They simply could not get used to the treacherous cold which never let up, nor the blizzards and snowfalls which occurred with monotonous regularity. But they had all learned to suffer in silence.

Then, when at last they had all begun to hope that they really must be approaching the end of the winter, an entirely new threat emerged. The Warden was taken ill and removed to hospital. Ginger Cat disappeared at the same time – presumably to a well-wisher. The Lodge fell empty and there was no longer any restriction to human access to the Nature Reserve. When the fact became known to the local human population, it was not long before gangs of boys with skates and toboggans were invading the Park, shattering its peace and quiet and destroying the freedom of its inhabitants. But, worse still, at night came poachers.

The first sounds of a gun came late one evening when Fox and Vixen were on the prowl. They stopped dead in their tracks, heads up sniffing the air, ears cocked for every slight sound.

'It can't be,' muttered Fox, looking at his mate. They waited. Then another bang convinced them of their suspicions and they dived for cover.

Under some shrubbery they listened with racing hearts, their bellies pressed to the frozen ground. They were a long way from their earth. As each second passed their nerves quivered in trepidation. There were no more shots, but then they saw two dark figures moving like shadows across the snow, not twenty yards from where they lay. Instinctively their heads went down in an attempt to render themselves even less conspicuous. But they could see what the figures were carrying and at the sight of it they both gasped.

'A deer!' they both hissed under their breath.

'And a large one, too,' said Fox, watching how the men were bent beneath its weight. 'Poor creature.'

'Is there nothing these humans won't stoop to?' Vixen said furiously. 'They know the very purpose of this Park is to preserve wildlife.'

'More to the point,' Fox reminded her, 'it was created a Nature Reserve to protect the very White Deer herd they are attacking.'

'Oh, where can our Warden have gone?' Vixen wailed.

'That we shan't know,' Fox said. 'But it is enough to know he is absent, and we are all unprotected.'

'The deer must be in a panic,' said Vixen. 'They've no experience of guns or of being hunted. And why *are* they hunted?'

'They're rare animals. Who knows what value the skin might have to a human who possesses one?'

'Then can *we* take that as some consolation? If the humans are only hunting the deer, maybe the other creatures here are not at risk.'

Fox laughed hollowly. 'It is my experience of such humans that all creatures are at risk as long as they have a gun in their hands.'

'Will they be back, do you think?' Vixen asked.

'As long as they know there is no Warden around, I think we can expect them,' Fox replied grimly.

His words were proved right. Although no guns were heard the next night, on the ensuing one they returned. The deer herd was frantic. Unlike their cousins in the unprotected wild and rugged areas of the country, they had nowhere to run to; no means of escape. What had been a haven of peace to them had now become a death-trap.

The other animals of the Park, who had always enjoyed a security from human intervention which was owed principally to the existence of the White Deer herd, forgot any obligation they should have felt. They only counted themselves lucky not to be the hunted ones. But the animals of Farthing Wood – the newcomers – were of a different mettle. From many different loyalties in their old home they had forged themselves into a unit

on their long march across country. They had learnt
during that period that the good of the individual usually
meant the good of the majority. The Park was now their
home, as it was the deer's, and they all of them felt some
responsibility towards their fellow inhabitants in fighting
their common enemy. But none of them could think of
anything they could do to prevent the poaching.

Fox and Vixen were again out foraging when the next
visit of the men with guns took place. This time they
were in a position to see everything. The deer herd were,
as usual, in the open part of the Park. In the absence of
the Warden they had lost their supplies of hay, and were
now reduced to digging beneath the snow with their
hooves as best they could to reach the grass and mosses
underneath. From the cover of a nearby clump of trees,
two men were creeping stealthily towards them.

The noble figure of the Great Stag himself towered
over the other deer, making a clear target for the guns.
Fox saw the men raising their weapons to take aim.
Without thinking, he commenced barking with an
abruptness that startled the already nervous deer. They
began to mill about, sensing danger again. When Vixen
joined in, Fox started to run towards the deer barking
as he went. He hoped the deer would take alarm and
run. The trick paid off. The more nervous of the deer
bolted, which alarmed the rest and they were soon running in all directions. Even the Great Stag ran, with a
backward glance at Fox over his shoulder. But, although
Fox may have saved the overlord of the Park, which had
been his main thought, he unconsciously hastened the
end of another. Unfortunately some of the deer ran
straight towards the trees where the men were hidden,
and so on to their guns. One was shot as they approached, causing the others to veer away. Then the
whole herd raced in panic as far as they could go, away

from the noise. But the men were satisfied with their stalking, and another white deer was removed from the Reserve.

'I hope my motives won't be misunderstood,' Fox said ruefully to Vixen. 'It might have looked as if I was in league with the killers.'

'Nonsense!' said Vixen. 'Is that likely? You aren't a man's pet but a creature of the Wild. You saved the Great Stag and he knows it.'

'But they still had their taste of blood. The herd is yet one fewer in number.'

'What can we do against the intelligence of humans?' Vixen asked. 'If they decided to slaughter every creature in the Park we could do nothing to stop it.'

'I'm not so pessimistic,' Fox said. 'All we have to do is to think of a way of preventing them getting into the Reserve.'

'Utterly impossible,' she replied flatly. 'How could we achieve that?'

'I don't know. Perhaps we could, at least, arrange a warning system at their approach so that we're not to be found when the men arrive.'

'And what would you do with the deer herd? Take them all underground?'

'All right,' Fox said wistfully. 'I suppose it's just wishful thinking, but there must be something that can be done to make them less vulnerable.'

'Oh, I know you when you're in this mood.' Vixen looked at him, and her great affection shone out of her eyes. 'You won't rest now. But thinking for a party of small animals that can hide themselves away is a far cry from causing a herd of deer to vanish.'

'I think I'll go and have a talk with the Great Stag,' Fox replied.

'I'll leave you then,' said Vixen. 'You won't want me around.'

'You couldn't be more wrong, my beloved Vixen,' he told her. 'I need you with me. You are my partner in everything.'

The Great Stag had not run far. He had been trying to muster the herd together again after the alarm. 'I am indebted to you,' he said to Fox at once. 'We only lost one. There was no scent of Man. We could have lost more.' He did not have the conceit to own that it was he who had been the prime target.

'We have to devise a way of preventing any more deaths,' Fox said earnestly.

'I spend all my waking hours trying to do so,' said the Stag. 'The fact is, without our supply of hay we may lose more animals from starvation than from the gun.'

'I can see it must be very difficult for the older and weaker among your herd to cope,' Fox agreed. 'But I am convinced we've seen the worst of the winter. The threat from Man, in my opinion, is far more severe.'

'You talk wisely,' said the Stag. 'I know you to be the intelligent animal who brought your friends here last summer from a great distance. But you didn't have large animals like us to contend with. I'm afraid the problem of ensuring our safety is well-nigh impossible.'

'You are repeating almost word for word what I've said to Fox,' Vixen remarked. 'Although our hearts are with you I don't believe we have the power to be of assistance.'

The Great Stag shook his noble head. 'If the Warden does not return I have decided there is only one course of action open to us.'

'I think I know what's in your mind,' said Fox quietly, 'for it has occurred to me also.'

'I fear we must leave the Park,' the Great Stag pronounced.

'Yes. It's as I expected. But outside you would run the same risk.'

'However, we could scatter over a wider area.'

Fox was silent for some moments. 'No,' he said finally in the determined manner that Vixen knew so well. 'It mustn't come to that. I won't admit defeat. I have the germ of an idea. Will you give me a day or so?'

'My dear friend,' the Stag said feelingly, 'you are under no obligation to do anything. You have your own problems. Of course I will give you whatever time you wish. I had not planned to leave our home just yet.'

'The men don't return every night,' Vixen said. 'You should be safe for the time being.'

Fox was deep in thought. 'I need to work things out,' he said presently. He turned to the Stag. 'We'll leave you now,' he said, 'and I will return to put my plan before you.'

'You are a gracious and clever animal,' replied the overlord of the Reserve. 'I shall await your coming again with the utmost eagerness.'

As Fox and Vixen turned after their farewells, she questioned him. 'May I ask what you have in mind?'

'I'll tell you all eventually,' he replied. 'It's the Pond, you see – that's the key to the whole thing.'

—15—
The Trap

The following afternoon the Park was invaded again by
groups of young boys, most of them muffled to the chin
to beat the cold, who had come to skate. The home of
the Edible Frogs had been frozen over for months, but
there were signs that a slight rise in temperature had
occurred. In a few places the surface of the Pond had a
little water on top of the ice. The youngsters, however,
after inspecting thoroughly, donned their skates and proceeded to enjoy them selves.

From a snow-festooned bed of rushes Fox was watching their antics closely. He chuckled to himself as he
thought of the many times Adder had waited at the
waterside during the summer, patiently watching the

Edible Frogs disporting themselves. But his vigil was for a very different reason.

After an hour or so he had seen all he wanted to. Carefully avoiding any risk of being spotted by pairs of sharp young eyes, he made his way back to his earth. Vixen woke as he entered. She looked at him searchingly. 'Nothing yet,' was his only remark.

During the next couple of days the weather became noticeably milder, and for longer stretches the sun broke through the cloud formation that had loured upon the Park for so long. Each day Fox watched at the pondside. On the second night the men returned and another deer was shot. The Great Stag in this time had not seen Fox again. Once more he began to think in terms of leaving the reserve.

But the very next afternoon Fox saw what he had been waiting for. The children arrived, but found their skating restricted. Almost a third of the Pond now had to be avoided, and they soon left it altogether in favour of tobogganing. Fox knew it was time for him to re-visit the Stag.

The great beast listened silently while he unfolded his plan, then raised his head and bellowed a challenge to the air, 'Now let them come,' he roared. Fox waited no longer. There was much to do.

But first he wanted Vixen's approval. During the journey to the Park he had relied a good deal on her judgement and had learnt to value it. She heard his plan and looked at him in admiration. Her enthusiasm did not need to be expressed in words. The Fox gathered all his friends together and put them in the picture also. They were totally in agreement save, predictably, for Tawny Owl who only gave grudging support.

'Can't see why you want to bother so much with a

deer herd,' he muttered. 'As long as the humans are banging away at them, *we're* that much safer.'

'But safer still if they can't "bang away" at *anything*' Fox said coolly.

'Very well,' said Badger. 'Now we must arrange for the sentries.'

So a system was arranged by which the animals were to watch the place where the poachers entered, the boundary between the Park and the road, and give early warning of their approach. Tawny Owl, Kestrel and Whistler were stationed at intervals along the fence. Along the ground Weasel, Hare, Badger and Vixen waited. Midway between the boundary and the Pond, Fox was stationed, while in the region of the Pond itself the Great Stag was patrolling in readiness to play his part in the Plan.

The first night passed without event, and at dawn the animals and birds returned to their homes. On the second night they were back at their posts. Although it was still cold, there was no longer the viciousness in the wind that had cut through their fur and feathers like a knife-blade. The snow that had covered the ground for so long had softened and, on the road outside the Park, had been churned into slush by motor vehicles. It was the noise of the steady squelch of steps through this slush that was the first sign to the waiting animals of the men's approach.

Weasel's sharp ears were the first to detect the sound. His small body, so close to the ground, had not the stature to see into the road. He ran quickly to the fence-post on which sat Tawny Owl. 'I hear footsteps!' he cried. 'Is it them?'

'I can see something coming,' replied Owl. 'Wait – yes, two figures . . . Yes! Yes! Quickly! Tell the others! I'm off to Fox!' He flew up in a wide arc over the tree-tops and sped off in the direction of the waiting Fox. Weasel passed the word to the others and together they raced back through the Park. Fox saw Tawny Owl approaching him at speed and himself prepared to run.

'To the Pond!' cried Owl. 'They're on their way!'

At once Fox set off at a breakneck pace, his breath coming like small bursts of steam from his mouth. Whistler and Kestrel were first back to safety. Vixen, Weasel and Badger had a long run ahead of them to keep in front of the men. Only Hare was almost as swift overland as the birds through the air.

Fox had told them to hide themselves once he had received the message. Out of sight they were quite safe from the poachers' guns. The men had come for larger game. But it was not in the nature of the animals of Farthing Wood to disassociate themselves from such an important event – and one in which the leader was placing himself in danger. So the slower animals had condemned themselves to run across an exhausting stretch of parkland to be in on things. Of the three Vixen was by far the fastest and she outdistanced Weasel and Badger as quickly as Hare had outdistanced her. Weasel, although far smaller than Badger, was much more lithe and had a far more elastic and rippling running pace. But he moderated his speed to suit the older animal's comfort.

As his friends hastened back to join him, Fox was on his way to join the Stag. The scion of the deer herd had agreed to keep his station by the Pond each night until he saw Fox again. He lowered his head as he saw the familiar chestnut body racing towards him.

'Hold – yourself – ready,' gasped Fox, his tongue lolling painfully from his mouth. 'They're coming.'

'So tonight is to be the night,' the Stag intoned. 'Rest

awhile, my friend. You appear to be somewhat
distressed.'

'No, I – mustn't stop – I must complete the – task,'
Fox panted. 'I – have to make – sure they – find you.'
And he was off again, back in the direction from which
he had come – back towards the men with guns. He
passed a black poplar in whose boughs clustered Tawny
Owl, Kestrel and Whistler. But they did not interrupt
him and he did not see them. He did see Hare but there
was no time to stop and he went by without a glance.
Next he passed Vixen who gave him a longing look. He
half looked back as he ran, but even she had to be
ignored for the sake of the Plan. When he spotted Badger
and Weasel in the distance he dropped on all fours, for
behind them the two fateful shadows were approaching.

'Go to cover,' he told his friends as they reached him.
'No need to endanger more of us than necessary.' They
passed on and Fox waited to begin the gamble of his life.

Among the snow-coated sedges by the Pond lay Hare.
He was watching the White Stag nervously tossing his
head as he stood by the edge of the ice, his legs quivering.
Vixen found him and lay down. She was unable to speak.
Her heart was pounding unmercifully. Eventually
Badger and Weasel tottered in to join them. There they
waited and watched.

Twenty yards from the men, Fox stood up and yapped
loudly. The signal was heard and out from the nearby
copse came the White Deer herd, slowly, timidly, in
knots of three and four. The men stopped. One pointed
and their voices made themselves heard. They were looking among the herd and Fox knew who they were looking
for. But the one they wanted was missing. The human
voices were heard again – harsh, rough voices. The deer
paused. Fox yapped again and started towards them.
The deer scattered as instructed, running in the direction

of the Pond. The men shouted angrily, now pointing at the fox. This was the animal that had frustrated them before. Fox ran behind the herd as if driving them. His back was to the men, and every nerve-end along his neck, his spine and his haunches was strung as taut as a guitar string. The hackles rose on his coat for he knew he was courting death. At last he had to glance back. He saw one of the men raise his gun. It was aimed at him, the cause of their wrath. But Fox had no intention of being shot. He wheeled away at a right-angle, running fast, then twisted and swerved, twisted and swerved, like a hare followed by hounds. A shot rang out but the bullet found no mark.

Now the men were running, for their quarry was escaping. They would have one deer, if not the one they were after. The herd reached the brink of the Pond and spread out, screening its edge. In front of them, on to the ice itself, stepped the Great Stag. Cautiously he went, pausing at each step, until he reached the limit of safety. As the men came up, the herd swung away to the right, leaving the Stag exposed – solitary, undefended, alone on the ice. The men saw their passage was clear on the left side of the Pond. The Stag's head was turned away as if he were ignorant of their intention. They edged out, foot by foot, on the treacherous ice. They meant to have him this time. At the moment they raised their weapons Fox barked a third time. The Stag swung his great head round, saw the men and, with a tremendous bound leapt for the shore. But the poachers were committed now. They saw their target about to escape from their grip again. They ran forward to take aim at the retreating animal and then – crash! suddenly it was as if their feet were snatched from under them, and they were plunging down, down into black, icy water. Their guns were thrown away as they sought to save themselves, floundering and trying to find a handhold on something.

The Great Stag turned at the edge of the ice and saw the weapons meant for his death sink to the murky depths of the Pond's bottom, abandoned without a thought by their owners. At this clear evidence that Fox's plan had worked to perfection the Stag laid his head back and bellowed in triumph. Then Fox was surrounded by his jubilant friends – his old friends and the whole of the deer herd. The Great Stag joined them. 'That,' he boomed, 'is a piece of animal cunning never likely to be surpassed.'

While the animals were milling around, the men were striking out for the shore. The Pond was not deep and they were in no danger save that of a severe ducking and a bad chill. Their cries of anger had changed to cries of distress before they had pulled their frozen, dripping bodies clear of the water on to the shore. They cast one look at the bevy of wild creatures who had bested them, and then set off at an uncomfortable trot. Their misery would not be over for a while, for back they had to go across the Park and along the slushy road before there was any hope of being dry and warm again. At every step the icy coldness of their drenched clothing chafed at their bodies and neither of them could imagine a discomfort existed that could be more severe.

'I think we've seen the last of them,' said Hare. 'Fox, this is your greatest day. Even on our long journey you never reached these heights.'

Fox felt the admiration of all the creatures swell like a tide around him, but he was content to know that his plan had worked without mishap. Only Vixen, in all her fierce pride, felt a nagging doubt about what might be the reaction of two humans degraded and humiliated beyond belief by a fox.

—16—
One Good Turn...

Fox's courage and ingenuity were now the byword of the
inhabitants of White Deer Park. It was no new discovery
for his old friends from Farthing Wood, but he was the
acknowledged hero of the deer herd, and even those
creatures who had not been witness to the events at the
Pond heard the story and marvelled. Once again he was
brimful of confidence after his successes with the chickens and now the poachers. In both instances he had
pitted his wits against humans and each time emerged
triumphant.

So Fox had a special status in the Reserve and,
although still underweight from the rigours of the winter,
he carried his head more erect, his gait was looser and
the sparkle had returned to his eyes. Vixen was de-

lighted. 'You're your old self again,' she told him. Yet still that unnameable thought lurked in her mind.

For the next few weeks the weather fluctuated. Warm spells were followed by cold spells which then gave way to milder temperatures again. Most of the old snow had melted, but there were still heavy frosts at night and new, but slighter, falls of snow still occurred. But the Park no longer seemed to be deserted. The inhabitants were out and about again when it was safe, and all sensed the coming of Spring. Food was easier to find for all creatures and health and appearance improved.

One day in late February Whistler found Squirrel, Vole and Fieldmouse enjoying together some nuts which Squirrel had been able to dig up from the softer ground.

'I don't think you need me any more, do you?' he asked, referring to the trips the birds were still making to the general store's dump.

'Not really,' replied Squirrel. 'But we're most grateful. You may have kept us alive.'

'It's not quite Spring yet,' Vole pointed out, shaking his head. 'I wouldn't like to say for sure – '

'Nonsense,' cut in the more reasonable Fieldmouse. 'Whistler and Kestrel – and Tawny Owl too – have done more than enough for us. It's time they had a rest.'

Vole was outnumbered and conceded defeat. 'At any rate,' he persisted, 'if things should get difficult again I imagine we can still call on you?'

Whistler bowed elaborately and winked at the other two animals. 'Always at your service,' he answered with a hint of sarcasm. 'I'll tell Kestrel the news.'

The hawk had been on a similar errand to Rabbit and Hare. 'So we've both been released?' he said as Whistler concurred.

'I can't say I'm sorry,' Whistler admitted. 'The job

was definitely acquiring a considerable degree of tedium.'

'Well, I think we can say no-one ever heard a word of complaint from us,' Kestrel remarked. 'Though the same couldn't be said of Owl. His constant grumbling is enough to wear you down. Some days I simply can't bring myself to talk to him.'

'Oh, it's only his way,' laughed the good-natured heron. 'His heart's in the right place really.'

'D'you think so? I sometimes wonder. But I suppose you're right.' Kestrel gave Whistler a mischievous glance. 'Er – have you told Tawny Owl yet?' he asked.

'No,' replied Whistler. 'I suppose we'd better go and –' He broke off as he noticed Kestrel's expression. 'Are you thinking what I think you're thinking, Kestrel?'

Kestrel screeched with laughter. 'Undoubtedly,' he said.

'Well, I don't know. . . .' Whistler said hesitantly.

'Pah! Teach him a lesson!' Kestrel said shortly. 'He won't know we've stopped because he sleeps during the day.'

Whistler reluctantly agreed. He was not one for perpetrating jokes on others. 'But we mustn't let him continue for long,' he insisted.

So poor Tawny Owl carried on flying outside the Park at night to fetch what he could from the usual spot. The animals the food was destined for said nothing as they never saw him arrive with it, and assumed all the birds had changed their minds. Then one night, as he was flying over the road, Tawny Owl saw two figures which he thought he recognized. He paused with his load on a nearby bough to make sure. He did not need long to ascertain that it was the two poachers abroad again and seemingly on their way to the Park. He watched them long enough to see that they appeared to be unarmed, but decided to fly straight to Fox to warn him of their approach.

On his way he saw Badger ambling along. 'Good gracious!' Badger called up, seeing the bird with his load. 'Are you still doing that, Owl?'

Tawny Owl dropped what he was carrying at once and landed by Badger. '*What* did you say?' he demanded.

Badger unfortunately began to laugh. 'I think you've been the victim of someone's joke,' he chuckled. 'The other birds stopped flying to the dump days ago.'

Tawny Owl's beak dropped open. Then he snorted angrily. 'So that's it,' he said. 'That's how I'm treated for trying to help others.'

'Oh dear,' Badger muttered to himself. He thought quickly. 'No, no,' he said, 'they just forgot to tell you, I expect. Er – don't take it amiss,' he added hastily.

But Tawny Owl was in high dudgeon. He stalked round and round Badger, rustling his wings furiously and a hard glint came into his huge eyes. 'So they forgot, did they?' he hissed. 'We'll see how much forgetting *I* can do, then.' His last words were uttered with a menace that alarmed Badger, though he did not know that Tawny Owl was referring to the warning he had meant to bring. Then the bird flew off, climbing higher and higher in the sky until he was far away from any of his companions.

'Oh dear, oh dear,' wailed Badger. 'He's really angry now. I wish I hadn't laughed. Whatever did he mean by his last remark? I shall never know now, and it might have been important.'

'And after all,' he thought to himself as he trotted homeward, 'it wasn't a very nice trick. He *was* doing it for others. I wonder who's behind it?' He made his way to Fox's earth but Fox and Vixen were missing. Badger decided to wait.

When his friends eventually returned, Badger told them of Tawny Owl's feelings. Fox shook his head. 'He hates being made a fool of,' he said. 'He won't forget this for a long time. He's a very proud bird – and I think he's sensitive too, underneath. We've not been very kind to him.'

'*I* didn't know he was still collecting food,' Badger said.

'Neither did we,' said Vixen. 'It must be Kestrel's idea. He and Tawny Owl don't always see eye to eye.'

'But he'll be blaming *all* of us,' Fox said. 'He'll feel we've ganged up on him. I know him.'

'What can we do?' Badger asked. 'He flew a long way off. We may not see him for days.'

'Kestrel must apologise,' Fox said firmly. 'I shall tell him so.'

'Poor old Owl,' said kindly Vixen. 'It's not fair.'

As they conversed, none of them was aware that the poachers had entered the Park once again. It was Weasel who saw them approaching, but he stayed to watch. He knew where their guns lay and thought the men no longer posed a threat.

They seemed to be searching for *something* though, Weasel was sure, it could not be for the White Deer. He followed them, and was relieved to see they were going away from his and his friends' area of the Park. Suddenly one of the men nudged his companion and pointed. An animal was trotting briskly over the snowy patches only some ten yards away. Weasel could see plainly it was a fox. He knew it was not his fox because of the gait. Both men had pulled pistols from their pockets. One of them fired immediately at the animal but missed. The fox stopped in its tracks and, for a second, glanced back. It saw the men and started to run. But it was not quick enough. Another shot, this time from the other pistol, brought it down.

Weasel, keeping well out of sight and with a fiercely pounding heart, saw the men walk over to the stricken creature and examine it. One of them put a boot under its body and turned it over. It was quite dead. But the men were not satisfied. They did not turn back as if intending to leave the Park, but continued on their way in the same furtive, searching manner. Weasel followed them no longer. He needed to see no more to recognize the men's purpose. It was imperative to find Fox and Vixen.

Luckily the two distant cracks of the pistols had been heard by them and Badger, and they were debating what the new sounds of guns could mean when the breathless Weasel found them.

'It's the same two men,' he told them. 'But they're not after deer. They've got small guns and they've just shot a fox.'

Fox and Vixen both gulped nervously.

'You *must* take cover underground,' Weasel went on. 'They – ' he broke off as another shot was heard. The four animals looked at each other in horror.

'They're after all the foxes,' whispered Vixen. 'I dreaded this.'

'No,' said Fox grimly. 'They're after me. It's revenge they want for the trick I played them. They'll kill every fox they can in the hope that one of them will be me.'

Weasel nodded miserably. 'That's exactly the conclusion I came to,' he said. 'Please, Fox, take shelter.'

With a dazed expression, Fox allowed himself to be led to his earth where he numbly followed Vixen underground.

'We'd better make ourselves scarce, too,' Weasel said to Badger. 'We must have been seen at the pond-side along with Fox. We can't be too careful.'

In his den Fox was shaking his head and muttering, 'What have I done? What have I done?'

'You did what you thought best,' Vixen soothed him. 'And it was a brilliant plan.'

'But what have I achieved?' Fox demanded. 'I've set our enemies more firmly against us. The deer might be saved – they can't shoot *them* with pistols – but now I've brought even greater danger to *us*.'

'You weren't to know this would happen,' she assured him. 'You acted with the best intentions.'

Fox stood up. 'But how can I skulk around here while innocent creatures are being shot?' he cried. 'It's *me* they want. How many other foxes have to die while I hide away? I'm putting every other fox in the Park at risk.'

'And what do you intend to do?' Vixen asked angrily. 'Run up to the humans and offer yourself as a sacrifice?'

'At least if they killed me they would be satisfied. Then the Park *would* be safe again.'

'Don't talk such foolishness, Fox,' Vixen said in desperation, seeing the look on his face. 'Will they recognize you as the fox who made fools of them? To a human we all look the same. You would be killed and still they would hunt for others.'

'Then they *will* kill every fox,' he said. 'Only in that way can they be sure they have got rid of me.'

'Is it likely with the sounds of guns again, that any wild creature will stay abroad? By now they'll all be lying low,' Vixen said.

Fox looked at her and marvelled. '*You* are the wise one, dear Vixen,' he said, 'not I.'

'Pooh, you're merely blinded by your concern,' she replied.

'But what can I do?' he moaned.

Vixen knew how to handle her mate. 'You devised a

plan before. Now you must use your wits again,' she said. 'It's your brain that's our safety measure.'

Fox smiled and was already calmer as he settled down to think. 'Whatever did I do before we met?' he murmured. 'My brave counsellor.'

——17——

...Deserves Another

Tawny Owl, feeling very aggrieved, had flown as far away from his friends in the Park as he could without actually flying over its boundaries. His pride was hurt and, as he moodily munched his supper, his indignation grew with every mouthful.

'Serves them right if they never see me again,' he muttered. 'And a fat lot they'd care if they didn't.' He went and hunched himself up on a sycamore branch and brooded. With each minute he felt more and more unwanted. He had done the worst possible thing for himself by disassociating from all those he knew. For, on his own, he had nothing to do but brood over his misery; whereas in company a cheery word or two from someone would have made him forget his hurts far more quickly.

However, in his own company, he had no appearances to keep up; no risk of losing face. He began to wonder after a while if he had over-reacted. He sat and thought.

It was probably not true that all the animals had collaborated to make him look a fool. Fox, he was sure, would never be a party to such a thing. And neither would Badger, although he had chuckled at his discomfiture. The more he thought of Fox, of whom he was genuinely fond, the more guilty he felt. To what fate might he have consigned Fox and Vixen by not warning them of the return of the poachers? They surely had been on the way to the Park, and who could say for what purpose? He shifted about on the branch, feeling more and more uncomfortable and nervous. If anything had happened, he could never forgive himself. In the end he could stay put no longer. He leapt from the bough and sallied forth in the direction in which he had first spotted the men.

The darkness was fading as he flew over the Park, and he spied the poachers in the act of clambering back through the fence before they jumped the ditch. He was glad they were leaving, but was fearful of what they might have left behind them. A little further on he saw something that made his stomach turn over. The body of a fox lay crumpled on the snow, its red blood mingling with the white ground. Tawny Owl, of course, immediately thought the worst. He had murdered Fox. He fluttered to a tree and sank down, overcome by weakness. Drained of all feeling, he contemplated his own selfishness. It was a long time before he could force himself to approach the body. At length, with a heavy heart and wings of lead, he managed to fly over to it.

As he came close he knew it was not Fox; neither was it Vixen. His spirits lifted, but only for a few brief minutes. Because, not very much further away, a second

fox corpse greeted his sight. This time he examined it at
once. A second time he was relieved. But now he wondered how many deaths had occurred. Was his friend
lying dead somewhere after all? He flew off again, combing the ground afresh as he went. He went this way and
that, and then back again, frantically searching the Reserve yard by yard for the sight he dreaded to see. None
of the night creatures watched Tawny Owl's agony. For
a long time they had been in refuge. But as the sun came
up, Tawny Owl dropped with exhaustion. And there —
high, high up in the glittering blue of the winter sky
Kestrel soared, and saw him fall.

Later in the day Mole, whose joy in tunnelling had been
unindulged while the ground had been at its hardest,
now found his freedom restored. Where the snow had
melted the ground was very soft once any overnight frost
had disappeared. Mole had made a new shaft that ran
up to the surface, and was poking his head into the open,
his pink snout quivering excitedly. As it happened he
was almost squashed by a hoof of the Great Stag who
was walking that way.

The giant animal looked down at the tiny velvet-clad
body beneath him. 'I beg your pardon,' he said. 'I didn't
see you at first. I'm looking for your friend Fox. I understand the humans returned to the Park last night.'

'Yes, Badger told me of it,' replied Mole. 'We all
thought we'd seen the last of them.'

'Your leader is very brave and doesn't always think
of himself. It appears that he may have piled up some
trouble for his efforts the other night. It is now our turn
to assist him. Hence the reason for my visit.'

Mole gave the Stag directions to Fox's earth, and went
to tell Badger of his encounter.

Fox and Vixen were not in their den. They were out foraging, for it had now become unsafe to leave shelter at night. So the Great Stag, having assured himself of their absence, passed the time by grazing where he could until they should return. Eventually he saw them coming as he chewed a mouthful of moss.

'Greetings,' he said simply. 'I've come to inform you that the entire deer herd is at your disposal if you need us in your *new* dispute with the human killers.'

Fox listened to the Stag's gentle tone of irony. 'I fear there's nothing new about it,' he replied. 'I have always looked upon them as our enemies as well as yours.'

'Have you decided on any course of action should they return again?'

'Oh, they'll be back,' Fox said. 'I hardly think they'll be satisfied with their work so far. Kestrel tells me there are two dead foxes. The men must know there are many more than that still living.'

'My advice would be for us to stay under cover every night until they decide to come no more,' said Vixen, 'but Fox won't listen.'

'Simply because we have no way of knowing their intentions,' he explained. 'How long would it be before they came looking for us in our earths? Then there *would* be no escape.'

'You have a plan then?' the Stag asked.

'Only a poor one, I'm afraid. But it may work.'

'I am all ears.'

'To be honest,' began Fox, 'it isn't really a plan at all. I've merely been thinking along the lines of finding the safest spot in the Park and then going there. It occurred to me that there is one place these poaching humans might perhaps not care to venture to, and that is the grounds of the Warden's own garden, around the Lodge. If we holed up in there we might avoid them.'

'Hm,' the Stag murmured, considering. 'And what of the other foxes in the Reserve?'

'My immediate concern, naturally, is for my mate and my friends,' Fox said. 'But it would, no doubt, be possible to pass the word to them, in case they should feel like joining us.'

'I can foresee problems,' the Stag commented. 'These other foxes haven't the same feelings for your friends as you have. I should imagine they would look upon the presence of your mouse and rabbit friends as a ready-made food supply.'

'There would be no need for the voles and fieldmice to leave their homes,' answered Fox. 'The humans are not interested in small fry like them. But it's true; the question of the rabbits needs some thought.'

'Well, I have an idea that might make yours unnecessary,' the Great Stag told him, 'if you are willing to go along with it. It is perfectly simple. If the humans return, and appear to be bent on killing again, I have orders for the whole of my herd to charge them *en masse*. With that sort of force arraigned against them, I don't think they will need a lot of persuading to leave.'

'What if they use their pistols on the deer?' asked Fox.

'We're quite prepared for the possibility,' answered the Stag. 'But it's a risk we must take. We feel it is time we repaid your good turn to us. In any case, I honestly doubt if these wretched humans will stand still long enough when they see us all thundering towards them. There will be more than a few pairs of lowered antlers for them to negotiate.'

Fox and Vixen could not help but chuckle as they pictured the scene. 'I think it's an admirable and very generous idea,' said Vixen.

'It's certainly that,' agreed Fox. 'The only thing that comes into my mind is, that it could only work once. If they are still determined to enter the Park after that, they would make sure of the herd's whereabouts first. You can't cover every corner.'

'Then we must make sure our charge is so terrifying that they are dissuaded for good from coming back,' the Stag said. 'Are you willing to give it a try?'

'Assuredly, yes.'

'Then I'll go to make preparations.'

'I will arrange for sentries along the perimeter as before,' Fox said. He turned to Vixen. 'I wonder what happened to Tawny Owl?'

Kestrel knew. He had found the exhausted owl on the open ground, without even the strength to fly up into a tree.

'I'm glad you've come back,' said the hawk, 'but sorry to see you in this state.'

Tawny Owl slowly shook his head, too weak to reply.

'I have an apology to make,' Kestrel went on. 'At Fox's insistence. I'm afraid I'm to blame for not telling you to stop flying to the dump. It was a rotten trick and I very much regret it.'

Tawny Owl blinked once or twice and nodded. 'All – for – gotten,' he gasped.

'You need something to eat to restore your strength,' said Kestrel. 'I'll see if I can – '

'No,' said Tawny Owl. 'Just rest.'

'But you can't stay on the ground – too vulnerable,' insisted the hawk.

'Can't – fly. Too – weak,' came the reply.

'I see. Well, I'll keep a look-out until you've recovered a bit.'

From the sky, where he floated effortlessly on air currents or hovered in his inimitable way, Kestrel could see

Mole, the Great Stag, Fox and Vixen. He wondered what was afoot. After checking once or twice on Tawny Owl's progress, he swooped down to speak to Fox.

'I've found Owl,' he said. 'Goodness knows where he's been. He's completely exhausted.'

'Where is he?' Fox asked. 'I need him tonight.'

'Don't know if he's much use at the moment,' said Kestrel. 'What's astir?'

Fox explained the Great Stag's idea.

'I understand,' said the hawk. 'I'll take you to Tawny Owl.'

The sight of Fox approaching him across the parkland was the best medicine for Tawny Owl that could have been produced. Now, at last, he knew his friend was safe. He tottered to his feet and stood, a little unsteadily.

'My dear Owl,' Fox said in great distress. 'Whatever has happened? You look dreadful.'

'It's all right – now,' said Tawny Owl. 'Thank heaven you're still alive, And Vixen too?'

'Yes. She's well.'

'I'm so glad. I saw the men last night – with guns. I meant to tell you, but – well, you know how I react when my pride takes a blow. I'm sure Badger has told you he saw me carrying the – er – well, you know,' he finished lamely.

'I understand perfectly,' said Fox. 'I won't question you any further. None of us will. But you must rest all you can. I shall need you as a look-out again tonight. Will you be able?'

'By then I shall have recovered,' Tawny Owl assured him. 'I think I can fly a little now. I'll go home and sleep properly. Where will you need me?'

'The same place as before. Our friends the deer are preparing a little reception committee.'

Tawny Owl nodded and, still bleary-eyed, took his leave.

'Kestrel,' said Fox. 'I'm relying on you to get the others to their places by the fence. They must be there by dusk.'

'Your wish,' answered Kestrel, 'is my command.'

'Very well,' said Fox. 'And tonight I, for once, shall stay firmly in the background.'

Sure enough, Fox's belief in the poachers' persistence in revenge was proved well-founded. This time they were spotted early on in the evening and the message was passed back along the lines to the Great Stag who quickly mustered his herd. It was then necessary for Fox, Vixen, Badger and Weasel to make themselves scarce before the advance of the men. Along with Hare and the birds, they decided to watch events from the Hollow from where, if necessary, they could make a quick escape to their homes.

The poachers seemed to be in a very ugly mood. Any sign of movement anywhere was enough to set them shooting and, at each report, the watching Farthing Wood animals shuddered at what might have been the fate of some unsuspecting night creature.

Foot by foot, the men entered further into the Park. Foot by foot they decreased the distance between themselves and the White Deer. The deer waited in some agitation. They disliked standing still as danger approached. Some cropped the grass nervously, while others tossed their heads and flicked their short tails. Only the Great Stag, at their head, stood impassive.

They saw the men getting closer from behind the line of trees that helped to screen them. The Great Stag's eyes narrowed as he waited for the right moment. The men remained ignorant. Then he threw his head back and roared like a stag in rut. The deer herd bounded through the trees and raced towards the poachers. The men looked up, startled, at the white mass that galloped towards them, their hooves thundering as in a stampede; a forest of antlers lowered in line. With shouts the men turned and began to run hell for leather back across the grassland. Neither paused a second to take aim. They could only run and run, as fast as they could, away from the white animal tide that threatened to engulf them. Fear lent wings to their feet, for otherwise they must have been caught.

As they neared the Park fence, the deer slackened their pace and swept round in a circle, back towards the open land where they usually stayed, the Great Stag still leading them. The men had gone.

From the Hollow came excited voices.

'Did it work? Have they gone?' asked Hare.

Tawny Owl flew to see. 'Yes, they've gone,' he reported.

'And this time for good,' said Badger.

'How are you so sure?' Weasel wanted to know. 'We all believed that last time.'

'Twice they've been defeated by animals,' said Badger. 'Are they prepared to risk a third tussle?'

'Only if,' said Tawny Owl slowly, 'they are sure they can win.'

Fox looked at him. 'Well,' he said, 'we still have my idea in reserve.'

—18—

Two Friends Return

All was quiet again in White Deer Park for some days. But in the last invasion by the poachers another of the Farthing Wood rabbits had lost its life – this time by the gun, for the men had shot indiscriminately. Fox felt this loss more deeply than any, for he knew that it was he that had, indirectly, caused the death of one of his friends. Rabbit had come to inform him of the death.

'Another one of our does gone,' he had said after explaining how he had found the body. 'And this Park was to be a haven for us! What sort of a haven is it when we rabbits have been thinned out to a mere remnant of those that lived in Farthing Wood?'

'I know, I know,' Fox answered miserably. 'I've had the same from Vole and Fieldmouse. It's very distress-

ing. We couldn't have expected such a terrible winter
– nor this other threat to our survival. The idea of a
Nature Reserve is that it should be a sanctuary for all
wildlife within. These murderous humans seem to have
no respect even for their own laws.'

'Well, let's hope the winter has sent its worst,' rejoined
Rabbit. 'But what can we expect from the humans?'

'Who knows?' Fox answered frankly. 'They may be
back again. They may not. Shall we try and be optimistic
about it?'

'I suppose it's all we *can* do,' agreed Rabbit.

'At any rate,' Fox said brightly, 'you rabbits will soon
be back at your usual numbers, I'll warrant. Your powers of recovery, you know . . . .'

'Why is it the only thing we seem to be renowned for
is how fast we breed?' Rabbit wanted to know. 'I bet
we're no more prolific than the mice. But, you see, Fox,
any danger that's around inhibits our desire to breed.
You know how timid we are.'

'I do indeed,' Fox said. 'Never ever will I forget the
river crossing.' He referred to an incident during the
animals' long journey to the Park when the rabbits had
panicked badly and caused a disaster.

'All right, all right,' nodded Rabbit. 'Neither am I
ever likely to, even if allowed.'

'No hurt intended, I assure you,' said Fox quickly.

'Don't mention it,' was the reply. Then Rabbit smiled.
'Where else in the Wild would a fox talk so politely to
a rabbit?'

Fox smiled back, and Rabbit turned to go.

The afternoon brought an excited Kestrel to Fox's
earth. His piercing cries brought Fox and Vixen hurriedly to the surface.

'What is it, Kestrel? You *do* seem in a state,' Fox said.

'I've just spotted that ginger cat walking in the Warden's garden,' he shrieked.

Fox misunderstood the motive for the hawk's excitement. 'Calm down, calm down,' he said. 'You just make sure you don't go in too close, and he won't attack you again. Your scars healed perfectly, didn't they?'

'No, no, it's not that,' Kestrel said hurriedly. 'I hadn't even thought of it. You don't seem to have grasped the significance of the cat's reappearance. The Warden must be back!' He looked triumphantly at the pair of foxes, as if he had brought the man and his cat back personally.

'Of course!' said Fox. 'The cat disappeared at the same time, didn't he? Oh but, Kestrel, can we be sure?'

'I would have hovered around a little longer to *make* sure,' said Kestrel, 'but I wanted to bring you the news.'

'It's marvellous news,' said Vixen. 'It means we can all breathe again. The poachers won't dare come back now.'

'I'll fly straight back and see if I can spot our protector,' Kestrel offered. 'Then we can spread the word.'

'Oh, this calls for a celebration,' said Fox happily. 'If the Warden is indeed back with us our worries are over.'

The Warden *had* returned and, to prove it, was seen on his rounds later in the day by many of the animals. Badger and Fox stood together by Badger's set talking.

'What changes will he see since he went away?' Badger mused. 'If only we could tell him of those who have been killed.'

'If he counts the head of white deer he will see their numbers have dropped,' said Fox. 'But he may not be suspicious of it.'

'How I wish those slaughterers could be brought before him,' growled Badger. 'Why should they escape their punishment?'

'Well, we're helpless in the matter,' said Fox. 'But, at

least, no more creatures will meet their fate in the Park at *their* hands.'

Little did Fox imagine then that Badger's wish was to be fulfilled, and that the animals of Farthing Wood were to be the instruments of bringing the offenders to justice. For the poachers, ignorant of the Warden's return, were about to make one trip too many to the Nature Reserve.

Fox's own cunning, which perhaps led him to anticipate better than other creatures the way humans might behave, was to be proved right again in his doubts expressed to the Great Stag. The poachers, it seemed, were still determined to wreak revenge where they could, although they now knew they must avoid the deer herd. That very evening they entered the Park at a different point, intent on redressing the balance in their favour by the work of their pistols.

Relieved, as they thought, of the need to stay under cover at night, a lot of the animals, as well as Tawny Owl, were abroad at the time on their various errands. But, separated as they were, they all stopped in their tracks at the same instant as they heard once more the report of a gun.

Fox and Vixen were, as usual, together. 'I don't believe it,' Vixen whispered. 'They can't have come back again.'

'The noise came from that direction,' Fox indicated. 'We haven't heard it from there before.' He scowled. 'The murdering scoundrels,' he said thickly. 'Come on, Vixen, we'd better get back.'

But Vixen did not move.

'What's the matter?' Fox asked. 'We can't stay here.'

'Perhaps it would be better *not* to go back,' Vixen said cryptically.

Fox looked at her in astonishment.

'Do you recall your latest plan?' she reminded him.

'The Warden's garden?' he asked. 'But it's not necessary, now he's back. These men are *his* quarrel now.'

'Exactly,' replied his mate. 'And we can lead him to
them – or rather *them* to him.'

'Phew!' gasped Fox. 'That's a little ambitious – even
for us.'

'Yes, it is,' she acknowledged. 'But don't we all want
these men caught? Well, we *could* make that more likely.'

Fox, as so often, looked at her in sheer admiration.
'You are a wonder,' he said. 'I'm sure we *could* do it.
But we must be very, very careful.'

At the sound of the gun Tawny Owl had automatically
played his part. He flew straight to where the shot had
been fired to locate the danger. He saw the men and,
this time, no victim. The shot had gone astray. Back in
the direction of the home area he winged his way and,
spying Fox and Vixen from the air, told them what he
had found. Fox sent him to warn Badger, Weasel and
any of the others around to exercise the utmost caution,
and to tell them of Vixen's suggestion. Silently Tawny
Owl flew off.

'I want to handle this myself,' Fox said to her. 'I don't
want you at risk too.'

'I'll stay well clear,' she replied. 'But I'll be right
behind you.'

Fox slunk off through the shadows to offer himself as
bait to the poachers, while Vixen crept in his wake,
twenty yards distant. The men were easily spotted, stirring up the dead undergrowth with sticks for any hapless
creature cowering beneath. But Fox, safe behind a broad
oak tree, yapped as he had yapped before in their hearing. The men looked up and saw a shadowy figure under
the trees. At once they gave chase, both firing haphaz-
ardly. Fox, his body close to the ground, sped away
through the copse towards the Warden's Lodge. Behind

the men ran Vixen, nervous, frightened, but with every nerve tingling.

Tawny Owl had rounded up Badger, Hare, Weasel and Rabbit. Then he went on to inform the Great Stag and the deer herd. Together all these animals began to converge from different directions on the focal point. No-one wanted to be left out of the adventure, and Rabbit had a particular wish to see himself avenged. The lights were on in the cottage, for the Warden also had heard the gunfire and was preparing to investigate. Badger even spotted Ginger Cat roaming outside the door. All seemed to be set for the finale.

Fox ran swiftly on a looping course for the cottage lights, making himself moderate his speed to keep the men within distance of him. As he neared his goal, he saw the Warden framed in the doorway and, to the left of the Lodge, the deer herd milling about in spectral array. Too late the poachers saw where they were running and stopped. As they tried to swing away to run from their fate, the deer herd rushed towards them, surrounding them, and buffeted them off their feet. The Warden raced over and shouted back towards his open door. While Fox and Vixen delightedly mingled with their watching friends a second man, whom Badger recognized as the animal doctor, ran out of the house. The poachers were collared and marched indoors. For a moment, in the doorway, the Warden turned back. He looked at the array of wild creatures strangely gathered together before his home. Each one of them looked towards him, and an expression came over his face of a wonderful compassion and affection that lit an answering flame in their own hearts. The moment passed, but there was a timelessness about it that was never to be forgotten. When he had gone, the most complete and utter silence reigned.

Finally the Great Stag spoke, rather stumblingly and inadequately. He was greatly moved. 'My friends, today we have formed a new bond of companionship,' he said. 'Today we are at one with Nature – er – and humanity.'

No-one else spoke or moved. The air above, the ground beneath were shot with magic; a strange echo of an Ancient World that none of them could comprehend had sounded in White Deer Park.

—19—
Thaw

The spell was broken by the movement of Ginger Cat who walked nonchalantly over to Badger. He seemed quite undeterred by the memory of their fight.

'We meet again,' he purred enigmatically.

Badger nodded. 'I hope in happier circumstances?' he ventured.

'Certainly,' came the reply. 'I'm quite aware I owe my life to your forbearance. Er – how is your friend the hawk?'

'Perfectly well,' answered Badger. 'And yourself?'

'Oh, couldn't be better,' the cat said. 'But I must say I'm relieved to be back here. I was taken to a spot miles away and shut up with a lot of other cats in cages while my mast – ah, I mean the man, was treated for his illness.'

Badger smiled at the cat's slip of the tongue, and Ginger Cat smiled back. He and Badger knew each other pretty well.

Fox and Vixen came over for a word, and the Great Stag led the deer herd away.

'Well, you all look a lot happier since I saw you last,' said Ginger Cat. 'And I'm glad to see, Fox, you've put on a little weight.'

'Oh yes,' said Fox. 'We've had some hard times, but we've come through all right.'

Badger recalled Toad's last words before hibernation when he had wished they would all 'come through' the winter. How long ago that seemed. And now, with the temperature steadily rising, they could all look forward to their friend's re-appearance. But, of course, they had not all 'come through'. What changes Toad would see in their numbers.

'You seem very pensive, Badger,' remarked Ginger Cat. 'What is it?'

'Oh, nothing really,' he said. 'Just thinking of old friends.'

Weasel, Tawny Owl, Hare and Rabbit joined them.

'Three times we've overcome those humans,' Rabbit said proudly. 'They must think the Park is jinxed.'

'The ones we've just seen caught?' Ginger Cat enquired. 'What happened before? You must tell me your news.'

'I will,' Badger offered. 'But another time, my feline friend. It's been quite a night.'

Hare felt inclined to mention to his cousin Rabbit that he had not seen *him* much in evidence on the two previous occasions, but decided against it. It was not a time for needless criticism.

The animals and Tawny Owl bid Ginger Cat farewell and, together, wandered slowly away from the cottage.

'I think we're entitled to have that celebration now,' Vixen said to her mate.

'Yes, I think so too. Now, truly, our troubles are over.'

'But our party is incomplete,' said Badger. 'It would be churlish to ignore the hedgehogs and, most of all, Toad.'

'Pooh, there's no knowing when *they'll* be back with us,' said Rabbit. 'And in any case they've played no part in our adventures.'

Now Hare felt he must intervene. 'I think some of us here present could hardly be said to have played much more of a part than they have,' he said pointedly. The remark was not lost on any of the others, Rabbit included. He looked a little foolish.

'Well, well, that's as may be,' said Badger, smoothing things over. 'But I don't think any of us need to have particular qualifications to enjoy ourselves together.'

'Why don't we make it a double celebration?' suggested Vixen. 'To mark our survival through our first winter and also to rejoice at seeing our hibernating friends again.'

'I think that's an excellent idea, Vixen,' said Badger. 'Don't you, Fox?'

'I do. Incidentally, does anyone realize we've none of us thought of Adder?'

'Certainly a case of out of sight, out of mind,' Tawny Owl remarked. 'But then, he's never the most genial of characters.'

'Nevertheless, it would be unthinkable not to have him with us,' Badger declared. 'In his own way, he's been a loyal enough friend.'

'As I have cause to remember,' murmured Vixen.

'Then it's postponed until the spring?' Weasel summarized.

'Perhaps not quite that long,' said Fox. 'The first

really mild spell will bring the hedgehogs out. And probably Toad, too. I'm not exactly sure how long snakes need to sleep.'

As February progressed to its conclusion, the final traces of snow and ice disappeared completely from the Park. The long, hard winter, which had begun so early, released its grip at last. Everything pointed to the fact that a warm spring was approaching, perhaps sooner than usual. Mild breezes blew and, underfoot, the ground was soft and spongy with water where the snow had melted. Most days were blessed with sunshine, however, which prevented the Reserve from becoming too waterlogged.

Already the earliest buds were swelling when the hedgehogs climbed out of their beds of thick leaves and twigs. Their first thought was food, and insects, slugs and spiders were in such abundance because of the mild weather, that they could never have guessed that for months previously their friends had battled against starvation. The hedgehogs' elected leader, having feasted grandly, went to look for signs of his old travelling companions.

As always, Kestrel was the first to spot this new movement on the ground. He dived downwards to intercept his recently emerged friend. 'Hallo, Hedgehog! Hallo!' he called as he hurtled down.

'Kestrel! It's good to see you!' said Hedgehog enthusiastically. 'How have you been?'

'Better than most,' Kestrel informed him. 'How did you sleep?'

Hedgehog laughed. 'Like a log – as always,' he replied. 'And the others? Have they fared well?'

'Not all of them, I'm afraid. You have been well out of the troubles we've experienced since we last saw you.'

'Dear, dear,' said Hedgehog. 'Has it been a bad winter, then?'

'The worst any of us can remember,' answered Kestrel. 'And that includes Badger.'

'But tell me,' Hedgehog said, looking concerned, 'have any lost their lives?'

'Many,' said the hawk simply. 'The voles are reduced to a single pair – Vole himself and his mate – and the fieldmice only one better. The rabbits have suffered badly, too. And the squirrels have had their losses.'

'This is shocking,' responded Hedgehog. 'I never expected anything like this. But Fox, Badger, Vixen . . .?'

'The larger animals have all survived – but only just. I tell you, Hedgehog, you can't conceive how near to death we all were. I think this winter has left its mark on everyone.'

'Is little Mole then – ?'

'No, no. He's all right. I think he suffered less than anyone. It appears his beloved worms are easier to find in cold weather – it restricts their movements.'

Hedgehog nodded. 'And the other birds?'

'Yes, Owl and Whistler have made it, too. But the winter hasn't been the only thing we've had to contend with.'

'Good gracious! What else?'

'Well, come along. Come and see the others and you'll hear all about it. I'll meet you at Badger's set.'

So Hedgehog made his way along and soon was surrounded by a number of the other animals. Together they told him of the harrowing events during the preceding months. At the end of it, he felt glad and relieved that *some* of his friends were there to greet him.

'And I've slept through it all in blissful ignorance,' he said wonderingly.

'Best thing to have done,' Hare told him. 'You've had a happy release.'

With the re-appearance of the hedgehogs, the animals knew that their party, although reduced, would soon be together again. One particularly warm morning in early March they all decided to make the trip to the Pond, as Badger was quite convinced that Toad and Adder would be tempted by its pleasantness from their burrow.

As they approached the water, the scene of such a dramatic occurrence during the winter, there were already signs of activity. The Edible Frogs had woken and were splashing about furiously, or sitting by the water's edge, croaking. And nearby, on a sunny slope, basking delightedly in the warm rays of the sun, who should they find but Adder?

'Mmmm,' he murmured dreamily as he spied the company, 'don't talk to me. I'm not really awake yet.'

The animals laughed but ignored his request.

'Certainly not alert,' Fox corrected him, referring to his proximity to the frogs, 'but definitely awake.'

'Where's Toad?' Badger asked. 'Did you leave him behind?'

'Oh no,' drawled Adder. 'When I awoke the hole was quite empty. He must have decided to greet the sun before me.'

'I wonder where he is,' said Badger. 'We couldn't have missed him.'

'I've no idea,' said the snake. 'But please – leave me. Let me doze.'

'Unsociable old so-and-so,' muttered Tawny Owl. 'We'll get no sense out of him for the moment.'

Fox was looking for the patriarch of the Pond, the large frog that knew Toad best. Perhaps he could throw some light on Toad's absence. He found him, newly glistening, surveying the scene from a piece of flat rock.

'Oh yes, I saw him,' he answered in reply to Fox's question. 'Two days ago. He was making off towards the Park boundary.'

'*What*!?'

'Yes – there, in that direction.'

The animals were stunned. What could he be up to?

'Perhaps he's lost his memory,' piped up Mole. 'During his long sleep, I mean,' he added, thinking he may have sounded silly.

'You all seem to have lost yours,' rejoined Adder in his lazy lisp. 'It's obvious what's happened. It's Spring. Toad's returning to his birthplace.' His red eyes glinted in the sun as he looked at their astonished faces contemptuously. 'He's on his way back to Farthing Wood.'

—20—

Whistled Off

The rest of the animals and the birds were dumbfounded. They looked at each other with blank faces. It was too incredible. Yet it had happened before. They all owed their knowledge of the Park's existence to Toad, who had discovered it and travelled across country for the best part of a year to bring news of it to the beleaguered Farthing Wood. On that occasion, however, he had been returning to his old home – Farthing Pond – only to find it had disappeared; destroyed by humans.

'But *this* is Toad's home now,' said Squirrel. 'He led us here. His old home no longer exists. How can he have forgotten all that?'

'I think he can't help himself,' observed Kestrel. 'It's his homing instinct. In the Spring it's like an irresistible urge that draws Toad and creatures like him back to their birthplace to spawn and reproduce themselves. And Toad's birthplace was Farthing Pond.'

'It's quite true,' agreed Tawny Owl. 'None of us can forget when, on our journey here, Toad started doubling back because the pull of his old home was still so strong.'

'Well, he can't have gone far,' said Fox. 'Not in two days. We must find him and reason with him.'

'No time like the present,' said Badger. 'He may not even have left the Reserve yet.'

'I'll see if I can spot him,' Kestrel offered. 'But his camouflage is so good it might be difficult.'

'There's no need for us all to go,' said Fox. 'That would only delay things. Badger and I will go with Vixen and, Whistler, perhaps you can assist Kestrel in the search?'

'I shall be delighted to do anything in my power,' said the heron, flapping his wings and making his familiar whistling noise.

'We'll visit you again, Adder,' Fox told the still motionless snake. 'I hope by then our party will be complete.'

'You can visit if you wish,' replied Adder. 'But I can't guarantee to be in the same spot. I have other things to do apart from lying around here waiting for your return.'

'Ungracious as ever,' said Tawny Owl loudly, but Adder was quite used to such remarks and only flicked his forked tongue in and out in a derogatory manner.

While the other animals dispersed, the two foxes and Badger trotted off in the direction of the Hollow. It was here they had all spent their first night on arriving in White Deer Park, and it was close to the hole in the fence through which they had first entered. Fox was quite sure Toad would be travelling on the same route if he had, indeed, intended to leave the Reserve.

Fox and Vixen skirted the Hollow while Badger entered it to make quite certain Toad was not safely there, all the time waiting for his friends at the traditional meeting-point. But he was not, and when they arrived at the boundary on this side of the Park they found Kestrel waiting for them.

'No sign as yet,' he announced. 'I think he must be outside.'

'What a nuisance he is,' said Badger. 'Now we'll all be exposing ourselves to risk on his behalf.'

'It's obvious we can't stay together outside the Park,' said Fox. 'We shall be far too conspicuous. But he can't possibly be far away, travelling at his pace. Kestrel, can you scout around in the immediate area for a bit? He may only be a matter of a few paces away.'

But when Kestrel alighted again the answer was the same. Whistler, too, had had no luck. 'There seems to be a distinct dearth of toads in the area,' he informed them in his droll way.

'There's nothing for it, then,' said Fox, 'but that we'll have to go through the fence. We'll split up and try a separate patch each.'

'Wouldn't it be wiser for you to leave it until nightfall?' suggested Kestrel.

'Safer, yes,' admitted Fox. 'But more difficult. Toad is a small animal and would be even harder to locate in the dark.'

'We'll keep our eyes open for you all, then,' said Kestrel. 'And we can warn you if necessary.'

'Thanks,' said Fox. 'Well, Vixen, Badger, shall we go?'

The three animals passed singly through the broken fence and Fox allotted them each their areas. 'If you find him,' he said to them, 'make the birds understand and they can round up the other two of us.'

So they each went their different ways, using sight and scent in their search.

It was Vixen in the end who found their lost friend. Perhaps half a mile from where she left the Park a narrow and normally shallow little brook ran bubbling across country. On its banks sat two small boys watching the water – now swollen by the thaw – run gurgling past them. Occasionally they would dip their nets into the stream, for they were collecting sticklebacks and water-bugs and anything else that came along. By their side on the bank were some big jars full of water into which they were emptying their nets whenever they caught a new specimen. All this Vixen saw as she approached as close as she could before having to hide herself among some gorse scrub. From this vantage point she could watch securely and see everything. What she saw in one of the jars made her heart skip a beat. For it was a toad, and she knew that, as likely as not, it was her toad. But then she was not so sure, for another of the jars also contained a toad, and this one was considerably larger than the other.

The two poor entombed creatures were jumping up and down in the water inside the jars, banging their blunt noses against the glass in frenzied and utterly useless attempts to escape. Their exit was firmly sealed by metal lids. Now Vixen was in a dilemma. For there was nothing she could do to free the toads. Yet she knew she must prevent the boys taking the jars away with them before she knew if her friend was one of the captives. She certainly needed Fox's advice and as quickly as possible, because the boys might choose to leave at any time.

From the safety of the gorse-bushes she barked, hoping one of the birds might be close. She saw the boys look up at the noise, and peer all about them. But they could see nothing, and soon turned their attention to the stream again.

Neither Kestrel nor Whistler heard Vixen's call, but Whistler had seen the stream and the boys while on the wing and now came looking for the three animals to warn them of the presence of humans. Luckily, as Vixen was closest, he found her first.

'I've seen them,' she nodded as he landed awkwardly beside her. 'And I think I've seen Toad.'

'Perfect!' cried the heron. 'Then we can collect him and make a hasty retreat.'

'It's not as simple as that, I'm afraid, Whistler,' she answered, and explained what was in the glass jars.

'How awful! Whatever can we do?' he boomed.

'I don't know. But you must bring Fox. He'll think of something. And tell Badger, too.'

'At once,' said the heron and flapped noisily into flight again. Vixen shuddered as she saw his huge form rise above her, immediately catching the attention of the two fascinated little humans who began to point and chatter excitedly. Fortunately, however, they did not move from the stream bank.

Fox and Badger came quietly and cautiously to join Vixen behind her prickly screen. They listened to her news.

'Of course it may not be Toad,' said Fox, 'but, naturally, we can't take the chance.'

'Oh dear, oh dear,' said Badger anxiously. 'Poor creatures. This is just the same way he was captured in Farthing Pond and brought all this way from his home.'

'A blessing in disguise, as it turned out,' Fox reminded him. 'Otherwise there would have been no White Deer Park for *us*.'

'I know, I know,' Badger nodded. 'But it is no blessing this time.'

'Well, there's only one thing to do,' declared Fox resolutely. 'We must rescue both these toads.'

'Of course. But how?'

'We'll take the captors by surprise. They're young. They may scare easily. If we all rush on them together, barking and snarling, they may run. To take them by surprise is our only hope. Hallo, here's Kestrel!'

Whistler had also informed Kestrel of developments. No sooner had he heard than the hawk had flown close to the brook, hovering as he examined the jars' contents with his phenomenal eye power. He came swooping up to the three animals. 'One of them is Toad all right,' he screeched. 'The smaller one.'

'Get Whistler back here,' Fox ordered peremptorily. 'I have need of his great bill.'

The heron came wheeling low to listen to the plan.

'As we make our charge you must sail in and snatch the jar up in your bill. Make sure it's the one with the smaller of the two toads inside,' Fox told him. 'Right, all ready? Together then!'

Across the grass hurtled Fox, Badger and Vixen making the utmost racket possible. The two boys jumped up, uncertain what to do. As they hesitated Whistler soared over and plummeted downward like a dive bomber. Barely giving himself time to land, he snatched at a jar and lumbered away, surprised at the object's weight. The boys seized the other jars, including the one containing the second toad, and made off along the bank, leaving their nets behind as the fierce animals approached them. Then Fox, Badger and Vixen heard Kestrel screaming at Whistler in the air. 'It's the wrong jar! You've got the wrong one!'

Partly in alarm and partly because his bill was already aching dreadfully at the unaccustomed weight, Whistler let go of the jar, which crashed to the ground and in-

stantly shattered. Out jumped the strange toad, none
the worse for the experience, having been buoyed up by
the water. 'Thank you! Thank you!' it called in its croaky
voice and began to hop away as fast as its legs could
carry it.

Now Whistler felt he must atone for his error. He
came sailing back after the frightened boys and stabbed
at them with his pointed beak, with the idea of making
them drop Toad. So vicious were his attacks that this
ploy met with quick success. All the jars were dropped
by the shrieking boys, the one carrying Toad rolling
down the bank and landing with a plop in the stream.
There it was buffeted and swept along by the current,
the jar pivoting end to end as it spun away.

Inside the jar Toad was stunned, dazed, stupefied.
One minute the jar had been standing on end on the
bank, then it had been grabbed up in the air and he had
bobbed up and down while the boy ran with it; then it
had fallen with a thud to the ground, rolled over and
over and now was racing along on the water, the reeds
and rushes shooting past on either side of his clear glass
prison. He did not know that any of his friends were
involved in the events, for all had happened too quickly.
The next thing he knew the jar came to rest against a
submerged barrier in the water. He looked out of the
glass and saw two stilt-like legs pressed against the side.
Then down came a huge beak and Toad, jar and all,
was hoisted up, higher and higher and higher still into
the sky.

'Don't drop him!' shouted Fox. 'Carry him to the
Park!'

'And back to the Park with us!' cried Badger. 'The
party is complete!'

—21—

Home or Away?

Once safely inside the Park fence again, the five friends made for the Hollow. Whistler carefully deposited the jar on the ground and they all stood looking at it. By now Toad had recognized the faces and was leaping about desperately.

'Now what do we do?' Kestrel queried. Whistler was resting his aching beak and was unable to speak. The three animals stared at Toad and frowned. Toad settled down and stared back.

Eventually Whistler said, 'The other toad came to no harm when I dropped it. May I suggest a repeat performance?'

Fox shook his head. 'No. We can't risk it. The other

toad was lucky not to have been cut by the glass. But it may not be such a lucky drop again.'

'Well, I'm afraid if that lid doesn't come off soon, Toad might suffocate,' Badger said worriedly. 'We don't know how long he's been in there.'

'What if we found a large stone and dropped it on the jar?' Kestrel suggested.

'Who could carry such a stone?' Fox asked. 'And it would be even more dangerous for Toad inside.'

'I think there's only one way he'll get out of there,' Vixen said.

'Well, Vixen, what is it?' Fox asked quickly.

'The Warden,' she replied.

'Bravo!' cried Badger. 'We'll take the jar to him. He can open it.'

'Well, Counsellor, you've done it again,' Fox smiled at her. 'Whistler, are you up to portering a little further?'

'The heart is always willing, my dear Fox. But my poor bill does the carrying,' he answered. 'However, if it's a case of life and death. . . . '

'I'm afraid it is,' said Fox. 'We'll meet you at the cottage.'

So once again the baffled and desperate Toad was hoisted into the air, and once again the ground rushed away from beneath him. The next time he was set down he was terrified to see a cat's face come and peer at him, and he became more frantic than ever. Whistler stood by the side of the jar enigmatically. His large size made him quite fearless of the Warden's pet. He knew Fox, Badger and Vixen would be a long time arriving for, even without snow on the ground, the journey was a considerable one. Kestrel discreetly stayed well out of the way.

'Whatever have you got here?' Ginger Cat whispered, prowling all round the container.

'An old friend of mine,' answered Whistler, 'who's got himself into a spot of bother.'

'He has, hasn't he? He won't get out of there very easily.'

'Not on his own, no. Is your master within?'

'I have no – ' Ginger Cat began, then shrugged. 'I believe so,' he finished. 'I see now. You want his assistance. Bring that object outside the door, and I'll try to attract his attention.'

Whistler complied, and Ginger Cat commenced an almighty howling outside the cottage door. There was no response. 'I'll have to fetch him,' he said, and squeezed through the cat flap. Whistler heard more miaowing and wailing going on inside and then, at last, the door opened. Ginger Cat stepped daintily out, followed by a puzzled Warden.

The man looked down and saw a sedentary heron guarding a large glass jar with something inside it. He did not know what to make of such a sight. Whistler decided to give him a clue. 'Kraaank,' he cried raucously, and pushed the jar towards the man's feet. The man bent and picked up the jar and saw the toad inside. Whistler snapped his bill excitedly, producing a sound like a castanet. The man looked at him and looked back at the jar. He knew herons ate creatures like frogs and could only surmise it had discovered this titbit and could not get at it. He unscrewed the lid and gently tipped Toad out, intending to save him from the two predators at hand. But before he could pick up the small creature, Toad leapt away as fast as he could, making for cover.

Ginger Cat saw the movement and made as if to pounce. But Whistler forestalled him. 'Leave it all to me, Toad, my friend,' he said and carefully lowered his beak. The Warden watched enthralled as the heron, instead of gobbling the morsel straight down its gullet as he had expected, gently took it up and flew away into the centre of the Park.

Fox, Badger and Vixen saw Whistler coming, carrying Toad, and ceased to run. Then they made a circle round Toad as he put his feet hesitantly on the ground, and gave him encouraging licks.

'Dear old Toad,' said Badger, almost overcome. 'What an adventure you've had! Oh, it's good to have you safe with us.'

'Thank you, Badger, thank you,' said Toad. 'And, Whistler, thank you most of all. I never thought I would see any of you again.'

'Why did you do it? Why did you leave the Park?' Fox asked. 'We came looking for you this morning at the Pond and Adder said you had gone.'

'I just can't stop myself, Fox,' Toad answered. 'I know it's silly, but in the spring I feel I have to go home. I seem to lose all control over myself. It's like being taken over by some kind of Power, much greater and stronger than I am.'

'But this is your home now,' said Badger. 'There *is* no other home for you. Your birthplace no longer exists.'

'I know. I know it. But I *have* to go.'

'Well, you see what happens when you stray outside the safety of the Reserve,' Fox admonished him. 'You're lucky to be back here.'

'Oh, don't you think I know it? You're all so sensible. Everything you say is true. You'll have to restrain me.'

'Perhaps we should have kept you in the jar until you can see sense,' Badger said and laughed.

'If only Adder had been awake when I woke,' Toad said, 'he might have dissuaded me. Oh, it's wonderful to see you all. Where are the others? Are they all right?'

'Not all of them,' Vixen said quietly. 'It was a cruel

winter, Toad. Some of your friends are no longer around to welcome you back.'

'But – but – surely – ' he stammered, 'there are – more – than just – you four?'

'Oh *yes*,' Fox said reassuringly. 'You've already seen Kestrel. And there's Mole and Hare and his family – well, less one actually – and *most* of the rabbits and squirrels and Weasel, of course. And Tawny Owl – he's indestructible.'

'And all the mice?'

'Er – no, not all. Well, not many, really. They took it the hardest.'

'The hedgehogs?'

'Yes, yes, the hedgehogs are all right. They slept through it all, just like you and Adder.'

'And then, Toad, off you were going to go without even coming to see if we were still alive?' Badger said pointedly.

'Oh, Badger! I feel so guilty,' said the wretched animal. 'How could I? Never to know what you've all suffered!'

His friends fell silent as they watched Toad's anguish.

Badger, compassionate as always, spoke first. 'What can we do to help?' he asked.

'I don't know,' croaked Toad miserably. 'Except not to let me out of your sight – at least until the mating season's over.'

'Well, well, perhaps we can keep shifts,' Badger said jokingly.

'We've a lot more to tell you about our months without you,' said Fox. 'And Adder hasn't heard the tale yet. You'll both want to meet up with all the others again, won't you? I think we should all meet in the Hollow just like we used to. We haven't all been together since last autumn.'

'An excellent idea,' agreed Badger. 'We must pass the word. Er – Toad, I want you to stay with me for the time being. For safety's sake, you know. Would you care to climb on my back?'

While his friends had been thus occupied, Kestrel had continued in his usual pastime of skimming over the Reserve on effortless wings, soaring and diving again. But he saw something that made him drop earthwards in curiosity. Through the gap in the fence where Fox, Badger and Vixen had recently passed in and out of the Park now came a solitary, plump toad – the very one Whistler had rescued and then dropped. Kestrel landed and spoke to the stranger.

'Are you seeking sanctuary here now?' he asked. 'You'd be wise to do so.'

'In a way,' replied the toad. 'This is my home. I was born here in the pond. It's spring and I've been travelling towards it since I came out of hibernation. During the summer I wander quite a way and last winter I hibernated outside the Park.'

Kestrel was struck by the irony of the opposing directions Toad and the stranger had taken to return to their respective birthplaces, meeting in the middle, as it were, by the brook-side. 'How strange,' he murmured. The toad gave him a quizzical look which prompted him to explain.

'Yes, that is the way of things,' said the toad. 'We didn't speak. I was already in a jar when the young humans caught your friend. I believe he'd been swimming in the stream.'

'So you are returning to mate?' Kestrel asked.

'Yes. I'm full of spawn at this time of year,' replied the toad, revealing that she was a female. 'When I'm paired the eggs will be released in the water and fertilized by my mate.'

Kestrel glared at the toad. An idea had struck him. 'I beg your pardon,' he said. 'I'm not an expert on amphibia. I hadn't realized you are a lady toad. What are you called?'

'Paddock,' she replied.

'I'm delighted to have had this talk,' said Kestrel. 'And I think our friend will be interested to hear about it.'

'May I say how grateful I am for my rescue,' said Paddock. 'Now my babies will be born in safety.'

'I hope we may meet again,' the hawk said courteously. 'But now I'll leave you to continue your journey.' He spread his wings again.

In the air he floated blissfully on warm currents, thinking hard. Unexpectedly, he had perhaps discovered the one thing that might keep Toad in White Deer Park. The pull of Farthing Pond could perhaps be surmounted by Toad's desire for a mate.

—22—

Life Goes On

No sooner had Kestrel come to this conclusion than he went in search of Fox, who told him that Toad had been restored to them. The hawk described his discussion with Paddock and asked Fox's opinion of his idea.

'Kestrel, I really think you've hit upon something,' he replied. 'After all, the sole reason for these journeys of toads and frogs to their home ponds is to breed. We'll introduce a dash of romance into our friend's life.'

'Where *is* Toad?' asked Kestrel. 'Perhaps we should intercept Paddock's journey to the pond before any other male shows interest.'

'A good point,' acknowledged Fox. 'Come on. He's with Badger.'

'By the set they found Toad talking to an excited

Mole. Badger was doing the rounds of the Farthing Wood animals, now back in their individual homes, to tell them of the meeting in the Hollow.

'Isn't it grand to have Toad back?' Mole chattered. 'It's just like old times.'

'Did Badger get tired of carrying you?' Fox asked Toad with a grin.

'He made me get down,' Toad said ruefully. 'He said I was tugging at his coat so. It's my grasping pads, you see.' He held up his horny front feet, one at a time, to demonstrate. 'They become very developed at this time of year. That's so that we males can hang on tight to our mates and not get separated.'

'Well, I think we can find something else for you to grasp on to,' said Fox, delighted that Toad had unwittingly introduced the subject himself. 'But first, you must hang on to me.'

'Now it really is like old times,' chuckled Toad. 'Remember how you used to carry me on our journey here, Fox?'

'Of course I do,' said Fox. 'Now, up you get. Ouch!' He winced. 'I see what Badger means. Ow! Well really, Toad, you didn't grip as hard as this even when I rescued you from the fire.'

'I'm sorry,' said Toad. 'I'll try not to tug too much. Where are we going?'

'Wait and see,' was the mysterious reply. 'Now, Kestrel, which way please?'

The lady toad had not progressed very far into the Park. She had paused to refresh herself with some insects and seemed to have settled down to digest them.

Toad dismounted of his own accord by leaping from Fox's back. 'My, what a beauty!' he exclaimed as he saw Paddock. He looked at Fox with a wry grin that seemed to express better than words what he thought of his friend. Fox grinned back and only stayed long enough to see Toad grasp the unprotesting Paddock firmly round her middle. He was amused to see how much larger than Toad she was as she waddled off with her affectionate burden on her way to the Pond.

'Well I never,' Fox laughed to himself. 'And not a word exchanged! I wonder how Vixen would like me to be so matter of fact?'

Kestrel also had been watching from the air. 'I thought so,' he muttered. 'Easy as pie.'

Some days later Adder was seen sunning himself in the Hollow.

'Hallo, stranger!' cried Weasel. 'We've all been waiting for you to put in an appearance. We're having a get-together.'

'Very nice, I'm sure,' remarked Adder. 'But you are mistaken if you believe I came to this spot out of any gregarious tendency. The fact is I could no longer witness the shameless scenes in that Pond with equanimity.'

'What *are* you talking about, Adder?'

'The length and breadth of the water is alive with courting couples,' he replied, 'whether they be frogs, toads or newts.'

'Well, naturally – it's Spring,' said Weasel. 'Or hadn't you realized?'

'I'm quite aware of that,' Adder snapped. 'But they seem to have no regard at all for others in the area with the way they're carrying on. Even Toad has been affected by it,' he added primly.

'This sounds to me like a touch of jealousy,' Weasel remarked pointedly.

'Rubbish,' returned Adder. 'It's not a touch of anything except perhaps good breeding.'

'More like a lack of breeding, in your case,' Weasel rejoined wickedly.

'If you'll excuse me, I don't care to converse in this manner,' Adder told him, and began to slither away.

'Don't go!' cried Weasel, who now regretted his unkind remark. 'I didn't mean what I said. I'm sorry. Please stay. We hardly ever see you.'

Adder, never very susceptible to overtures of friendship, flickered his tongue in an uncertain manner. He hated to give signs of weakness. In the end he compromised. 'I'm going on a hunting trip,' he told Weasel. 'I haven't eaten for five months. But when I've managed to put a little plumpness behind my scales I'll be back.'

Weasel had to be content with this vague promise, and went to convey it to the rest of the community.

'Well, at least he doesn't intend to shun us completely,' said Fox.

'Best thing for him to do is to hunt himself up a nice female adder,' Tawny Owl observed crustily. 'She would take some of the starchiness out of him.'

'Isn't he a character, though?' Vixen laughed. 'He really is quite unique.'

'Thank goodness for that,' said Hare. 'Just imagine two like him around.'

'So it seems as if our celebration is to be delayed once more?' said Badger. 'I wonder when Toad will leave the Pond?'

'Not till the mating season's over,' answered Fox, glancing a little coyly at Vixen. 'And we know how long that goes on.'

Back in White Deer Pond, Toad and Paddock were still united as she dived underwater to lay her eggs. Other toads had already done so, for strings of eggs could be seen wound round weed and plant-stem. But the offspring of Toad and Paddock were destined to start their tadpole life in a different setting. For these eggs, as they descended in the water, attached themselves to some very different objects sticking up from the mud: the rusting remains of two quite harmless shotguns.

At last the day dawned when all the animals were ready to hold their celebration. Fox and Vixen made their way to the Hollow where many of their friends had already gathered. They could see Badger and Weasel chatting lightheartedly with Kestrel, while Hare and Rabbit exchanged views from the midst of their families. Toad, Adder and Tawny Owl had assembled on the lip of the Hollow and looked towards the pair of foxes as if awaiting their arrival.

'Dear, dear friends,' murmured Fox. 'How glad I am to see them together again. I think we should count our blessings that so many of us are still here to take pleasure in each other's company.'

'Yes, indeed,' said Vixen. 'It's due to our ties of friendship more than anything else that we were able to survive our troubles. Alone, it could have been another story.'

Fox nodded. Now they could see the smaller animals bunching together in a corner of their meeting-place. Mole was there with the mice, the squirrels and the hedgehogs. In the air a familiar whistle heralded the arrival of their friend the heron.

'A fond greeting to you all,' said Whistler joyfully as he landed amongst the sprouting bracken. 'This is a wonderful day!'

'Then let's make it one we shall always remember,' said Fox. 'So that, whatever may happen in the future, whatever fate may befall us, we shall remember that this day, together, we rejoiced to say that WE ARE ALIVE.'

The Siege of White Deer Park

Adder could see nothing of his attacker. He was unable to turn to look behind, and the pressure was so great on his body that he thought his bones might break. There were no animals in the Park who ate snake and so Adder was in no doubt that he was trapped either by a human foot, or, more likely, by the very creature he had intended himself to surprise. There was a momentary easing of the pressure and Adder at once tried to turn. As soon as he moved, a huge paw swung round and patted at his head. Luckily for him the claws were retracted.

The Siege of
White Deer Park

Contents

For Sarah, Rachael, David
and Ruth

—1—
What Sort of Creature?

In the Nature Reserve of White Deer Park the animals were looking forward to the bustle of Spring. It was the end of February and dead Winter's grasp was loosening little by little with each spell of sunshine. The survivors of the band of beasts and birds who had travelled to the haven of the Park from their destroyed home in Farthing Wood had passed their third winter in the confines of the Reserve. Only a few still survived. The short life spans of most had run their course. But now their descendants populated the Park, and they knew no other home. These voles and mice, hedgehogs, rabbits and hares mingled and mated as natives with others of their kind whose forefathers had always lived within the Park's boundaries. Yet they were still conscious of a sort of allegiance to the few stalwarts of the old Farthing Wood community who remained alive.

Foremost among these were the Farthing Wood Fox and his mate Vixen, venerated almost as mythical beings to whom the animals turned for advice and counsel. They were the doyens of the Park's inhabitants, along with the aged Great Stag who was still supreme among the deer herd. Fox's oldest companion, Badger, was also a counsellor who tried to promote harmony between birds and beasts where it was feasible within their own natural order. Badger was very ancient now and never strayed far from his own set. He was slow, dim-sighted and rather feeble, but his kindly ways made him, if less respected, more loved even than Fox.

Tawny Owl, Adder, Toad, Weasel and Whistler the heron still lived and were occasional companions of Badger's extreme old age. But the old creature missed Mole, who had been his special friend. Mole's offspring – the result of his union with Mirthful, a female born in the Reserve – tended to live their own lives. So Badger suffered the loss of the wonderful bond that had existed between the two underground dwellers. Mole's allotted span of existence had reached its end during the winter. As he had lived, so he died – underground. His home had become his grave, and his tiny body went unnoticed in the labyrinth of tunnels. But he was remembered and mourned.

The descendants of Fox and Vixen now stretched almost to the fourth generation, for in the spring the cubs of their grandchildren would be born. From their own first litter Friendly and Charmer survived. Their cub Bold, who had left the Reserve and died outside it, had mated with Whisper who had journeyed to the Park for the safe birth of her own offspring. Now they, too, would become parents. So each season the Farthing Wood lineage was extended.

Badger and Tawny Owl had never paired off in their second home. They were too old and set in their ways – at least, so they said. As for Adder, who vanished altogether for long periods – well, no one was quite sure about him . . . .

It was dusk on one of the last days of February when the first signs of some strange influence in their lives appeared to one of the old comrades from Farthing Wood. Tawny Owl had been quartering the Park's boundaries where these adjoined the open downland. He noticed an unusual number of rabbits converging on a hole scraped under part of the fencing. The timid animals were jostling and bumping each other in their attempts to reach this entrance to the Reserve before their fellows.

'Hm,' mused Owl. 'This is odd. What's their hurry, I wonder?' He was not thinking of the possibilities for himself in this sudden abundance of food. His first thought was for the cause of their fright. He flew out of the Park a little way, following the rabbits' trail backwards – all of the time expecting to discover what was driving them. But he saw nothing, however much his night eyes scanned the ground.

'*Something* scared them,' he murmured to himself. 'Yet why haven't they dived for their burrows?' Tawny Owl knew all about the behaviour of rabbits.

He flew back and hooted a question at them. 'What's all the fuss about?'

Some of the animals looked up but, when they saw the owl, they scuttled ahead even faster. They were certainly not going to stop still to talk to a hunter! And, by the time Tawny Owl remembered his stomach, they had disappeared into the undergrowth.

He perched in an ash tree and pondered, his great round eyes staring unseeingly through the bare branches. He rustled his brown wings.

'No point brooding on it,' he muttered. 'Things reveal themselves eventually.' He flew off on his noiseless flight into the gathering darkness.

A few days later, again in the evening, Fox and Vixen were emerging from their den to go foraging. In the winter months there was often carrion to be found and recently they had been subsisting chiefly on that. Fox paused as a clatter of wings broke the stillness of their home wood.

'Pigeons,' he remarked.

But there were other noises. Birds' cries, and the sounds of sudden movements in the tree-tops as many took to flight, made the pair of foxes listen intently. There was a general disturbance that went on for some minutes.

'The whole wood's been alarmed,' said Vixen. She stayed close to her bolt-hole in case of trouble.

Fox gazed fixedly at the night sky. At last he said: 'I think I see what it is.'

Vixen waited for him to explain. He was still looking up through the fretwork of naked branches.

'Yes,' he said. 'I'm sure of it.'

'Well – what?' Vixen prompted, a little impatiently.

'There are a lot of birds flying in from beyond the Park. They seem to be wheeling about, uncertain where to go. They must have unsettled those at roost here.'

'They sound very panicky,' Vixen observed.

The foxes watched a while longer. Eventually many of the birds from outside found perches in the Reserve.

Others flew onwards, and gradually quietness was restored. Fox and Vixen went on their way.

Occurrences such as these became more frequent in the ensuing weeks. All the inhabitants of the Park became aware that something, as yet unknown, was bringing change to their little world. Animals from all over the countryside came flooding into the Park. Sometimes the creatures stayed; sometimes they passed right through or overhead; sometimes they returned again whence they had come. But it was obvious that the wildlife around was in a state of real alarm, and these continual movements to and fro brought an atmosphere of disquiet to the Nature Reserve. Weasel, running through the carpet of Dog's Mercury under the beech trees, noticed a sudden increase in the numbers of wood mice. These mice appeared to have thrown their inbred caution to the winds – most of them were running about quite openly, inviting themselves to be taken. Weasel was not one to refuse the offer and he had quite a field day or, rather, night. It was only later that he realized that the mice had been thrown into a state of panic by the arrival of dozens of hunting stoats and weasels like himself, who were closing in on their quarry from every direction. The poor mice simply did not know where to run next. But where had these hunting cousins of his suddenly appeared from? They were certainly not the ordinary inhabitants of White Deer Park.

Squirrel and his relatives found themselves competing for their hoards of autumn-buried acorns and beech mast with strangers from elsewhere who watched where they dug and stole where they could.

Hare's first-born, Leveret, who was still called so by his Farthing Wood friends from old association (though he

had for long now been an adult) saw more of his own
kind running through the dead grass and bracken than
he had ever done since his arrival in White Deer Park.

Finally the friends began to gather to compare their
opinions. It was now March and a shimmer of green was
slowly spreading through the Park. New grass, tentative
leaves on hawthorn and hazel, and ripening sycamore
and chestnut buds gave glad signs to the animals that
Winter was over. But they were puzzled and a little
worried by the recent influxes.

'Where do they come from?' asked Squirrel.

'What's bringing them here?' asked Leveret.

Badger had no comment to make. He was only
acquainted with the facts by hearsay. He had seen
nothing himself.

'It's as if they've been driven here,' Tawny Owl
said.

Fox had been doing a lot of thinking. 'You could be
right, Owl,' he remarked. 'Birds and beasts are being
driven here to the Reserve in the hope of shelter and
then – '

'Finding themselves cornered?' Vixen broke in.

'Exactly! Then they'd be ripe for rounding up. It's like
part of a deliberate plan by some clever creature.'

'Or creatures,' Weasel observed.

'Yes,' said Fox. 'It couldn't be just one. Unless . . .'

'Unless of the human variety,' finished Whistler the
heron drily.

'Wouldn't make sense,' Tawny Owl contradicted him.
'What purpose could there be in this for Man?'

'How should we know?' asked Friendly, Fox's son.
'Who else is so clever?'

'I don't like this rounding up idea,' Leveret said
nervously. 'It stands to reason – *we'd* be caught up in it
too.'

They fell silent while they digested the implications of this.

'From what you say, Fox,' Badger wheezed, 'it sounds as if some animal or other is planning to use the Park as a sort of larder.'

Fox looked at him. 'You've gone straight to the point, Badger. But what sort of creature . . . .' he muttered inconclusively.

'A sort of creature *we* know nothing about,' said Owl.

'The deer are very uneasy,' put in Vixen. 'You can tell they sense something.'

'It's horrible waiting around,' said Charmer, her daughter, 'for this . . . this . . . *Something* to make an appearance. There are young to be born and looked after.'

'We mustn't get too jittery,' said Fox. 'Perhaps there *is* no "Something". There might be a more simple explanation. And a less alarming one.' But he could not convince himself.

Tawny Owl said, 'We mustn't fool ourselves either, Fox. We should prepare for the worst.'

'That's very helpful,' remarked Weasel sarcastically.

'I meant it for the best,' Owl defended himself. 'We don't want to be caught napping, do we?'

'No, but there's a reasonable chance in your case,' Weasel murmured wickedly. It was well known that Tawny Owl spent most of the daylight hours dozing. Owl pretended not to hear.

'Oh!' exclaimed Fox. 'How I wish our brave Kestrel was still around to do some scouting for us!'

'Yes,' said Whistler the heron. 'If anyone could have spotted the danger he could have done. But can I be of any service? I don't have Kestrel's piercing vision, but I *do* have wings, and there's a deal to be seen from the air which you creatures would likely miss.'

'Of course,' said Fox. 'Thank you. Any help is most welcome.'

'You know long flights are awkward with your bad wing,' Tawny Owl pointed out to the heron. He referred to the bird's old wound from a badly aimed bullet, which had caused him more trouble as he grew older. 'It had better be me.'

Whistler, whose name derived from the noise this wing made as it flapped through the air, knew perfectly well that Owl felt he had lost face by not offering his services first. But he was too polite to mention it. 'That's all right,' he said. 'I know you night birds have to catch up on your sleep while my sort are active.'

His intended tact misfired. Tawny Owl's feelings were hurt. He was very conscious that his advancing age made him sleep longer than he used to. His feathers ruffled indignantly.

'Nonsense!' he said. 'I'm quite capable of flying by day. And more accurately than you, I might add.'

'As you say, old friend,' Whistler said readily with his constant good humour. He was quite unaffected by Owl's sharp retort.

'We'll share the search then.'

'Very well,' replied Owl huffily.

Weasel looked at Owl with distaste. 'He gets worse as he gets older,' he murmured to himself.

— 2 —
The Pond is Deserted

The two birds made long flights over the surrounding area; the heron by day, the owl by night. Neither was able to see anything that might explain the recent developments. But some of the creatures who had taken refuge within the Reserve talked to the animals they met there. Word spread of a large, fierce beast who made raids in the night. No animal had seen it and survived, so none of the refugees could give even the vaguest description of it. There were rumours of terrible slaughter. Tales of its unnerving hunting skills were rife. It could climb; it could swim; it could catch creatures underground. Some even suspected it could fly, since birds also suffered from its depredations. Soon the whole Park was in a state of suspense.

But it was Spring and, despite the suspense, the activities of Spring went on. Pairing and mating, nest-building and preparing dens for imminent births overrode any other consideration. For a while the threat of the unknown seemed to recede. Then, with startling suddenness, a change in the usual absorbing routine shocked the animals out of their preoccupation. In the midst of their mating season, the colony of Edible Frogs made a mass exodus from their pond. They were not content to hide themselves in the waterside vegetation. They hopped away in all directions as far as they could go, apparently desperate to get right away from the pond. Other aquatic creatures such as newts were seen in great numbers leaving the pond, and the ducks, coots and moorhens who had built their nests on or near the water deserted them entirely. It was obvious that something very alarming had happened to drive them away. The animals and birds did not need to ask each other what this could be. They knew. The Beast had arrived in the Park.

Toad, who had acted as guide to the Farthing Wood animals on their long journey to White Deer Park, was eager to talk to Fox. He had not been in the water himself when the eruption of the Edible Frogs from the pond had occurred. But he had witnessed their panic.

'It was pandemonium,' he told Fox. 'They couldn't scramble away fast enough from that water. There was something *in* the pond.'

'Did you see what it was?' Fox asked quickly.

'No, no. It was too dark for that,' replied Toad. 'But I didn't want to stay around myself to find out!'

'Of course not. I can well see why.'

'I don't know what the Frogs will do now,' Toad croaked. 'The pond is their gathering point. How can they carry on their lives now – and in the middle of the most important time of the year?'

'I wonder how any of us will cope,' Fox returned. 'You can't deal with something unseen.'

'I'd like to stay around here for a while if I may?' Toad murmured. 'There's comfort in company and I haven't seen Badger in a long while.'

Fox spoke quietly: 'I'm afraid he's failing, Toad, little by little. We're all much older than we were, but Badger seems to live in his own little world. He only does what's necessary – can't be bothered with anything else.'

'I think Mole's sadly missed,' Toad murmured. 'And Kestrel too. What an acrobat *he* was in the sky! But our old life, back in the Wood, and the great trek here that seemed as if it would go on for ever – doesn't it seem so long ago?'

'An age,' Fox agreed. 'Vixen and I often talk about the past. A sign of *our* age, no doubt,' he mocked himself.

'Yes. We always overcame troubles together before, didn't we?' Toad went on. 'But, you know, this new menace – I have a feeling it may be too much for us.'

After this, life in the Reserve went on as if on tiptoe. The whole community held its breath – and waited. One morning the remains of three adult rabbits were found close together under some blackthorn. It was obvious this was not the work of a fox. The other rabbits spoke of a hint of soft footfalls around their burrows. As usual they had seen nothing. But each of them seemed to have been aware of a Presence.

At intervals other carcasses were discovered. Their killer had great stealth and cunning. It was never seen during the day, and at night, although every animal and bird stayed alert for it, nothing positive was heard.

The inhabitants of White Deer Park, many of whom were chiefly nocturnal in their habits, began to feel as if they were under siege. Yet they had to eat. They went about in fear and trepidation, trying to stay as close to their homes as possible. But deaths still occurred. The mystery continued to hang balefully over the Reserve.

The creature's amazing silence was a constant talking point. The hunters among the Park's population began to feel a sort of grudging respect for its expertise. Some of the young foxes harboured ideas of emulating its methods.

'That sort of skill would make any animal the most respected of predators,' remarked one youngster, a nephew of Friendly's called Husky.

'Do you admire it?' his uncle enquired.

'Of course. Don't you? If I were like that I'd be the envy of all.'

'You'd have to learn a little more quietness then,' Friendly chaffed him. The point was not lost on his young relative who was something of a chatterer. 'And,' he went on, 'can you climb trees?'

'I can climb a bit,' the youngster declared. 'I'm not sure about trees.'

While this conversation was proceeding, the elders of the Farthing Wood community were meeting specifically to discuss the threat from the super-predator. The talk seemed to go round and round in circles, without anything being resolved. At last Badger, who had held his peace for most of the time, murmured, 'I can't help thinking of cats.'

'What? What did you say, Badger?' Fox asked sharply.

'Well, you see, Fox,' Badger went on in his rather quavery voice, 'I'm reminded of Ginger Cat. I spent a lot of time with him in the Warden's home after my accident. You'll remember that winter when I hurt my –'

'Yes, yes,' Fox cut in hurriedly. He knew how Badger was apt to wander off the point. 'We all recall Ginger Cat. Now what about him?'

'Well, the thing that struck me most about *him* was his stealth,' Badger explained. 'He could be so quiet in his movements, you wouldn't know he was about. And . . . and . . . he could *climb* like anything. So I wonder if this stranger in our midst might be a cat?'

'Oh, Badger, don't be absurd!' Tawny Owl scoffed. 'How could a cat have slaughtered as this beast has done? It wouldn't have the strength.'

'I didn't necessarily mean a cat like the Warden's cat,' Badger continued doggedly. 'But – er – another sort of cat . . .'

Weasel said: 'It makes sense, doesn't it, Fox?'

'I don't know,' said Fox. 'What other sorts of cats are there?'

None of them had an answer to that.

'It's *not* a cat,' Tawny Owl declared peremptorily. 'It's a larger animal altogether.'

'But if it's so large, Owl,' Weasel said cheekily, 'why haven't you been able to spot it?'

Tawny Owl looked awkward. 'I don't know,' he said, and shuffled his feet. 'But Whistler looked too,' he added quickly as if that helped his argument which, of course, it did not.

'The fact is,' said Toad, 'we're all completely in the dark. And we shall remain in the dark until one of us – or another animal – comes face to face with the creature.'

'If that should happen, he won't live to tell the tale,' Fox reminded him.

'He might – if he had wings,' Toad suggested.

'Wings haven't been of much use so far,' Whistler said. 'Birds have been taken from their nests.'

'Then the bird in question should remain in the air,' Toad answered.

'I think Toad has something,' Vixen remarked. 'Another search should be made. Tawny Owl and Whistler didn't actually search the Reserve itself because the beast was believed to be outside it.'

'Very true,' said Fox. 'No use looking by day, though. It keeps itself well hidden. Owl, if you were very clever and very quiet, you might catch a glimpse of it. It has to hunt.'

'Oh, I can match the beast itself for quietness,' Tawny Owl boasted. 'No question of that. My flight is utterly noiseless. You see, my wing feathers – '

'Yes, we're all aware of your abilities,' Weasel cut in, rather sourly.

'Will you have another try?' Fox asked hurriedly, before Owl reacted.

'I certainly will,' the bird answered at once. He was delighted to be relied upon, and flattered by Fox's confidence in him.

'I still think it's a creature of the feline type,' Badger muttered obstinately.

Tawny Owl stared at him. His hooked beak opened on a retort, but he closed it again without speaking. He would very soon prove Badger wrong about that.

The gathering began to break up, when Fox suddenly asked: 'Has anyone seen Adder?'

It appeared that none of them had. Toad was usually the first to set eyes on him in the spring, for they often hibernated together. But even he had no idea where he was.

'I don't like to leave him out of our discussion,' Fox remarked. 'But he knows where *we* are so it's easier for him to seek us out.'

'Perhaps now it's warmer he'll turn up soon?' suggested Whistler.

'Huh! I suppose he might deign to show himself,' Weasel retorted. 'But as time goes by Adder gets crustier and crustier or, perhaps I should say in his case, scalier and scalier.'

'He'll be around,' Toad affirmed. 'I think I know him better than you do, Weasel. You've always taken his offhand manner too much to heart. It's just his way. After all, he is a snake, not a warm-blooded mammal. And I can tell you, he's just as loyal as any of us.'

The little group split up and went about their own concerns. As it turned out, talking about Adder seemed, though quite by chance, to hasten his arrival. The very next day Vixen found him coiled up by the entrance to her earth.

'Ah, Vixen,' said the snake. 'Another spring and yet you look just the same.'

Compliments from Adder were few and far between. Vixen was conscious of the unusual distinction. 'How nice to be greeted in such a charming way,' she said graciously. 'And how good to see you after all this time.'

Adder uncoiled himself and slid towards her. His thin body was blunt at the tail where some time ago he had lost about two centimetres of his length in a tussle with an enemy fox.

'The Reserve is alive with frogs, it seems,' he remarked with his infamous leer. 'I must try to work up an appetite and make the most of them.' His tongue flickered in and out as he tested the air.

'That won't be very difficult after your long fast, I should think.'

'Oh, my cold blood needs time to heat up properly,' he

answered. 'I'm always a bit sluggish at first.'

Vixen explained what had happened at the pond.

'Yes, I've heard rumours,' the snake drawled. 'There seem to be all kinds of strange stories about. Some monster or other on the prowl, I believe?'

'I think that's an exaggeration,' Vixen said. 'But there *is* a fierce creature roaming the Park. None of us feels safe. And the worst of it is – we don't know what this creature *looks* like.'

Fox, hearing Adder's voice, had emerged from the earth. 'Tawny Owl is keeping a lookout on his night travels,' he added, after he and Adder had exchanged greetings.

'Hm. Well, I've seen nothing,' the snake said. 'Except –'

The foxes waited but Adder seemed to have forgotten what he was going to say.

'Except what?' Fox prompted.

'Oh, it's of no importance,' Adder hissed. He had quickly decided that something he had detected might alarm them further. 'Have you seen Toad?' he asked to divert them.

'Oh yes. He steers clear of the pond too,' Vixen told him.

'Mmm. I hope I come across him,' Adder murmured. 'Well, I'm off to sun myself,' he added abruptly. 'Then I'll be ready for those frogs.'

He disappeared rather hurriedly and Fox and Vixen looked at each other with wry expressions.

'He doesn't change,' Vixen observed.

'No, he doesn't,' Fox concurred. 'And I wouldn't want him to. But he's keeping something from us. I know him.'

*****

Adder *was* keeping something back. Before he would say more, he wanted his suspicions about what he had seen confirmed or allayed. Toad was the one to do that. So the snake went in search of him.

He had not been misleading the foxes about sunning himself. He needed the warmth from a long bask in the sun to get his muscles working properly in case there should be a bit of travelling for him to do. He found a patch of dead bracken which faced into the spring sunshine. The spot was dry and the ground felt quite warm. It was ideal for him. While he enjoyed his sunbath Adder reflected that it was just the opposite of the sort of place Toad would be seeking. Toad liked dampness and shelter from the sun's rays, and preferred to move about after dark.

When Adder felt thoroughly warm and sufficiently lively, he moved off. He was still in the part of the Park originally colonized by the band of Farthing Wood animals, and so he hoped he might meet some old companions. As he rippled through the dry dead stalks of grass he saw an animal rise from the ground a few metres in front of him. It was Leveret who, in a typical attitude, was standing on hind legs to look about him. Adder hastened forward, calling in his rasping way. He knew that if Leveret bounded off there would be no hope of his catching him again. No animal in the Park could move so swiftly. Luckily Leveret detected the snake's movement and dropped on all fours to await him.

'I thought it must be you,' he said when Adder came up. 'Well, it's a sign Spring has really and truly arrived when you are seen moving about.'

'I'm looking for Toad,' Adder stated bluntly, without offering a greeting.

'Yes. I see.'

'Well, can you help me?'

'I hope so, yes. What's the problem?' Leveret asked. The snake's tongue flickered faster than ever, a sure sign of his exasperation. It was always the same with this maddening animal, he thought. Everything had to be said twice. 'Can you help me find Toad?' he hissed slowly and emphatically.

'If you wish it, Adder. Now where shall we begin?'

'Oh, don't bother!' said the snake angrily. 'Perhaps I'll manage better on my own.'

Leveret looked surprised. 'But I thought – ' he began.

'Look,' said Adder. 'I'm going towards the pond. If you see Toad tell him to meet me there. I need his advice.' He slid away in a bad humour. 'Mammals!' he muttered.

Leveret watched his departure. 'Funny he should be going *to* the pond when everyone else has been moving away from it,' he said to himself.

— 3 —

Footprints and Eyes

Adder took a roundabout route to the pond. Always one of the most secretive creatures in his movements, he now used extra care in view of the new air of uncertainty in the Reserve. It was a while before he reached the pond and his progress had been arrested twice on the way by two plump frogs who had presented to him irresistible reasons for delay. But once near the water's edge in the early dusk, Adder was still able to see the strange signs he had detected before. He settled himself down amongst the reeds and sedges for what might prove to be a long wait. The surface of the pond was undisturbed in the evening calm and no sound – not a single croak or chirp – arose from the vegetation clothing its banks.

Toad had soon been rounded up by Leveret. He was puzzled by Adder's message but, since he well knew that the snake was not prone to seek another's company without a definite purpose, he agreed to set off for the rendezvous. It was with some considerable misgiving that Toad found himself returning to the scene of so much recent agitation. He decided to run no risks – even though he suspected a small creature like himself might be beneath the notice of the mysterious fierce hunter. He covered most of the distance to the pond in daylight, but as soon as he got close to the danger area he hid himself in some thick moss to await darkness. Then, with the benefit of its screen, he continued rather more confidently. However, he was still wary, and he paused often to listen. He reached the pond without noticing any evidence of an unusual presence abroad that night.

Toad gave a muffled croak once or twice in the hope that only the waiting Adder would recognize it. The snake had expected him to arrive after dark and had remained alert, so the ploy worked.

'Well, you've taken a chance,' Toad said in a low voice as he pulled himself into the waterside screen from which Adder hissed his position.

'Only a slender one if there's no chance of discovery,' Adder observed wryly. 'I want you to look at something, Toad, I'm at a bit of a disadvantage.'

'What do you mean?'

'That patch of mud,' Adder indicated in front of them. 'What do you make of it?'

Toad looked where he was bidden. After a while he said, 'Nothing much. Unless you mean – oh!' a little croak of alarm escaped him involuntarily.

'You see them then?'

'Paw prints!'

'I thought as much,' hissed the snake. 'But, you

understand, Toad, someone who relies on my sort of locomotion can't claim to be an expert in such matters.'

'I take your point,' said Toad. 'But there can be no doubt. The frightening thing is – '

'I know – the size of them. I suppose they've been made by a mammal?'

'Oh yes. No frog or toad in existence could make marks like that.'

'I first saw them a day or so ago,' Adder said, 'and didn't pay much attention. It's only now I realize their significance.'

'Do the others know?'

'*I've* said nothing. I wasn't sure. Well, Toad, this will put their fur into a bristle.'

'I wonder if we should tell them? I mean, LOOK! What size must the creature be?'

'Big enough to kill a deer. No, we can't leave them in ignorance. They should be prepared.'

'Prepared for what, Adder? What can they do?'

'Nothing, I imagine,' the snake answered bluntly, 'except – keep their wits about them.'

Toad recalled the birds' mission. 'The animal might have been seen by now. Tawny Owl is combing the park.'

'This creature's too clever to be found by an owl,' Adder remarked with a hint of contempt. 'It's a master of concealment.'

The notion entered Toad's head that the Beast might be lying hidden nearby at that moment, and keeping them under observation. He became very nervous. 'I – I –think we shouldn't stay here,' he chattered. 'It might come back at any moment and – and – we know it's active at night. Let's separate.'

'I think we're safe enough,' Adder drawled affectedly,

'But all right, Toad. Thanks for your advice. My fears were well founded.'

Toad muttered something about seeing Adder again 'in the usual place' and hopped hurriedly away. The snake made up his mind to stay awhile in case he might be able to add some more evidence to the existing clues.

In the meantime Tawny Owl was on his second reconnaissance flight. He combed the park methodically, concentrating on the areas most fitted to an animal who wanted to hide itself. But, like the first, this second night of searching produced nothing. Before dawn, Tawny Owl flew wearily to a favourite perch in a beech copse. He was very tired indeed, but was pleased with the way he had carried out his mission. He felt he had left, as it were, no stone unturned. He settled his wings sleepily and, little by little, his big round eyes closed.

The Moon shone brightly over the countryside. White Deer Park shimmered in its glow. Once or twice the owl shifted his grip on the beech bough. It was a bright night, and each branch of the tree was picked out sharply in the moonlight. Tawny Owl dozed. But something – some influence or other – prevented him from sleeping properly, despite his tiredness. He opened one eye and, from his high perch, looked down towards the ground. What he saw nearly caused him to fall from the branch. A huge face, with eyes glinting in the moonlight like live coals, stared up at him.

Tawny Owl lost his grip, overbalanced, flapped his wings frantically and just saved himself from plunging downwards head first. He let out a screech and fought his way awkwardly up through the branches, at last gaining sufficient height to feel safe. He veered away from the copse· and steadied himself as he recovered from his sudden shock. The Beast!

As Tawny Owl calmed down he wondered if any other creature had seen his frightened reaction. He looked all round to see if he was watched and then alighted elsewhere, far enough away from his first spot to be comfortable. Now he wondered if he had imagined what he'd seen. It was so sudden – had he been dreaming? He did not think so, but he knew he ought to go back for a second look. After all, he was quite safe in the air. He thought about it for a while, trying to find valid reasons for not going back. But he could not think of any.

'Still. It's probably moved by now. Not much point,' he told himself unconvincingly. Then he thought of his friends. He owed it to them to make a proper report. He hesitated. Tawny Owl was not lacking in courage, but he really had had a bad fright. The Beast had been so close! At last he stiffened his resolve and took to the air once more, flying on a circular course which eventually brought him back to the borders of the beech copse. He fluttered to and fro uncertainly. Actually to enter the little wood again was extraordinarily difficult.

When he finally did fly in, he went cautiously from one tree to another, stopping each time before moving on. When the tree from which he had seen the Beast came into view, of course there was no sign of any animal, large or small, in its branches. A feeling of great relief flooded over the owl and now he flew right up to the tree for a closer look. Nothing!

'I shouldn't have delayed,' he muttered. 'It was wrong of me. Two great eyes – *that's* not much to go on. Now I suppose the thing's got well away from this place.' He flew about the copse, examining everything that might yield a clue. But there were no clues, not even footprints, for last year's dry leaves were still thick on the ground. And not the slightest rustle disturbed them.

Tawny Owl left the copse and directed his flight towards Fox's earth. He began to feel quite proud of his news. He, alone of all the Park's inhabitants, had had a glimpse of the stranger who had come to dominate their lives. It made him very important.

Day broke as he arrived. He called to Fox and Vixen peremptorily. Already his mind was beginning to exaggerate the little he had seen. There were stirrings in the foxes' den. Vixen peered out.

'Oh, hallo, Owl,' she murmured and went promptly back inside again.

'Wait!' cried the bird. 'I've news that – '

But Vixen was not listening. Tawny Owl could hear voices inside the earth. He hooted with frustration. He was bursting to tell them of his experience. Then Fox emerged on his own.

'Have you had any luck, Owl?' he asked nonchalantly.

'Luck!' spluttered the bird. 'I – I – I've SEEN it!'

Fox looked at him sharply. 'The Beast? The hunter, you mean?'

'Yes, yes. I came to tell you. I was in a tree and – and it was *enormous*.'

'Did it attack you?'

'No. Oh-ho, no. I was too quick for that,' Tawny Owl boasted. 'I was asleep, you see, Fox. I awoke and – there it was.'

'You were asleep? Oh, I understand. And what did the creature look like?'

The suspicion in Fox's voice was unmistakable and Tawny Owl noticed it at once. Did he think he had imagined it? Well!

'If that's your attitude,' he said resentfully, 'why should

I continue the story?'

'Now don't get in one of your huffs,' Fox pleaded. 'But sleep's a funny thing. We can all – '

'*All* doesn't come into it,' Owl interrupted haughtily. 'I alone have seen this thing. No one else was around. I was merely dozing after tiring myself out looking for the creature. I tell you I looked down and saw a massive head with gleaming eyes just below me. It was watching me! Do you think I invented it?'

'No, of course not,' Fox assured him. 'But – what was the rest of it like?'

'Ah well,' Owl mumbled, 'now you're asking. I wasn't able to see the *rest*.'

Vixen joined them. 'I overheard most of it,' she said. 'There's to be a meeting in the Hollow. Why doesn't Tawny Owl tell *everyone* about it then?' She was addressing Fox.

'A wise idea. It's tomorrow at dusk, Owl. Friendly and Charmer will come, and Weasel and Badger. And Whistler, of course. Perhaps he might have seen something too.'

'I doubt it,' Tawny Owl remarked jealously. 'The Beast doesn't reveal itself in the daylight.'

The Hollow was the traditional meeting place of the Farthing Wood community. It had been their first resting point on their arrival in the Park after their months' long journey. They had returned to it ever since when important matters were to be discussed, as a place of significance to them all.

The party assembled as darkness began to fall. Leveret and Squirrel were among the numbers. Toad arrived last, unwittingly bringing news to corroborate Tawny Owl's statement.

When Owl finished giving his description, which by

now he had embellished with all sorts of additional dramatic references, Toad croaked out what he and Adder had seen.

'I can vouch for the truth of Owl's remarks about size,' he added afterwards. 'The prints we saw could only have been made by a monster. Your feet, Fox, would have fitted into one corner!'

There was a silence and some of the animals looked at each other in consternation. Tawny Owl felt that his experiences were not getting the attention they deserved.

'Pooh,' he said, struggling to find words to bring his own experience back into the limelight, 'what are marks in the mud compared to a sight of the entire beast?'

Fox and Vixen looked at each other with wry amusement at the bird's childishness. But Toad wished Adder had been there to supply one of his caustic retorts. Owl could be very trying and silly at times. He had already admitted that he had seen only the head of the Beast clearly.

Badger asked if the prints had been like a cat's.

'Neither Adder nor I are qualified to tell you that,' Toad told him.

Badger turned to Tawny Owl. 'What about the head? Did it resemble a cat's?'

'Not in the least,' the bird answered immediately, without thinking about it. 'I told you you were on the wrong track.'

'But what other creature can climb a tree?' Badger persisted. 'Apart from our friend Squirrel.'

'None I know about,' Squirrel remarked.

The young foxes, Friendly and Charmer, were becoming impatient with the obtuseness of the ageing comrades.

'What does it signify whether it's a cat, a dog, a – a –

horse or a giant rat?' cried Charmer exasperatedly. 'It hunts. It kills. And it's very dangerous. Surely all that matters is what we can do to protect ourselves?'

Her brother Friendly supported her. 'Charmer's quite right,' he agreed. 'Whatever it is, we've got to think of a way to get it out of the Park.'

'But that's impossible,' Leveret said nervously, 'if we never know where it is.'

'We can track it,' Friendly declared. 'We foxes. It must have a scent.'

His father intervened. 'You're getting carried away, Friendly,' he said. 'Even if the scent could be picked up and then followed – which I doubt – what would the object be? What would you do if you came up against the creature?'

'Er – well, I – er – *we*, that is, would, I suppose – ' Friendly stopped in embarrassment. What *would* they do?

'You see, you haven't thought it through, have you?'

'All right, Father. But we must do *something*, mustn't we? Otherwise we could face extinction.'

'I only know what we mustn't do,' Fox returned, 'and that is confront it. This is a cunning, powerful animal quite beyond our experience. We're not dealing this time with rivals of our own kind.'

Now the attention of all the animals was fixed firmly on their old leader. Fox was the one to whom they had always turned when in trouble or danger. They respected him and trusted him. He had never yet failed to find a solution. They waited for him to go on. But the words of wisdom they expected to hear were not forthcoming.

'I'm afraid I've nothing to add to that,' he said finally.

The animals looked crestfallen.

'We have to defend our home – don't we?' Friendly whispered uncertainly.

'We can't,' said his father. 'I told you – it's beyond us.'

The little group exchanged glances unhappily. This defeatist Fox was unknown to them. They depended on him so much and he had never let them down before. Fox knew what they were thinking.

'I'm no longer a young animal,' he told them. 'We've all grown older. We can't indulge in the sort of escapades we used to do in the old days. We're no match for this Beast.'

'It's true,' sighed Badger. 'It's as much as I can do to get myself out of my set to feed sometimes.'

The young animals – Friendly, Charmer and Leveret – felt like intruders into an assembly of veterans. Friendly began to realize his father was, as always, trying to be realistic about their abilities. Perhaps it was time for the younger generation to take up the fight. But Fox was speaking again.

'To be blunt,' he said, 'there are some animals more at risk in the Reserve than others. Rabbits and, I'm afraid, hares, too, are the most vulnerable, as well as the smaller game such as mice, frogs and so forth. Foxes and badgers and snakes are not generally hunted for food. Birds, of course, have the perfect escape mechanism. So what I'm saying is that most of us are safe if we ensure that we don't antagonize the Beast.'

'That's a lot of comfort for me,' Leveret said morosely.

'I'm certain Fox didn't mean we'd turn our backs on you,' Vixen reassured him. 'The Oath of Mutual Protection still survives.'

'Of course,' said Fox. 'All of us are available to help another animal who gets into danger. But that's rather different from setting out to court it.' He looked meaningfully at Friendly.

Friendly said nothing, but he was eager for the meeting to break up. After what his father had said about foxes not being so much at risk, he had started to formulate some ambitious plans of his own.

—4—
A Waiting Game

The animals did not stay together much longer. The meeting had been inconclusive and the only message to come out of it was that they each needed to take extra precautions for as long as the Beast chose to make White Deer Park its hunting ground.

After Tawny Owl's fright no more was seen or heard of the stranger. Adder had seen nothing more, although he had waited for a long time at the pool's edge. This state of affairs continued for quite a while, and once again the Park's population returned to its main concern – the business of raising families. Even the Edible Frogs forgot their alarm and, in dribs and drabs, returned to the water.

Friendly had been down to the Pond in the meantime to see the reported footprints for himself, and to use his nose in the hope of finding a scent. But the stranger had moved on. The fox could find nothing useful and the mud where the stranger had left its pug marks now betrayed no hint of the unusual.

The animals started to hope again, although they still dared not believe that they were to be left in peace.

Then the Beast announced its presence with an emphasis that ruled out all their hopes. An old and infirm member of the deer herd that roamed the Park was killed. Its remains – and they were scanty – were found some time afterwards, lying under a screen of budding elm scrub. It chanced to be Friendly who came across them. He was shocked at the discovery but, in a strange way, excited too. For it meant that the heroic plans he had laid might still be adopted. At first he told no one about the evidence except his contemporaries. These younger foxes and their descendants formed quite a large group, all of whom were related to each other through the blood of their common ancestor, the Farthing Wood Fox. Whilst the females amongst them were occupied at the moment with their new offspring, the males had time to gather and listen to Friendly's news. The older animals were kept in ignorance for the time being.

'There was no mistaking the odour all round the carcass,' Friendly told them. 'It was a sharp, thin smell – quite detectable above the smell of the rotten meat. And it was an animal smell I've never picked up before in this Reserve!' He brought the last words out with an air of triumph.

'Did you try to trace it?' asked one of his own male progeny, who was now entering his second season.

'Yes, Pace. I followed it for a way back. Then the trail

lost its scent. But, between us, we should be able to pick it up somewhere else.'

'Then what would we do?' asked a nephew, one of his dead brother Bold's cubs.

'I want to trace it back to its lair,' Friendly explained. 'Once we've found that, we can choose our time to assemble together and corner the Beast. We'll make it understand it's not wanted around here. It can't fight all of us, however big it is.'

The other foxes were quiet. Friendly allowed them a while for his words to sink in. Some of them did not appear to be very comfortable with this plan. Others, the more adventurous among them, were enthralled at the possibility of routing such a remarkable predator.

'When would we begin this tracking down?' one asked.

'We'll let the Beast make the first move,' Friendly answered. 'Let it show itself. If it's too clever to allow itself to be seen, let it reveal its whereabouts by its activity. That carcass was an old kill. What we want to find is a fresh one. Then *that* would be our starting point.'

The foxes dispersed, most of them enthusiastic about the venture. The days passed. It seemed as if the stranger had an inkling of the plan, for no carcass was found. The Beast was taking great pains not to advertise itself.

There had been births in the White Deer herd, just as there had been births amongst all the other species that inhabited the Park. The stranger, having tasted deer flesh, was particularly interested in the new arrivals born to the herd. These babies promised an even more succulent meal than the first victim. So it had been stalking the deer in its silent way, waiting for the right moment to strike.

The moment arrived. The opportunity was taken. In the darkness the fawn's mother knew little about her loss.

The stealth, the swiftness of the stranger worked with a sweet harmony. It was a harmony that was also ruthless. The fawn was taken, carried off and devoured with a quietness that was bewildering. The tenderness of the hapless young deer enabled its killer to leave very little evidence in the way of remains. So it was easily overlooked by the foxes who were searching for clues while they hunted for themselves and their mates.

Friendly was baffled. He had expected the Beast would have given a hint of its hideout by this time. Now the animals were back to wondering if it was still around.

But now the Reserve Warden began to suspect that something was amiss. He was the last to become aware of the existence of a fierce killer in the vicinity. He knew how many births had taken place that season in the deer herd, and when he discovered the loss of one and, later, a second, he became suspicious. There was no sign of their bodies. So their deaths were not from natural causes. When on his rounds he discovered the rotting remains of the old animal that had first fallen prey to the Beast he knew at once a killer was hunting his deer. His first conclusion was that it was a dog, and he was well aware that such an animal, having once killed deer, will return again and again to the attack.

From that time on, the Warden kept a careful watch on the herd, making regular evening and early morning circuits near the deer's position. He saw and heard nothing at all. This puzzled him because he knew that a dog is not the most silent of animals, and he was an experienced and careful observer. What he did not know was that he had become watched: the killer the watcher.

So long as the Warden continued his daily rounds, the killer wisely contented itself with smaller game. But it had inexhaustible patience, and it knew that eventually there would be another opportunity to eat raw venison. The Warden had patience too. He expected the creature to strike again, and that this lull was a temporary one. He was quite sure it was still close by and he waited for its return. He carried a gun while on his rounds, since he had the authority to use it if necessary to ensure the protection of the rare white deer. And so a waiting game developed that was played by both sides.

Naturally the other animals were also interested in the frequent appearance of the Warden. They realized that human endeavour was now ranged against the intruder and the older ones were comforted. Friendly and the more daring young foxes had mixed feelings. They were heartened by the man's presence, but really they wished to have the glory of defeating this unknown enemy all to themselves.

Fox and Vixen had gone one day, as they sometimes did, to talk to the Great Stag, the leader of the deer herd. Like them, he had suffered the changes wrought by Time. It was a matter for speculation how long he would continue to lead his kind. By now Fox had heard of the deer losses.

'Can you add anything to the little we know of the killer?' he asked.

'I only know of its speed and its strength,' the Stag answered him. 'It's approach was unnoticed and its retreat unmarked.'

'What *can* we be up against?'

'An extremely efficient predator,' observed the Stag. 'Certainly one to worry our human friend as well as ourselves.'

'I have a sneaking feeling,' Fox declared, 'that he will meet with the same lack of success.'

'I can't comment on that,' was the reply. 'He has his

methods, I believe. But we must certainly hope otherwise. Because *we* have no defence against it.'

'None at all,' agreed Fox. 'I've already accepted that.'

'Oh, it won't be any concern to you,' the Stag went on. 'I think it unlikely it will show any interest in foxes.'

'We're only worried about some of our young friends being foolhardy,' Vixen told him. 'I'm sure Friendly sees himself as a sort of successor to Fox. He has a lot of confidence and courage.'

'Well, it must be in his blood, I suppose,' commented the Stag. 'But it would be a foolish enterprise, I fear, to attempt to tussle with this supreme hunter.'

'Yes. I prefer to respect it from a distance,' said Fox.

'And hope that before we're all much older it'll choose to go away,' Vixen added.

'I wouldn't hold out a lot of hope for that,' the Stag returned. 'The creature has had no opposition so far. I feel that, as long as there is a deer herd here, it will choose to stay. That is, unless it is persuaded otherwise.'

'It's a sobering thought,' Fox said solemnly.

'My hinds are in a proper turmoil about it. Their nerves are all strung up. And I can offer them no assistance.'

'Not while the Beast remains hidden,' Fox acknowledged. 'But you stags are about the only animals in the Reserve who might successfully oppose it in a fight. Surely one day it's going to make a slip and be seen?'

'Don't count on it,' the Stag advised him.

The three talked more. Then, with the Warden once again coming into view, Fox and Vixen departed.

*****

Adder had returned to his home area after quitting the pondside, using the secluded route that was habitual to him. He liked to enjoy as much of the spring sunshine as he could, and he lay amongst the bracken very often, sleepily absorbing the sun's rays. The first new fern shoots were just pushing their heads above the surface and the pale green tightly-curled heads carried a promise of the fragrance that was to come in the summer. One day Adder was lying in this way, his red eyes glinting in the sunlight. He was thinking about his next meal but he was in no hurry to look for it. His reptilian stomach did not require to be filled with the mechanical regularity of a bird's or a mammal's. Because of his proximity to the stream that ran through the Park, he happened to be the first recipient of news brought by a very flustered Whistler.

It was early morning and the heron had been standing in the shallows in his usual sentry-like posture. As he watched for the rippling movement of a fish, out of the corner of his eye he saw an animal move slowly along the bank away from him. It was some twenty metres away and appeared to be looking for the best spot to descend for a drink. Whistler's immobility had kept him unobserved. He noted the animal was large, with sleek brown and black fur in blotches of colour which merged into stripes on its back. Its body had a powerful but streamlined appearance, with a long, thin, furry tail. It got down to the water's edge and, leaning on its front legs, lapped thirstily. As it drank, it maintained a watchful eye on its surroundings. It paused two or three times to look about. When it was satisfied it raised itself, shook one front paw in a kind of fastidiousness, and moved away with an unhurried, loose and undulating motion. Whistler was impressed by the creature's graceful movement. It looked round once more and he caught just a glimpse of a round whiskered face with two green eyes, and small ears and nose.

Whistler had held himself quite still during this entire episode. But now he hastened to fly off. He flapped his long wings and, with his stilt-like legs trailing beneath, he gained height and turned in the direction of his friends. A few seconds later he spied Adder sunbathing. He dropped down briefly to tell him what he had seen.

'What do you think it was?' he asked the snake.

'Oh, the creature we've all been looking for,' Adder answered nonchalantly, without even shifting his position. 'No question about it.'

'I wondered the same myself,' Whistler replied. 'I must go and spread the word.' He gave a farewell 'krornk' and flew away.

Adder's feigned lack of interest turned into action as soon as the heron was gone. He slid furtively from his couch in the bracken and made for the stream side. There would be footprints by the water and he wanted to compare them. He went along the bank and his eyes soon picked out the place where the animal had drunk. Yes, there were the marks! He examined them for a while to make quite sure.

'Just as I thought,' he lisped to himself. 'Identical.'

Now his curiosity was aroused. He wanted to see the creature for himself. He debated whether it was safe to follow in its wake along the bank. There was very little cover at that spot and he wanted to remain undetected. Only in that way could he hope to have a chance of surprising the stranger. He slithered hastily into the nearest patch of vegetation. As he lay hidden his mind began to concentrate itself on a grand scheme.

Some seasons ago, Adder had been the chief victor in a battle that the Farthing Wood animals had fought against some foxes. These had resented the animals establishing a new home for themselves in the Reserve. The snake had a weapon more telling than any of his friends possessed – the weapon of poison. He had used it before to rid them of a dangerous enemy. Now he began to entertain thoughts of doing so again – and with much more purpose. For the stranger who had come to dominate their lives was more powerful and dangerous than any fox. And, as long as it lived amongst them, it was a potential enemy of every animal in the Park. Adder had no way of knowing if his poison was sufficiently potent to immobilize such a big hunter. So there was only one way of finding out.

The snake glided through the plant stems, intent on his secret pursuit. Surprise was everything. There was a patch of bare ground between the clumps of vegetation he needed to cross. But, once across it, the cover was thick and tangled again. He slid into the open. All was quiet. His head was about to enter the next mass of growth when the breath was driven from his body. A heavy weight came down in the centre of his back along his vertebrae. He was pressed against the hard ground so tightly that we was unable even to wriggle his tail. Adder was securely pinioned.

—5—
Strangers

Whistler sped on, his great steel-grey wings beating rhythmically. He began to call as he neared Fox and Vixen's earth.

'News! News! Sensational news!'

He made such a noise, and the noise was so unexpected from the normally dignified heron, that animals and birds came out of their burrows and holes and boughs, or stopped what they were doing, to look up at him. He hastened to land.

Fox and Vixen were all agog and an indignant and sleepy Tawny Owl flew to a nearby perch to hear what all the unwarranted (in his opinion) commotion was about.

'The Beast is seen!' Whistler cried by way of a preliminary. 'Drinking, as boldly and openly as you like, from the stream.'

More animals and birds were gathering to listen. There was a chorus of demands to know what it was like, in voices of many varied pitches and registers. The heron waited for the hubbub to die down. He was familiar with the ginger cat belonging to the Warden and so this was the obvious comparison to make.

'It was like,' he told them, and at once there was a hushed silence, 'a much larger version of the cat our Badger got to know so well.'

Tawny Owl blinked his great eyes in disbelief.

'The colouring was quite different,' Whistler added. 'But there was the same litheness of movement, the same suppleness, the same silent gait.'

The owl prepared himself to give a sharp retort if Badger should start saying 'I told you so.' He looked around, but Badger was not in the throng. Owl was glad – but felt he would have to defend his own argument sooner or later.

'Where did the creature come from?' Fox wanted to know.

'I didn't observe its approach,' replied Whistler. 'It was already on the bank when I first saw it. Then it drank and made off towards the nearest cover – thankfully in a direction away from this part of the Park.'

Friendly had been listening eagerly. He knew where Whistler preferred to fish and now at last he had the evidence that he needed. He did not wait to hear any more but ran off at once to round up his confederates.

'So we're dealing with a large, powerful cat,' Fox summed up. 'Well, it could be worse. But what kind of cat can it be? Certainly not a human's pet. It's something none of us have ever seen or heard about before.'

'Excuse me,' Tawny Owl interrupted in his pompous way. 'Aren't you jumping to conclusions, Fox? How do we know this is the animal that has been doing the killing?'

There was a pause while his words were considered. Tawny Owl felt he had produced an effect and he was much gratified.

'We don't *know*,' admitted Fox. 'But everything points to it.'

'Adder was quite clear about it as soon as I told him,' Whistler remarked.

'Adder?' Owl scoffed. 'Adder? What would *he* know about it?'

'Its very size, as Whistler describes it, must be a sufficient clue.' Squirrel said. 'And it's an animal that's quite new to us.'

'Just how big *was* it, Whistler?' Tawny Owl demanded, enjoying his position as the cautious dissenter.

The heron tried to give as vivid an impression as he could of the powerful body, the shape of the head – even the eyes. 'They had a cold gleam in them,' he said, 'just as you would expect to see in the eyes of a calculating, ruthless killer.'

'Stuff and nonsense,' Tawny Owl returned. 'There's a lot of your imagination gone into that description, Whistler. They don't sound a bit like the eyes *I* saw in my tree. It's certainly not the same beast.'

Tawny Owl had caused quite a stir, which is what he had intended. Were there *two* powerful strange animals roaming the Park? The animals started chattering all at once in a nervous way so that it was quite impossible for Whistler to make himself heard. Fox tried to think constructively, but that was impossible too.

Vixen said to him quietly, 'At least none of us is immediately threatened. We've got the time to think more about it, but now's not the right moment.'

'Just so,' agreed Fox, and they indicated to the heron that they were returning to their den.

'Someone should tell Badger your news,' Weasel said to Whistler. 'No one should be kept in the dark.' He ran off towards Badger's set.

Leveret mentioned that Toad was not present, but Whistler thought it likely that he might be found near the stream.

'And that takes care of everyone,' he summarized. He had no more to add and flew back to his usual haunt, though with the necessary circumspection.

Tawny Owl found himself surrounded by a miscellany of birds who bombarded him with questions about his experience with the Beast. He did not much relish this position, now that his close companions had gone on their way. It was daytime, he was sleepy, and he was never very comfortable in the company of a host of songbirds who sometimes chose to mock him during his periods of inaction in the daylight. Whilst he was trying in vain to disentangle himself, Weasel arrived at the entrance to Badger's home.

The first thing he noticed as he went in was the sound of voices. Badger lived alone and Weasel wondered to whom he was talking.

A voice, very like poor Mole's, was distinguishable. Weasel paused some way down the tunnel to listen to the conversation.

'You don't know how happy you've made me,' next came the gruff sound of Badger's voice. 'I really had given you up for lost.'

'But, you see, Badger, you're getting muddled,' said the Mole-like voice.

'Muddled?' Badger repeated. 'Oh yes, at my age – I

suppose you're right. I expect I do get muddled. But what does all that matter? What's important to me is that my dear old friend has come back. I *have* been rather lonely, Mole. Now we can have our cosy little talks again just like we always did. And I – '

'No, no,' the shriller voice interrupted. 'I'm not who you think. Oh dear. What can I say?'

Weasel detected a tone of helplessness in this voice and he began to put two and two together. He went on towards Badger's sleeping chamber. It was very dark deep inside the set so he could not see either of the other animals. He hurriedly announced himself.

'Oh! Weasel,' said Badger. 'What brings you here?' He did not wait for an answer but went on immediately with unmistakable excitement: 'This is a wonderful moment. Mole has returned! We've just been — '

A wail from the animal cut him short. It was a sound Mole had never been heard to make in *his* life. 'I am a mole,' said the unhappy creature. 'But not the one you want. *He* was my father!'

Weasel was glad he could not see Badger's reaction. He would have found it too distressing.

'I – I blundered into your set through one of the passages. I know my father used to use these tunnels,' the young mole explained. 'I can be company for you, and willingly, if you wish it. But I can't be the mole you want – only myself!'

Weasel thought he had never been witness to such a pathetic encounter before and he heartily wished he was elsewhere. He tried to divert the conversation.

'I've come to tell you, Badger,' he said awkwardly, 'about a discovery. Whistler has seen a great cat, and we think it must be the Beast.'

There was a deep silence. Weasel wondered if he was understood. Then Badger said, 'Cat? A great cat? Well, I wonder what we should do about it. What do you think, Mole?'

Weasel stared into the darkness in disbelief. Was Badger's mind wandering? He seemed not to have grasped what the little animal had told him. And this time the young mole remained quiet. Perhaps he had decided it was futile to make a further denial. Or perhaps he was too stunned to speak.

'You suggested, didn't you, Badger, that the stranger seemed to have feline characteristics?' Weasel prompted.

'What? Oh, oh yes, Weasel,' Badger murmured. 'I did. I recall it. But I don't think I can do anything for you, you know. I'm really getting very feeble now . . . .'

'No one expects you to do anything,' Weasel assured him. 'I merely brought you the news. It helps to know what we're up against.'

Suddenly Badger's mind seemed to have a moment of startling clarity. He said, much more briskly, 'No doubt Tawny Owl has refuted the notion of a cat, straight away?'

Weasel was impressed. 'Well, yes, he did, in a way. How did you guess?'

'Oh, Weasel,' Badger chuckled, 'don't you think I know our Owl after all this time?'

Badger's shrewdness did not tally with his previous confusion. Weasel began to realize that the old creature had wanted to believe Mole had returned and was rejecting the truth. He had shut out the idea that Mole was gone and was going to use his youngster as a substitute.

'Well, where's the harm in it, if it gives him comfort?' Weasel said to himself. He had an idea. He whispered to the young mole whose velvety fur his whiskers had located nearby, 'Go along to the outer tunnel. I'll join you there.'

When Weasel was sure they were alone he said to
Badger, 'I haven't any more to tell you for the present.
I'm sorry you've been lonely. We can't expect you to go
visiting so much now, so we must come to you. And I, for
one, promise to do so.'

'Thank you, Weasel. How very kind,' said Badger
joyfully. He seemed to be quite moved. 'Do, please. I
should enjoy it.'

They bade each other farewell and Weasel made haste
to find the perplexed young animal who had, quite
unintentionally, got himself into such a pickle.

'Come to the set entrance,' he said to him.

The youngster obliged.

Now Weasel was a last able to see him properly. When
he had a good look he was astonished to note just how
much the young mole resembled his father. 'What do
they call you?' he asked him.

'My father used to call me Mossy,' was the answer. 'I'm
not quite sure why, unless it had something to do with
the texture of my coat.'

'Well, listen – er – Mossy,' Weasel said. 'From now on
you can allow yourself to be called just plain Mole. It's for
the old badger's sake, of course. He won't know the
difference, as you must already be well aware. It'll mean
such a lot to him, and what does it matter? Will you
mind?'

'Er – well, no, I suppose not. But won't it be
confusing?'

'Not at all,' Weasel answered. 'I can soon explain the
situation to the others. Thank you, my young friend.
And, by the way, do drop in to Badger's set now and then.
I know you offered.'

'I will. I meant what I said, Weasel. I feel sorry for him
and he's always been such a kindly creature.'

'Good. Well, I'll leave you. Oh, and remember, if he

starts to talk about 'The Old Days' – which you know nothing about – just agree with him. That's all he expects, really.'

Mossy watched Weasel's pencil-slim body make its retreat and sighed. 'Ah well,' he murmured, 'I suppose it's not much to ask.'

Tawny Owl had managed to disengage himself from the attentions of the other birds and was now trying to doze, away from interference, in a hollow tree. But since all of his friends knew this favourite place, the exasperated owl was disturbed again by Weasel.

'I just dropped in to tell you I've seen Badger,' Weasel explained.

Much irritated, Tawny Owl snapped, 'Is that all you've woken me up for? How kind of you!'

'No, no, there's something you should know. I'm passing the message to everyone.' He went on to describe the scene in Badger's set involving Mole's offspring.

'Humph! So his mind's addled,' was Owl's comment on Badger. 'I might have known – the way he kept on about the strange animal being like a cat!'

Weasel refrained from pointing out that it looked as if Badger was correct in that. He contented himself with saying, 'I don't think his mind's addled at all. He's playing a sort of game with this young mole and I think we all ought to play along with him.'

'Pooh!' scoffed Tawny Owl. 'I'm past playing games. Badger ought to see sense. At his age too!'

'That's just it, Owl, "at his age". He's very old. I really don't think we'll have him around much longer. So why can't we humour him? I'm sure Fox and Vixen won't mind.'

'Oh, I can't be bothered with all that nonsense,' said Tawny Owl. 'Haven't we got more important things to think about?' He ruffled his feathers, re-settled his wings and closed both his eyes in a very determined sort of way. Weasel knew that he was dismissed.

As he had expected, Fox and Vixen and, indeed, all of his other friends whom Weasel managed to find, were agreeable to keeping up the pretence for Badger's sake. They were upset by the idea of Badger being in his dotage, and they tried to push to the backs of their minds the thought that it might not be long before they were without him.

Weasel's message did not get to Adder or Toad that day. But Whistler found Toad in the early evening and quickly told him of his important news, as well as that of Badger.

'And I have some news for *you*,' Toad said, 'while we're on the subject of the Beast. One of the frogs told me and *he* had been told by another and that one by another and so on. You know how fast news can travel through the Reserve. The upshot is that, despite the Warden's patrols, another deer has been killed.'

—6—
The Trail of the Beast

Adder could see nothing of his attacker. He was unable to turn to look behind, and the pressure was so great on his body that he thought his bones might break. There were no animals in the Park who ate snake and so Adder was in no doubt that he was trapped either by a human foot, or, more likely, by the very creature he had intended himself to surprise. There was a momentary easing of the pressure and Adder at once tried to turn. As soon as he moved, a huge paw swung round and patted at his head. Luckily for him the claws were retracted.

For the first time in his life Adder was really scared. He was scared in a way that he would not have been if the beast who was attacking him had been one he understood – such as a fox or a hawk. Fear of the unknown coursed through his sluggish blood. He felt he had no hope of escape. Then, abruptly, the great weight bearing down on his back was removed.

For a moment Adder's fear kept him frozen into immobility. He awaited the great blow that would crush the life out of him. But his paralysis lasted only a moment. Then he squirmed away painfully, in a desperate bid to reach the patch of vegetation. He was not permitted to. The paw descended again and knocked him back. The Beast was toying with him.

Adder kept moving – first this way, then that. Each time he was knocked back into place. Once a blow lifted him up into the air. He landed awkwardly. Pain racked his body but still he strove to get away. The Beast prodded him, tapped him and, finally, he felt its claws sear through his skin. He imagined he was going to be killed slowly in a form of torture, just as a cat will torment a bird or a mouse before the final kill. He wriggled in vain, like a creature in its death throes. Then a particularly heavy blow hooked him up high above the ground, over the vegetation, and suddenly Adder's scaly coils landed with a plop in the shallow part of the stream.

Like all snakes he was a good swimmer and, before he quite knew where he was, he instinctively rippled away into the deeper water. Only his head protruded above the surface. He looked back towards the bank and saw his assailant for the first time quite clearly. The Beast was staring out at the stream in an attempt to discover where its plaything had gone. Adder kept himself well hidden. After a while the Beast got bored and slowly padded away.

For a long time the snake dared not approach dry land,

although the water felt as cold as ice. He had to keep moving to avoid sinking to the bottom, but he merely swam through a cluster of weeds and then back again, until he was convinced the Beast would not return.

He made his way to the bank and slowly, painfully, drew his battered body into a cluster of rushes and reed mace. Here he rested and nursed his wounds. He was scratched, bruised and some of his scales were torn, but his bones were sound and for that Adder was profoundly grateful. All his grandiose ideas of performing the heroic act of ridding White Deer Park of this menace, seemed now to him piffling and nonsensical. A paltry creature like him trying to meddle with this great hunter from an unknown world! Why, he was no more than a worm who afforded a minute or two's distraction as a toy for such a powerful beast. Any animals who had made their homes in the Park had about as much chance of diverting it from its intentions as of learning how to walk on two legs. Adder would have chuckled at the absurdity of such a notion if he had been capable of it.

When he had recovered a little he moved carefully away from the stream, always keeping himself well screened, and slid with the utmost caution towards that quarter of the Reserve where his friends maintained their community. He had to make them understand about this Beast in no uncertain manner. But it was not until dusk that he approached close.

Toad was the first to hear of Adder's horrible encounter. He was full of sympathy.

'Oh Adder,' he croaked, 'my old friend! What a pounding you have had. Do come and rest yourself a little. There's a clump of moss I frequent which is as soft as thistledown. I'm sure if you lie there a while – '

'I'm much obliged, Toad,' Adder interrupted, 'and I'll take you up on your offer later. But I really feel Fox, at least, should know what we have to contend with.'

'I think he's aware of it already,' Toad returned.

'No. How could he be? He hasn't seen the creature. I tell you, Toad, we're all at its mercy. We're minnows by comparison.'

'Yes. Even the deer are suffering. Another one has been pulled down. I've just been telling Whistler. So despite the Warden's efforts – '

'Oh, the Warden!' hissed Adder. 'What can he do? Can he live amongst the deer herd? No. This hunter will take what it likes without hindrance. First it's at the pond, then it's by the stream or in a wood or choosing its prey in the open. It moves at will.'

'Is it the same creature?' Toad enquired.

'The same? What do you mean?'

'The same creature who caught you – did it make those footprints we saw?'

'My dear Toad, identical marks are all along the bank of the stream. That was how I was caught. I went to look.'

'It seems that Tawny Owl holds the view that there are two different beasts.'

Adder did not reply at once. Then he said in his driest lisp, 'If there are two, then our days are truly numbered. But I don't believe it. And now I must carry my warning.'

The snake's body was aching all over but he moved on. Fox's earth was empty. It was dark and, as usual, Fox and Vixen were on their evening quest for food. Their absence, however, at least gave Adder a chance of taking a proper rest. He awaited their return with patience.

As he lay, sleepily coiled up near the den entrance, another animal blundered into his path. There was an exclamation of surprise in a gruff, wheezy voice.

'It's only me, Badger,' Adder said evenly.

'Oh! So it is. I'm sorry. My sight was never very good
and it seems to get worse. But I'm glad to see you. We
don't often – '

'I'm glad to see *you*,' Adder butted in, 'because I'm
bringing a warning.' He described his alarming tussle in
dramatic terms.

'Goodness!' said Badger. 'You're lucky to be in one
piece. But are you all right? Are you in pain at all? I can't
see you very well . . . .'

'I shall survive,' Adder replied grimly. 'But I warn
others – don't meddle with this creature!'

'Oh, I'm sure there is no question of it,' Badger said at
once. 'That was Fox's advice before this happened. I
doubt if anyone is contemplating such a thing.'

Adder said drily, 'It might surprise you to know that
one was.'

'You?' cried Badger. 'But why? I mean, what could you
have done?'

'That's immaterial now,' Adder drawled. 'But if *I* had
the idea, another might too. That's why I'm here.'

Badger pondered this. He could not imagine any of
the elders of the Farthing Wood community being so
foolish. But he thought it would be tactless to say so, and,
to change the subject, began to talk about the Warden
and the recent deer killing.

Eventually Fox and Vixen appeared, and Adder told
his story to them with his attendant warning.

'This is timely advice,' Fox said, 'because I already
have a sneaking suspicion that something might be afoot.
Vixen and I have seen no other foxes around this night,
although we covered quite a lot of ground. Usually we
come across at least one or two of the youngsters out
roaming. I wonder if they are up to something?'

*****

Friendly had three young foxes in particular who looked up to him. There was his own son Pace, so called because of his speed; and there were two of his nephews. One was the son of Bold, known as Husky, who had his dead father's stout appearance. The other was Charmer's son, Rusty. Friendly's endearing qualities which had given him his name had attracted these youngsters and they were easily led by him. There were others, too, who had ties of one sort or another: Ranger, Charmer's mate; and a cousin of Ranger's, called Trip. Many of the vixens were fully occupied just then with their new litters, but Friendly had managed to gather together these five males – a substantial group – to join him on his expedition against the stranger who still threatened the peace of the entire Reserve.

He lost no time in leading them to the stream where the Beast had at last been seen in the open. None of these foxes knew anything of Adder's narrow escape, for that had happened while they were gathering.

Friendly soon noticed the Beast's spoor in the damp, soft ground at the edge of the stream. Working from there, he detected a scent and began to follow it along. The others ran behind. The youngest of them were both excited and frightened. Friendly had told them they were to track the stranger to its lair. He had not enlarged on what then was to be their purpose, but they were happy to be on an adventure and eager to prove themselves. Ranger and Trip brought up the rear of the party. They were about the same age as Friendly and of a cooler temperament.

The trail led through vegetation and then seemed to take a direction away from the water. The scent was fainter but Friendly was still certain of it, and it led them eventually into a wooded area.

'Now we must go very, very carefully,' he said. 'There's plenty of cover here and any scrub or undergrowth could be a hiding-place.'

A greenish light pervaded the enclosure. The young, newly-opened leaves made a thick screen which filtered the sun's rays. Last year's dead leaves and fallen twigs snapped and rustled underfoot, despite the animals' cautious movements. After a while Friendly lifted his head to listen, twitching his ears. He could find no unrecognized sound and bent his wet nose once more to the ground. He lost the scent and circled for a while before he picked it up again.

'Over here,' he called softly to the others, who had waited where they stood.

Friendly was moving slowly towards a mass of bramble which surrounded the base of an ancient hawthorn. Ranger had a sudden premonition.

'Take care!' he barked.

Friendly turned at the sharp sound and, as he did so, something stirred in front of him in the depths of the undergrowth. There was a muffled snarl and then the thing was gone, through some bolt-hole known only to itself, and with just the slightest disturbance of the low-lying foliage on the briars.

Friendly plunged after it, without stopping to think of the consequences. The other foxes hovered nervously, trying to peer in amongst the brambles. But they could see nothing. They could only hear their companion as he crashed through the undergrowth.

Now the youngsters turned to Ranger. 'What shall we do?' they asked. Pace said, 'Shouldn't we follow him? He's put himself in danger.'

'No. Stay together,' Ranger advised tensely. 'We're safer in a group and we might have to fight. We can't risk being picked off separately.'

'But what about Friendly?' asked Rusty.

Ranger did not answer.

The young foxes looked hesitantly from one to the other. They looked at Ranger and Trip who seemed uncertain of themselves. Without Friendly around, none of them had much confidence. The moments passed. A silence had fallen on the wood. The quietness seemed to them to be sinister.

'Sh – shall we wait a bit longer?' stammered Husky. It was obvious the way his mind was working.

'Yes. I think so,' Ranger answered, trying to sound calm. But their thoughts were all taking the same direction.

'I – er – don't see the point . . . .' Trip began, and then his voice petered out. He had caught a sound in the distance – a mere whisper, as of a brushed leaf. There was a soft swish of vegetation, nearer this time. The foxes' legs quivered. They were on the verge of scattering.

Then they heard Friendly's voice. 'It's no good – we missed him this time,' he called. They saw him approaching, but from another corner of the wood.

'There was just a glimpse,' he said as he came up. He was panting. 'A tail, I think.' He looked exhilarated. 'Anyway, we found its hideout – or one of them.'

'I don't think that's much help now,' Ranger said to him. 'Whatever was in there won't use it again, now it's known. The Beast is far too subtle for that.'

'*Was* it the Beast?' asked Pace in a whisper.

'Oh yes, I'm sure of it,' answered Friendly. He turned to Ranger. 'You're quite right, of course,' he said. 'No good looking here again. But the significant thing is – the creature ran! It didn't care to face all of us.'

The young foxes looked very pleased at this. They felt proud that Friendly had included them in the achievement, although they had not actually done anything definite.

'We can foil this beast,' Friendly continued confidently. 'We can drive it away from here.'

'Maybe we can,' said Ranger. 'But how do we ever get close to it? It's vanished again now, so I suppose we must start our search anew?'

Friendly considered for a moment. 'We could at least stay around this area for a while,' he said. 'It might not have gone far.'

The foxes stationed themselves at widely-spaced points so that they could cover quite a stretch of that part of the Park. They settled down for a long wait.

It was while they were waiting that the stranger killed its third deer. It was another fawn: only a few days old. The kill was sudden, silent and swift, just as before. Once again it seemed the Great Stag and all the adults of the herd were powerless to prevent it.

The meal was devoured in quite another corner of the Reserve and, by nightfall, the foxes themselves were feeling hungry. Ranger left his place and moved over to Friendly.

'I think we might as well call it a day,' he suggested.

'But it's the night when we should have the best chance,' Friendly replied. 'That's when this beast is most active.'

'Think of the youngsters,' said Ranger. 'Do they have the endurance? It could be a trial of nerves.'

'We shall be nearby – and Trip too,' returned Friendly. 'But perhaps I am expecting too much,' he added as an afterthought.

'I'm sure they must be famished,' Ranger remarked, 'if they feel anything like me.'

'Yes, very well. Let them refresh themselves,' said Friendly. 'But we'll wait on – shall we?'

Ranger looked glum, but his expression was hidden by

the dark. He kept his feelings out of his voice. 'Of course, if you think it will do any good.'

'It's worth a try,' answered Friendly. 'Will you tell the others then? And when they've fed they can come back. I have a feeling that, between us, we might be able to do something really worthwhile tonight.'

— 7 —

Trouble in Store

Fox and Vixen wondered what trouble Friendly and his followers could be getting themselves into. Then they discussed what, if there were to be trouble, *they* would be able to do about it. It did not take long for them to accept that there was nothing they – Fox and Vixen – *could* do. Friendly was no young cub to be reprimanded by seniors. He was a mature male into his third season who had strong ideas of his own and who, although he might listen politely to advice, would not necessarily act upon it. As for the younger foxes of a later generation, they were so remote in age from the elders that they might not even be prepared to listen.

'They must go their own way,' Vixen summed up.

'Yes,' said Badger who had remained with his old friends. 'Our day is done. All *I* hope for is sufficient peace and quiet to last me out.'

'I'm afraid we can't look forward to much of that at present, the way things are,' Fox said realistically. 'The Beast is still very much in evidence, as the latest deer killing shows. And Adder says it was done in daylight, so now there's a new dimension. The creature grows bolder. It seems to think nothing of stealing what it requires from under the nose of the Warden.'

'The problem does seem insoluble,' Badger agreed. 'But we know quite well humans are not fools. This brave hunter is likely to go one step too far.'

This notion comforted them all a little. Adder had left them to take advantage of Toad's proffered couch of moss. He had, so far, been the only surviving victim of an attack by the feared stranger. The others stayed talking a while, but Fox and Vixen were all on edge. They waited only for one of the younger foxes to put in an appearance. Eventually Badger went on his way. No fox came near.

Adder had barely made himself comfortable, after following Toad's directions, when he caught the vibrations of another creature moving along the ground nearby. His forked tongue flickered from his mouth as he tried to detect what sort of scent was given off. He was hoping for a tasty titbit in the shape of a frog, or maybe a shrew. His empty stomach felt like a cavern inside him. The leaves disturbed by the creature's progress crackled faintly. It was evident that it was something not very large. Adder was philosophical. Snails or large earthworms were all grist to the mill when you had not eaten for days.

The one thing he had not expected to come into view was another snake. But that was exactly what it was – and another adder, too. The snake came up quite close, slithering smoothly over the moss with an air of preoccupation. It did not speak to him.

Adder wondered if it meant to slide on past without appearing to notice him. For some reason, of which he was not quite sure, he felt indignant.

'I am alive,' he said sarcastically, 'not just part of the leaf litter.' Then he wondered why he had said it.

The other snake stopped and looked at him with the unwavering stare of their kind.

'Oh – yes. I see you are,' it replied phlegmatically. 'Have you been in a fight?'

'Well, I have. You're very observant.' Adder had not realized his scars were so obvious. Then he remembered his blunt tail. 'It's an old wound,' he added. 'It doesn't bother me.' He was a little surprised to discover that he was addressing a female.

'You're an old warrior, it seems,' returned the she-viper. 'There are scratches all over your body.'

Adder suddenly felt proud of his scars. For the life of him he did not know why. 'You're not often in this neck of the woods?' he ventured to enquire.

'Not very often. I've been looking for frogs. This is a good terrain for them when they're not in the water. But I was about to rest.'

'I'm doing the same myself,' said Adder. 'I can recommend this spot for comfort.' (What *was* he saying?)

'Well, since you recommend it, then,' said the female, 'I suppose I'd be a fool to ignore you.'

Adder did not know what to say next. He was quite unaccustomed to making pleasantries.

'There's been an abundance of frogs about this season,' the female went on. 'I've found them in all sorts of places.'

'Yes,' said Adder. 'And there's a reason for it.'

'A reason? Oh, I suppose you mean there was a glut of tadpoles last spring?'

'No, I don't mean that,' Adder hissed at her confidentially. 'It's a reason to do with a change of habitat.'

The other snake did not know what he was talking about and did not seem to be especially interested anyway. She made no reply.

Adder waited in vain. He was disappointed. He had been hoping to show off the depth of his knowledge. At length he said: 'You see, they took to the land at a time when they should have been in the water.' (He had an inkling this sounded rather foolish.)

'Really? Do tell me more,' came the toneless reply. It was obvious the she-viper was quite bored by the topic.

'You see, they were forced to leave the pond by a strange and powerful hunter.' Adder drew the words out slowly to heighten the dramatic effect.

'You mean the Big Cat? Oh yes, I know about that,' said the female. 'Have you only just heard the news? I should have thought every beast and bird in the Park would know by now.'

Adder was taken aback and, indeed, a little affronted. She had made him feel small and he did not think she was trying particularly hard to be polite.

'Er – yes,' he muttered. 'But how do *you* know about it being like a cat?'

'What a funny question,' she commented. 'Because I've seen it, of course!'

Her manner really was very abrupt, Adder decided. He did not know why he was bothering with her. Politeness was not something he normally cared very much about, one way or the other. He was preparing himself for one of his most sarcastic retorts when the female snake spoke again.

'I've just had a thought,' she hissed. 'Those scratches of yours. They couldn't be – '

'Yes!' Adder cried triumphantly. His attitude changed at once. 'I was mauled by the "Big Cat", as you call it.'

'I guessed as much,' she returned. 'You must have been very careless to have got in its way. It couldn't have been chasing you, because it doesn't feed off snakes!'

Adder had been mistaken in thinking his scars had impressed her. Now his anger began to kindle. Who was she to make comments about his carelessness?

'I'm afraid you're speaking from ignorance,' he said sourly. 'The stealth of this beast is more than enough to annul the most painstaking efforts at caution any other creature could make.'

The female snake looked at him for a few moments. She could tell she had annoyed him. 'Now don't get in a coil,' she said easily. She seemed to be preparing to rest, for she slithered away for a few centimetres. Adder heard her murmur to herself, 'Goodness, what a pedantic reply!'

His red eyes glared into the darkness. The mossy couch no longer seemed so soft and comfortable. He had not realized how offended he had been. He – the Farthing Wood Adder! What had *she* done to compare with his exploits? The more he thought, the more irritated he felt. In the end he could not bear to remain any longer in her company. Without another word he slid away, and it was not until he had put a fair distance between them, that he stopped again.

Before he quite sank into his usual nocturnal state of dormancy, Adder considered his reaction. *Why* had he been so irritated? What was this female to him that he should care so much as a fern-frond for her opinions? He was not sure he knew the answer. But he had half a mind, when daylight should arrive again, to return to Toad's clump of moss to see if she was still around – even if only to tell her what he thought of her!

The news of the deer killing was brought to Friendly by his young companions. Husky, Pace and Rusty had gone in search of food as had been suggested. They had kept close together to give themselves courage. Because of this they did not feel they had to restrict themselves in their range, and they wandered quite far. It was Husky who found the body. As usual, most of it had been consumed. The remainder was lying amongst some undergrowth, and there was no mistaking the freshness of the meat. The blood around it had hardly dried. Husky did not delay in bringing it to the attention of the other two.

'How could it have done that so quickly after escaping from us?' Pace asked rhetorically.

'Us?' Rusty echoed with a wry look.

'Well, Friendly, then . . . .'

'It moves as it pleases, doesn't it?' Husky said. 'It chooses its victim. It stalks it. And then it snatches it with the utmost ease.'

'I wish I had such confidence and such skill,' Pace remarked. 'I'd like to see the Beast in action. I can imagine the whole sequence – the smoothness, the stealth . . . .'

Husky was looking at the remains. 'Well, are we going to waste this?' he demanded of the others.

There was a silence. Then Rusty said, 'But we – we – *daren't*.'

'Why not?' Husky returned cockily. 'Can you see old "Stealth" around, or hear him?'

'No, but that's not to say he's not in the vicinity. How should *we* know?'

'We don't,' Husky declared. 'But I'm hungry – and there's more than one of *us*.'

'I – I don't think it would be wise,' Pace cautioned. 'The Beast might be planning to come back and finish this.' But as he looked at the meat and smelt again its freshness, he began to drool.

'Come on,' Husky urged him. 'We might not get another opportunity like this.' He bent and took a small piece of flesh from the carcass. 'You'll regret it if you don't,' he pronounced. 'Trust "Stealth" to choose himself the finest game.'

Pace did not need any more persuasion, and eventually Rusty too joined in the meal. It was an act of bravado, really, by these youngsters urging each other on. None of them were at ease as they ate. Their ears twitched to and fro constantly, trying to pick up the faintest of warning sounds. They chewed the meat stiff-legged, ready to dart away at the first moment. All the time their spines tingled and the hair on their backs rose slightly in a sort of awareness at the risk they were taking. But they were not interrupted and, when they had finished, they were all in agreement that they should return at once to the wood where Friendly and the older foxes awaited them.

They ran quickly, without any deviation from the route. They looked forward excitedly to Friendly's surprise when they would tell him of their audacity. As they loped along in high spirits, they were watched from a low branch of an oak by a pair of unblinking, gleaming eyes. Not one of them went unheeded. Not one of their actions was unperceived.

Friendly's reaction was not entirely as they had expected. He looked concerned at their news, and they thought they were about to be reproached for their daring. But he reminded himself how faithfully they had followed him and he had not the heart to issue a rebuke.

He even went so far as to remark that he liked their cheek.

Ranger, however, make them understand that he thought they had been very foolish. 'You don't know what trouble you might have stored up for yourselves,' he told them. 'If the Beast takes it into its head to teach you a lesson, don't come running to *me*.' He was ravenously hungry and the young foxes' foolhardiness only aggravated his general feeling of discomfort.

'You know you don't mean that, Ranger,' Friendly reasoned with him. 'We all stand together on this. We formed our group for a purpose and we can't back down now.'

'Well, there's no more to be done tonight,' Ranger asserted positively. 'We can't go off hunting now, we adults, and leave the juniors unattended. Not after what they've just told us. What do you think, Trip?'

'I agree with you,' said his cousin. 'There's always another day.'

'Of course there's another day,' said Friendly. 'But on another day we'd have to start from scratch again trying to pick up a trail. I still feel our best chance of success is *now*. I'm willing to ignore my stomach for the rest of the night if necessary.'

'Well, I'm not,' said Ranger bluntly. 'The situation's changed. We've lost the element of surprise. We might find that the Beast will decide to come looking for *us*.'

'Perfect!' was Friendly's reply. 'It would find it had made a grave mistake. How could it cope with the entire group of us?'

Trip decided the matter by siding with Ranger. 'It's too clever for that. Now let's go and feed. We can meet again tomorrow.'

Friendly saw he must succumb. 'So be it,' he said, trying to mask his exasperation. 'You youngsters must take us at dusk to this latest kill, and we'll begin to track it from there. We may find it easier next time, for we'll be following the taint of blood.'

—8—

New Measures

Toad returned to his mossy base later that night. He had
ed well on slugs and insects, and he was in a good
humour. He was keen to see if Adder had found the spot
because he was feeling rather talkative. When he saw the
mosaic coils of the snake at rest on his soft bed, he was
delighted.

'Well, you've certainly made yourself comfortable,'
Toad began, 'and – goodness! – it really looks as if your
scratches are healing already!'

The she-viper raised her head and regarded the small
amphibious animal who addressed her. Her eyes glared
greedily, for she thought at first she was looking at a frog.

But when she realized it was a toad she lost interest. She knew how unpalatable toads were and, without saying a word, settled herself once more.

Toad was surprised and a little disappointed at the snake's reaction. But he knew how unpredictable Adder was. You could never be quite confident that he would be in a friendly mood. Then he remembered his recent experiences and wondered if Adder were in pain or feeling unwell.

'Are you all right, Adder?' Toad asked with real concern.

The snake looked up again. 'I'm perfectly well,' she answered smoothly, 'though I must confess I'm somewhat puzzled at your interest.'

Now Toad realized his mistake and, quite unconsciously, hopped a little further away. A strange snake was always a potential enemy. 'I – I took you for another,' he muttered and began at once to move off.

'I think I met him,' was the unexpected reply. 'He won't be far off, I should say. He *was* here, but somehow I seemed to upset him.'

Toad was most intrigued, but his discretion kept him moving. He would have dearly loved to have known what had happened at the meeting. Adder had never been known to consort with females, though his private activities were largely a mystery. But Toad was well aware that, even if he found his friend, the snake would give absolutely nothing away. He plodded on in a reflective mood.

From his solitary resting-place Adder heard the toad's rustlings through the leaves. He waited until he was closer and then made himself visible.

'You needn't have come looking for me,' he hissed.

'I didn't,' said Toad, 'I've had to abandon my little roost temporarily. I expect you can guess why.'

Adder's face was a mask. His impassive features did not show a flicker of comprehension. He remained silent. Toad said no more, but started to dig himself down into the leaf litter. His back feet worked vigorously.

'Are you burying yourself?' Adder asked curiously.

'Oh no. But I never squat quite on the surface,' Toad explained. 'You don't know what creature might come along.' He shot a sly glance at the snake but Adder made no response.

Later, when it was still dark but in the early part of the morning, they were aroused by the sound of running feet. They soon discovered the cause. It was Friendly and his group of followers.

'They look as if they have some purpose in mind,' Toad commented.

'Yesss,' drawled Adder. 'And I don't think it's a hunting trip.'

They watched the band of foxes move on their way.

'They don't often travel together like that,' Toad said. 'They've been on some errand or other.'

They had seen five of the foxes. Ranger had broken away to search for much-needed food. Some time afterwards he came right past the two animals, quite oblivious of their nearness. He was not one of the Farthing Wood community of creatures, but Toad and Adder were both impatient for information. So they halted him.

'Oh,' said Ranger, when he saw them. 'I hadn't realized. My mind was on other things.'

'We've just seen Friendly with a group of youngsters,' said Toad. 'Quite a bunch of them. We've been pondering the meaning of it.'

Ranger had no qualms about waiving secrecy, particularly as he had lost a lot of enthusiasm on this night for the idea of cornering the stranger. 'Yes, we made a party,' he told them honestly. 'We've been tracking the Beast.'

'I suppose you had no luck then,' Adder lisped, 'since there is no sign of any injuries?'

'We did and we didn't,' Ranger returned cryptically. 'It's all Friendly's idea. He wants to get the Beast away from here and he thinks a group of us can do it. I doubt if he's right. It escaped us easily. But I agree with him that *something* has to be done.'

Adder displayed his wounds in an elaborate exhibition of what could happen to them too. But they were lost for the most part on Ranger who, even in the moonlight, could scarcely see their severity.

'Do you mean to go on with this?' Toad asked the fox.

'Friendly wants to. I'm beginning to have doubts,' Ranger replied. 'But I'll stay with him a while and see what turns up.'

'I've just shown you what will turn up,' Adder hissed acidly. 'You won't be warned. So try and think of your offspring.'

'Oh, I have done,' Ranger assured him. 'But I have no control, you must understand. They're not cubs – any of them.'

'You're all cubs in temperament,' Adder told him bluntly. 'Playing around with something that could be lethal.'

Ranger objected to Adder's tone of superiority. He – Ranger – was no refugee from Farthing Wood who was obliged to respect the foibles of his comrades. 'You're entitled to your opinion,' he told the snake, 'for what it's worth. But I think the subject of tracking and out-manoeuvring a mammal is best left to those who know about these things.'

Adder was not in the least put out. He had the patience to wait for his words to be proved true by future events.

Ranger did not tarry. He wanted to get back to Charmer and see that all was safe with their new litter.

Charmer greeted him with her customary sweetness. She soon allayed his fears and then asked him if he and the others had been successful.

'No,' said Ranger. 'Not successful. Only the Beast continues to be that. He is a proficient hunter and I think will always evade any of our stumbling efforts.'

'The deer herd is very much in peril then,' Charmer surmised. 'How glad I am fox meat is no delicacy.' She shuddered as she looked at her cubs.

Ranger looked too, and the sight of the tiny bundles of fur huddling together for warmth steeled his resolve. Yes, Friendly was right. They *must* go on. For what sort of future could there be for these little ones – or any of them – whilst they were all in this stranger's power?

'The white stags must long for their new antlers to grow,' he murmured. 'They are the herd's only protection.' He lay down next to his mate. Charmer nuzzled him comfortingly. Outside the den, dawn hovered on the horizon.

At first light Adder stirred. Toad was deep in his bower of soft soil and leaves. The snake slid noiselessly away. The she-viper was again in his thoughts. Adder found himself moving in her direction. He had not decided what sort of approach he would use with her and, as he went along, he endeavoured to compose a really choice remark. But the female had gone on her way, and Adder was left to wonder about her – and ponder, his hurts forgotten.

*****

Later that day the Park's inhabitants became aware that some new scheme was being put into action by the Warden. He and three other men were working by the perimeter of the Reserve, on a piece of open ground about half a kilometre from the Warden's cottage. They did not at first realize what was happening, for the sight of men and their tools and machinery frightened them and they kept well away. But as the day went on, birds who flew over the area were able to report on events. It seemed that part of the Park was being cordoned off. Using the boundary fence on one side, an enclosure was being erected with extra poles and bars which looked like a miniature reserve within the Reserve. The curiosity of the animals was profound but, naturally, they dared not go anywhere near the work. By late afternoon it was complete. Whistler decided to go and have a look for the benefit of his own particular animal friends.

When the heron flew over the construction, the men had left taking all their equipment with them. Already a few of the most inquisitive beasts were gathering to make an inspection. From the air the fencing could be seen as forming a circle. There was a single opening.

'Now what on earth is it for?' Whistler asked himself. He made sure he looked at it from all sides, so that he could describe it accurately to the others. 'Something is to be put in it, that's clear.' He flew away, racking his brains for a solution.

Fox and Vixen, Weasel and Leveret were waiting for Whistler's return. When he told them, in the greatest detail, what he had seen, they put their heads together.

'It sounds like a sort of cage,' Vixen said.

'Of course!' cried Weasel. 'It must be for the Beast!'

'I don't think that can be, Weasel,' Whistler remarked. 'It's too big for one animal. And, besides, can't the creature climb?'

'Yes, yes. It wouldn't hold it,' Fox agreed. 'Something much more subtle would be needed for that cunning character.'

'It's not – er – something that all of us could be put into, is it?' Leveret asked hesitantly, afraid he would sound a fool.

The others were amused at the idea but tried not to show it.

'There would be no point in that,' Fox reassured the hare. 'Don't worry Leveret.'

A familiar hoot sounded and they looked up to see Tawny Owl flying towards them. He seemed to be in a great haste about something. He landed awkwardly, bumping into the heron's long legs and making the tall bird rock.

'Sorry, Whistler,' he muttered in a flustered way. 'The deer – the deer — ' he started to say. Then he stopped. 'I must remember my age – shouldn't fly so fast,' he murmured to himself.

'What of the deer?' Fox asked eagerly. It was obvious something of import had occurred.

'They're being – rounded up,' Owl told them with an effort. He had tired himself badly.

'So that's it!' the others cried simultaneously.

'Yes, there are men on horseback and – and – a couple of dogs,' Tawny Owl went on. 'I don't know where they mean to take them.'

Fox enlightened the bird. Then he continued, 'The men must want the whole herd in one place. Easier to look after them, I suppose.'

'They'll have to feed them as well,' Vixen pointed out, 'if they're not left free to forage.'

'Well, one thing's for certain,' said Weasel. 'It will call a halt to our silent friend's activities.' He spoke with great satisfaction.

'Yes, indeed,' said Whistler. 'But wait – this Beast could *still* get at them.'

'I think we should give the humans credit for a little more sense,' Fox said wryly. 'They're not likely to leave a herd of penned-up deer unguarded, are they? They're to be protected from its ravages, not left at its mercy.'

'Of course,' said the heron. 'How silly of me.'

'*And*,' Fox emphasized, 'there's another aspect. The deer might also act as bait to lead the Beast on. Then our clever Warden and his friends will pounce and – the threat is gone!'

'Poor deer,' murmured Vixen, 'to be used in such a way. I hope the Beast will show its cleverness again by seeing sense and leaving this hunting ground.'

As soon as Vixen had finished speaking she and all the others realized at once the implications of what she had said. They looked at one another with serious faces. The thought had occurred simultaneously to them. The Beast might decide not to leave, but simply to change its diet!

Leveret knew that he was the most vulnerable of the group then present. 'The likes of me and the rabbits will be its fare again,' he said in a whisper, looking ahead with frightened eyes as if he could visualize this nightmare. 'None of you are at such risk from it – nor have you ever been.'

'We must try and look on the bright side,' Fox told him earnestly. 'If the Beast has developed a taste for deer, then it might not wish to forgo the treat. So, what happens? It is captured – or destroyed.'

'I'm not convinced,' Leveret replied. 'Thank you for your encouragement, Fox. I know you mean well. But, you see, there's something about this creature – a kind of – er – invincibility.'

'Well, we'll see about that,' Fox said grimly. 'In the

meantime, you and your family must lie low and not stray too far.'

'Oh, we've been doing that all along,' Leveret said. 'But *that's* no defence.'

'Leveret's right,' said Tawny Owl. He turned to the hare. 'I don't know why you can't take a lesson from your rabbit cousins and get yourself underground. You lie out in the open with no more than a depression in the ground to hide you.' He never was the most tactful of beings and Weasel gave him a glare that told him just that.

'We're not diggers, Owl,' Leveret explained simply. 'We have to rely on our speed.'

Tawny Owl stared back at Weasel, quite unrepentant. Then he went on in the same vein. He made a virtue of bluntness. 'You'd need some speed, too,' he commented, turning once more to the hare, 'to get away from the creature *I* saw.'

Weasel was exasperated. 'What do you know about it?' he demanded. 'Was the Beast running when you saw it?'

'Er – no, but I – '

'Well, don't talk such nonsense then,' Weasel interrupted him. 'Leveret's a timid enough animal as it is.'

Tawny Owl did seem to feel a twinge of regret. 'I just think it's better to know the facts,' he excused himself. 'I'm sure Leveret understands. I wasn't trying to frighten him.'

'It's all right,' said the hare. 'Don't let's argue – that won't help. We're all in this together, aren't we?'

'Of course we are,' said Tawny Owl promptly. 'If I can be of any assistance at all you know you can always count on me.'

'Except for any diplomacy,' Weasel muttered.

'Tell me, Owl,' Whistler said hastily, 'are you still of the mind that there is more than one strange beast about?'

Tawny Owl had forgotten his own theory on that matter. 'Oh – er – well, I can't be certain about it, Whistler. The facts are beginning to point, I suppose, to there being – er – perhaps just the one.'

He had been caught off guard and felt a trifle awkward about it. He tried to retrieve the situation. 'Anyway,' he said, 'I'll keep an eye open tonight by this – um – deer pen and see if I can discover anything.' The animals watched him fly away.

'Well,' said Fox. 'The next few days should tell us if the Warden's plan will work out or not. The craft of the Beast will really be put to the test.'

—9—
Captured

Before dusk, Friendly was ready and waiting for the evening's action. The three younger foxes – Pace, Rusty and Husky – arrived just as darkness began to steal across the Park. Ranger and Trip came last. No word was spoken. They all knew what they were going to do.

Husky took the lead, with Pace and Rusty behind him. They made straight for the fawn's remains they had found the night before. As they neared the place they slowed and went much more carefully. As usual, they paused periodically to listen. They reached the carcass. There were only bones and skin left. Friendly sniffed vigorously at the carcass and then at the ground all about. The others followed suit.

'The smell of blood is very strong,' Friendly said in a low voice. 'And there's something else – something recognizable.' He was thoroughly absorbed. 'Yes, it's the same as before. It's the creature's scent all right. The question is – where does it lead?' With his muzzle bent low, he moved about, this way and that, making patterns over the ground. Then he gave a bark of excitement. 'Come on,' he whispered. 'This way!'

He was following the strongest scent; the one made most recently. The other foxes followed him through the undergrowth. The youngsters' hearts were beating wildly.

'Keep your eyes and ears at full alert,' Friendly turned to say. 'Leave the tracking to me.'

They went on slowly. The undergrowth gave way to open grassy ground. Much of it was still soft from the frequent spring showers of rain. Suddenly, Friendly stopped. He turned round. His eyes were glistening. 'Look!' he said triumphantly.

Amongst the short grass there was a small patch of bare earth dotted with plantain. In the centre of it, almost as if left deliberately to assist them, was a huge pawprint.

'We're really on to something, this time,' said Friendly. 'Here's an unmistakable clue.'

They all stared at it. It seemed obvious that it had been made quite recently. Only Ranger seemed unhappy. 'I don't know,' he said. 'It could be a trap.'

'A trap!' cried the young foxes together.

'What are you getting at, Ranger?' Friendly asked him quietly.

'Isn't it too obvious a clue?' he returned.

'Nonsense!' was Friendly's immediate reaction. 'Do you mean it's trying to lure us –' He broke off. He looked at Ranger and considered. 'There may be something in that,' he murmured. 'How are we to tell?' He was pensive for a while. Then he shook himself out of his reverie. 'Anyway, if you're correct,' he said, 'then so be it.' Friendly looked determined. 'Our friend will find he has more than he bargained for.'

The foxes proceeded on the trail but with noticeably more caution. They crossed the open ground and now the scent led them under some trees. They found themselves in a small copse. It was not one they had been to before. Pace, Rusty and Husky were feeling the strain of having their eyes and ears as it were stretched to their limit. Ranger and Trip showed no sign of their feelings, but they all were expecting something to happen. Friendly came to a stop at the foot of a tree. He went round the tree, trying to trace where the scent led. Then he sat down, looking puzzled. The rest of the group regarded him, but could not find their voices. The skin on their backs began to crawl. Slowly they raised their heads.

Friendly followed their eyes and, as he did so, a most unearthly snarl ripped through the stillness of the copse. In the next instant a huge creature leapt from the tree and landed directly beside Husky. With a vicious blow from a front paw it tumbled the fox over. The beast's jaws fastened on the scruff of his neck and he was lifted helplessly, legs dangling, as with one bound the creature whirled around and vaulted back into the tree. Its claws raked the bark as it raced up the trunk to its vantage point in a broad lofty branch. The five foxes barked furiously from the ground. Their fur was raised, their lips curled back to reveal their fangs, while their eyes gleamed with anger. But they were helpless. The beast retained its grip on the struggling Husky as securely as if he had been no more than a rabbit. There was a look of malevolence about the creature as it glared down at them which made their barks sputter into silence. The foxes were helpless and they knew it.

'It was – a trap,' Ranger muttered almost inaudibly. They stared up through the darkness, aware of their utter powerlessness in the face of this monster. All they could see was its shining eyes – eyes that seemed to mock their weakness. For some time they remained rooted to the spot. They were unable to think of any action they could take. They felt as if the Beast's influence had frozen their limbs into immobility.

At last Friendly said hoarsely, 'We must get help.' He had no idea what help they could look for, nor where they could look for it. It was a blind reaction from their situation put into words.

'But we can't leave . . . .' began Pace. His voice faltered and he lapsed into silence.

None of the others spoke. They dared not look at each other. Then, with drooping head, Friendly began to move away. He knew that, even if they should stay there until dawn, they could achieve nothing. The others followed him forlornly. From his terrifying height Husky witnessed their departure with the keenest agony.

As soon as the Beast was satisfied that the foxes had gone on their way, it released its grip. Husky fell like a stone to the ground.

When they were some distance from the copse the foxes began to give vent to their feelings. The natural course was to look for a culprit to blame for what had happened. So it followed that Friendly became the target.

'It was very foolhardy to come on this venture,' said Trip. 'It was your idea, Friendly. You might have known it could only end like this.'

'I guessed it would be a mistake from the start,' Ranger

concurred. 'Now see what you've led us into.'

'How shall we tell Whisper?' murmured Rusty.

Only Pace, Friendly's own son, forbore to comment. Yet his thoughts matched the others'.

'Don't you think I regret it now?' Friendly said miserably. 'But how could I have foreseen what has occurred? I did this from the best of motives. And – you didn't have to accompany me; none of you.'

'It's true,' said Pace. 'We must be fair. And it's too late to regret our actions.'

'We have to think of finding help,' Friendly said. '*I* don't know where to turn. Perhaps my father – '

'Your father,' Ranger cut in, 'would have had more sense at the outset!' (Now he recalled Adder's words.)

'You're right,' Friendly said unhappily. 'He gave his advice, at the beginning. "Don't meddle," he said.'

'Grandfather is very wise,' said Pace. 'He may think of something that can be done.'

They carried on their way in silence. In their minds was the picture of Husky clenched in the fierce jaws of the Beast – the powerful beast they had tried to tamper with! For Friendly the image held the most horror, for he did feel responsible despite what he had said.

Ranger and Trip left the group as they came near the earth of the Farthing Wood Fox. They were of a different parentage and had not the same allegiance.

Fox and Vixen were absent. Friendly gave a yelp of frustration. Just when he needed them most! Of course, they were hunting. However his call of distress brought another animal's answer. Friendly knew it was Badger's cry. He dearly loved the old creature but – ironically – he was the one friend who was really too old and feeble now to be of any assistance.

'What is it, Friendly?' Badger asked after greeting him and the two youngsters.

The fox explained with a woeful expression. Badger was aghast.

'Oh dear, oh dear, oh my word!' he muttered continually. He swung his striped head to and fro. 'Oh, Friendly!' he said. 'Oh dear, oh dear!' He was trying to think how he could help. 'Poor Husky. Has he a mate?'

'No,' Rusty answered.

'Well, that's a blessing,' Badger murmured. 'But Whisper will be so upset! Vixens are all the same when their cubs are in danger.' A though struck him. 'She mustn't be told – not yet,' he said hurriedly. 'She might do something foolish, and we've had enough foolishness already.'

Friendly took the implied reproof without demur.

Badger was beginning to think of an idea. It depended on what the Cat would do with its victim. If it intended killing Husky, then it was already too late for any animal to act. But if it merely meant to keep him captive, there perhaps was a way out. Badger made up his mind. He knew he could not tell the foxes his plan. They would be sure to prevent it. So he gave no sign.

'I think you must wait and speak to your father,' he told Friendly. 'No doubt you intended to do that anyway. You must all stay here. I'll see if I can find him and then I'll send him back to you. Now, you mustn't stray – do you promise?'

'We promise,' said Pace and Rusty. Friendly was too dispirited even to answer.

Badger shambled away, his head full of what he must do. It was some time before the realization struck him that he did not know where he was going. He did not know where Husky was!

'Oh, you old fool,' he castigated himself. 'You forgot to

find out where it all happened.' Now what could he do? He could not traverse the entire Park in search of the elusive hunter. And he could not go back to Friendly with the all-important question. He would be suspicious at once and then his plan would come to nothing. He had not meant really to look for Fox. He only wanted Fox's three relatives to remain where they were, out of the way. He knew that Fox and Vixen would return eventually of their own accord. But now he could think of nothing better to do than to consult his old friend himself. So he shuffled about, going to all the places he thought most likely to find him, and calling at intervals in his gruff, wheezy voice. He even went up to the stream and along the bank for a stretch in case Fox was after a meal of water-rat. But he saw nobody, not even Whistler, who was comfortably at roost in a tall tree at that time.

Badger, thoroughly disheartened, made his slow way back again. He hoped to find all the foxes together now. He was so wrapped up in his thoughts on the matter that he did not see a small creature move quickly out of his path. But he heard it squeak.

'Mole?' he mumbled automatically.

'No. Er – yes. Here I am, Badger,' was the answer. It was Mossy.

'Oh Mole, what trouble,' Badger said. 'Things have taken a turn for the worse. Husky has been captured by that awful Cat.'

Mossy did not know who Husky was, but he remembered Weasel's advice and made a pretence. 'Poor creature,' he commented, wondering for what sort of creature he was showing sympathy.

'Yes,' said Badger. 'They shouldn't have gone near it. And he's only a youngster.'

'I know,' fibbed Mossy.

'If this had to happen to one of us, why couldn't it have been me – or – or – somebody like me,' said Badger. 'My life's as good as over anyway.'

'Don't say that, Badger,' shrilled Mossy, more genuinely. 'Your friends would be heartbroken.'

'Well, thank you, dear Mole,' Badger said warmly. 'But – oh! I must leave you now. There's no time to waste.'

Mossy watched Badger lumber away and he felt a surge of affection for the old animal. 'He was the truest of friends to my father, I know,' he murmured to himself. 'Perhaps I can help repay the debt.'

As soon as he was within sight of Fox and Vixen's earth once more, Badger noticed that they had come back. All five foxes were in conclave – Friendly, Pace and Rusty anxiously explaining what had happened. Badger paused awhile in order that the bad news would have been grasped, with all its implications, before he joined them. When he did do so, Vixen turned a miserably worried face in his direction. Fox was deep in his own thoughts. Only when Badger was amongst them did he see Tawny Owl looking on from a nearby perch. He wondered if Owl had had something to report too. Now he felt he must ask his question.

'Where is Husky? Where did it take place?'

In a low voice Pace described the copse. Badger pumped him for more information. What quarter of the Park? Was it near the boundary fence?

'Nowhere near that,' Tawny Owl chimed in. 'The Warden is in that area, guarding the deer. So the Beast is keeping well away. In any case, it would have no need to risk being shot.'

'No. There's other food,' Badger agreed. Then he wished he had not. He had been thinking of rabbits and such like, but now he wondered about Husky.

'Not only other food,' Owl continued, 'but its preferred food.'

Badger was puzzled. 'Preferred food?' he repeated.

'Oh yes. Not all the deer have been penned, you know. I've seen two hinds wandering free, quite on their own. They must have wandered off and become separated. Probably old ones past breeding.'

Now Fox looked up. 'You see, human ingenuity has failed too, Badger. What hope have *we* of ridding ourselves of this pest?'

'Well, we can't live life as if we're under siege,' Badger declared. 'And first of all we must rescue Husky.'

'Do tell us how you propose to do so,' Tawny Owl begged. He was convinced Badger was becoming senile and he waited to hear a stream of nonsense.

'I do have a plan,' said Badger uncertainly. 'But I – I – can't tell you it.'

Tawny Owl made derisive noises. But Fox was interested.

'Why can't you tell us?' he queried.

'You wouldn't approve,' Badger explained.

'He's got some madcap notion of challenging the Beast to combat, I suppose,' Owl remarked scornfully.

Badger remained silent. There was a grain of truth in what he had said but he had not quite hit the mark.

'I hope that's not – ' Fox began urgently.

'No, no, don't worry,' Badger assured him. 'I'm not quite the old idiot Owl takes me for.'

'I didn't say that,' Owl remarked, a little embarrassed.

Badger now pretended to have taken great offence. It suited his plan. 'And you're so sharp, aren't you, Owl?' he growled. 'You couldn't even recognize the creature as being a big Cat!' He made a great play of looking very hurt and indignant and turned his back on them all.

'Now look what you've done,' Fox said angrily to Tawny Owl. 'Do you have to make even more trouble? As if we haven't enough to contend with!'

'Well – I – I – never intended . . . .' the bird spluttered.

When Badger was sure he was hidden by the darkness, he put on speed. He knew he had to act quickly, because he was sure Fox would eventually demand that Friendly lead him and Vixen to the scene of Husky's capture. He could not simply do nothing. It was not in Fox's nature. So, armed with only the scant descriptions Pace had given him, Badger trundled forward in search of the copse. His idea was a simple one – to offer himself in exchange for the release of Husky.

— 10 —

A Common Aim

Fox had, indeed, accepted that there was no alternative
but to go to help, and at length the four male foxes went
on their way. Vixen left Tawny Owl for Badger's set. She
wanted to console him for the hurt she supposed he had
taken. The set, of course, was empty. As Vixen emerged
from Badger's dark labyrinth she found Mossy apparently
on his way there.

'Is Badger there?' he asked. He knew who Vixen
was.

'No, Oh – you must be – '

'I'm to be known simply as "Mole",' he twittered
informatively.

'Of course.'

Mossy began to ask Vixen about Husky. He soon discovered he was another fox. Then he told her what Badger had said about his life being almost over, and how it would have been better if *he* had been the captured animal. Vixen went cold. She recalled Badger asking Pace for directions. Yes, there was no doubt of his intentions – it would be typical of him. She must stop him!

She raced away. Her first idea was to use Tawny Owl as her messenger. Wings were faster than legs. But Owl was nowhere to be seen now and she had to trust to her own speed. Vixen was no longer the swift-footed, lithe creature of her youth. She loped along for a while, then eased down to a trot. If she could catch up with the other four, one of the young foxes could be sent on to forestall Badger. But her breathing became laboured and soon she had to stop altogether, her sides heaving, to bring it under control.

Badger's lead had been cut considerably by Friendly's faster pace. But the old animal lumbered on persistently, full of dogged determination. He was not absolutely sure of his destination and, because of this, the foxes on their direct course arrived at the scene first. Friendly led them, with much trepidation, towards the tree where the killer had lurked. Husky's body lay where it had fallen, all life crushed out of it. Friendly stared at it in horror and disbelief. The others surrounded him.

Fox looked at his dead grandson. He remembered, with a sharp pang, another occasion when he had found one of his own cubs in just such a state. The only difference this time was that the body was full grown. And there were no marks on it.

Pace and Rusty were looking fearfully up into the tree. No sound, no sign hinted at the presence of the hunter.

The Cat had done its work and had moved on – who knew where?

Vixen was next to arrive. Fox looked at his mate without speaking.

'Are – are we too late?' Vixen whispered. Then she saw the still form of Husky.

'He never had a chance,' Fox rasped. He was racked by helpless, impotent anger. 'I will get even,' he intoned in a growl to himself.

Vixen understood. She could find nothing to say. Her heart ached.

'It was a desire to get even that began it all,' Friendly muttered. 'I didn't think – oh how ignorant I was!'

'Let's get away from here,' Rusty suggested. The sight of Husky's body frightened him. He knew how easily it could have been himself lying there.

'Yes – it's a hateful place,' said Fox.

'We must wait for Badger,' Vixen said hurriedly as they began to move.

They looked at her questioningly. 'He – he thought he could help,' she explained lamely. There was no need now to go into detail.

'So that was why he wanted the directions,' Pace remarked. 'Dear old Badger – this is no quarrel of his.'

'Of course it is,' Fox told him surprisingly. 'Any quarrel of mine has always been Badger's too. He'll soon tell you that.'

Badger came at last, grunting, and out of breath. He saw, in his turn, the young animal he had set out to save. 'It really has gone too far now, hasn't it?' he muttered.

'But what are we to do, Badger?' Friendly wailed.

'Wage a war,' was the old animal's reply. His voice suddenly seemed to have lost its wheeziness. It sounded crisp, assertive and younger.

'*I* tried,' said the fox. 'Look what I've achieved.'

'You should not have acted alone,' Badger admonished him. 'There are those who are wiser and more experienced than yourself. They should have been consulted.' He named no names.

The Farthing Wood Fox spoke. He was unaccustomed to finding himself put in the shade by Badger and he admired his resolution. 'Well, old friend,' he said, 'this isn't the first time we've faced danger. Where do we begin?'

Vixen did not like the tone the talk was taking. She saw the cause as hopeless. 'How can you begin anywhere?' she cried. 'How can you fight an enemy you can't see and know nothing about? None of us, separately or together, is a match for this beast.'

'Are we to wait about then, all of us, to be picked off one by one?' Fox demanded. 'Is that what you want?'

'No, no,' said Vixen. 'But I don't want any more deaths either.'

'Deaths are inevitable,' Fox declared. 'There will continue to be killings until this threat is eradicated.'

'Oh, you've changed,' she told him. 'You said yourself, before, we shouldn't meddle . . . .'

'Yes, I've changed,' Fox admitted coldly. 'That pathetic sight at the foot of the tree changed me.'

Vixen knew her mate. His mind was made up. Now, she feared, there would be no end to their troubles. She clung to one faint hope. Human intelligence. Somehow the Warden would find the Big Cat before they did.

The animals left the copse. Fox was already formulating ideas for a campaign. He would need all the help and support he could muster. – not just from the old community of Farthing Wood, but all their dependants;

all the birds he could find willing to scour the Reserve by day and night; the other larger mammals of the Park – every creature who could play a part. Before anything else they *had* to locate the Cat and note its movements; otherwise there might be a massacre. How he wished he could count on the strength of the white deer herd. The stags, with their antlers grown, would be formidable contestants. But they were out of the reckoning now, bottled up in one corner in a fruitless attempt by Man to frustrate the Beast's activities.

They reached their home territory. 'Put the word about,' he told the other foxes. 'All the animals in the park must be united in this. I want to have any slightest clue reported. Whistler and Owl must speak to the birds. We ourselves must assemble in the Hollow tomorrow at dusk – every one of us. That includes the vixens. Every animal will be needed. We *must* involve everyone from the largest to the smallest. We all know the risks. But risks are preferable to subjection. And that's what we're experiencing.'

Fox was his old self. Like Badger, he seemed suddenly to have thrown off the seasons. He was a leader again. The younger foxes marvelled and ran off unquestioningly to do his bidding. Fox waited for Tawny Owl to put in an appearance and, when he did, told him what he wanted. Owl recognized the urgency in his voice and the note of command. He respected Fox above all others and bowed to his authority. He noticed Badger watching and regretted that they were at loggerheads.

'Oh – um – Badger,' he hooted, 'you know, I never meant to – um – give the impression – er – well, that you – '

'It's all right, Owl,' Badger called up to him. 'Think nothing of it. We're all apt to say things at times.'

'Thank you, Badger,' said Tawny Owl in an unusually humble manner. 'Are we still friends?'

'Oh, Owl,' said Badger. 'Have we ever been anything else?'

Tawny Owl gave a hoot of pleasure and flew away.

At dusk on the following day the Farthing Wood animals gathered with their kindred. Whisper, Husky's mother, had been told of his death and was near the front of the gathering. The other vixens, among them Charmer and Russet, Friendly's mate, were there too. Fox explained how the entire Reserve must be alerted. Together they could drive the stranger from their home. Whisper's loss was alleviated a little by the proposal for action. She wanted to have a leading role in avenging her cub.

Over the next few days and nights, the animals and birds of White Deer Park became aware that all of them were to be part of a concerted move to restore their habitat to safety. Despite day-to-day differences which arose from the natural order of things, they realized that on this issue they were as one. All of them knew of the existence of the stranger and feared it. They had needed something to be done and had only lacked a leader. Now in Fox they had been given one: a co-ordinator for their scheme. They were glad – and relieved – to be doing something positive. So all over the Reserve the animals and birds kept watch at all times for a sign of the Cat. They waited for it to make a move, some by day and some in the darkness.

Each night the Warden or another man patrolled near the deer pen, unwitting allies of the animal community. For a while there was nothing to report. There were no more killings. This lapse was unexpected. Had the Beast gone away of its own choice? Or was it using its cunning again to lull them into a false sense of security?

The deer still at loose in the Park were aware of their vulnerability and kept constantly on the move, never staying in one area for long, and ranging through the whole of the Reserve. One of them was found near the pen one night and persuaded, with the use of a stick, to join its fellows. Then the gate was securely fastened again behind it.

The deer herd did not relish their confinement. They had no escape route if their attacker should decide to put in an appearance by day. They suspected that the Cat could vault the enclosure and create havoc amongst them if it should choose. They felt unsafe and had no faith in the humans' ability to protect them. They would have preferred to take their chance and roam free when they at least had the use of their legs to run from danger. However, it was soon proved that *they* were not to be the target, but the one deer still at large.

Somehow the Cat had eluded every effort to locate it. Of course there was nothing to stop it going in and out of the Park at will, and none of the animals was quite sure just what its movements were. It never allowed even a hint to come their way. Then at last the solitary hind was stalked and pulled down as she drank by the stream in the evening. The Beast was hungry and ate a hearty meal, leaving part of the deer well hidden amongst a mass of waterside vegetation for its return later. The kill was not witnessed, but the carcass was discovered by a moorhen paddling about amongst the reeds. Whistler was soon made aware of it and gradually the Park heard that the Beast was back in action. They tried again – keeping eyes peeled, ears open for a clue.

Meanwhile the Warden had come to the realization that the ruse of penning the deer was not going to work. The hunter was too clever to come near and there was no benefit to the deer themselves, who were becoming fretful and difficult to feed. So the barricades came down and the nightly vigils were ended. The deer ran free again and exulted in the feeling. The Warden was reduced to tramping over the Reserve again in daylight hours. He was becoming convinced that the threat was over. Fox and his associates knew better.

'It's beaten us again,' he complained to Vixen. 'How does it manage it?'

'It's a superior creature,' she answered. 'Superior in cunning, superior in hunting, superior in every way. Husky's name for the Beast was "Stealth", and stealth is the essence of the animal. It has a sort of stealth that we cannot begin to understand.'

'And with all of us – every animal around – out looking for it! The humans are beaten too. Where *does* it go?'

With the deer herd available again as an unlimited food source, the Cat had no need to return to the place of its last kill. So the motley collection of birds and animals who had that corner under special scrutiny had no reward for their pains. However, at last a sort of clue did emerge from an unexpected source.

Adder had not encountered the surprising she-viper again. After their first meeting he had not felt that he had given a very good account of himself and he wished he could put that right. He felt she had somehow got the better of him and he could not feel comfortable about it. As time went on he did not think a lot about her but when he did she still intrigued him.

The weather was now quite warm. All the trees were in leaf; there was new greenery everywhere. Adder had his favourite spots for basking and one of these was a piece of sloping ground, not a great distance from the stream. It was well screened by fronds of bracken. The bed of last year's brown dead fern fronds underneath him made the ground warm and, among the new fast-growing green shoots, Adder delighted to indulge himself, particularly after eating. He had thought this place was his and his entirely. But one day, after swallowing a vole and feeling very sleepy, he had slid into the spot, only to find another occupant. This did not please him and he said grumpily, 'How long have you been coming here?' He was talking to the she-viper.

She stared at him in the snake's usual unblinking way. But her tongue tested Adder for smell. 'Oh – the scarred one,' was her response. 'But no,' she added. 'Am I mistaken? Or have the wounds healed?'

'Of course they've healed; they were only scratches,' Adder hissed. 'And you haven't answered my question.'

'Coming here? Not very long. I found this spot by chance.'

'Did you though? Well, I might tell you that I've been sunning myself here without interference from another for as long as – '

'I'm not going to interfere with your habits,' she interrupted. 'There's plenty of room for both of us.'

'I like solitude,' Adder asserted. (As soon as he had said it he wondered why he had.) 'And I have a prior claim.'

'You make yourself understood,' the female replied drily. 'I take the hint. There's plenty of room in the Park.' She uncoiled herself and began to slide away. Before she disappeared she said, 'You may like to know, Solitude-lover, that this isn't necessarily the safest of places for you.'

Adder checked her departure. 'How do you mean?' he lisped.

'I mean that, in view of your previous tussle, you possibly wouldn't want to risk another one.'

'Are you referring to the Cat?'

'Indeed I am,' she answered. 'I know for a fact that it

sometimes uses a large hole in the bank by the water's edge for concealment. The hole is well covered and not many know about it. Who can say if the creature is there now?'

'How do you know all this?' Adder asked, thinking of the way all the inhabitants of the park had been baffled by the stranger's secrecy.

'Quite by accident,' the female snake informed him. 'It can only be seen from the stream and I happened to be following a frog.'

'But why haven't you told anyone?' Adder demanded. 'I assume you've been involved in the general alert?'

'But I have told someone now, haven't I?' she answered disarmingly. 'Because I thought you needed to know.'

Her final remark had scarcely registered its message before she was gone. Adder was left to brood in his solitude, unsure whether he was glad or sorry she had left. He felt strangely restless. He had never experienced uncertainty about himself before.

—11—

United

Adder did no sunbathing that day. He pulled himself together and set off for the stream, but with the she-viper's caution very much in his mind. He wanted to investigate the lair in the bank. Once in the water, Adder felt he was safe. He swam in one direction, close to the edge of the stream, looking for places where the vegetation was thickest. He saw no hole large enough for the Cat to get into so, despite his feeling of chill, he swam across to the other bank and reversed his direction. He was becoming colder and colder and his movements slower and slower. He knew he would soon have to abandon the stream and search for warmth. Then he saw it – a dark opening in the bank almost obscured by reeds and rushes. He could see at once that its cavernous depths would easily accommodate a whole group of animals. Adder swam on by. He was not such a fool as to approach any closer. The darkness of the hole would comfortably hide whatever creature might be inside it.

When he was far enough away from the lair, the snake slid from the stream and up the bank. He was quite torpid from the cold, and allowed himself to revive in the sun's warmth, only a metre or so from the water. When he was ready, he rippled away at his swiftest pace to carry the news of his sighting. He was hoping to find Whistler the heron before anyone else. The bird could act as his messenger.

He found him without difficulty, and quickly explained about the hole in the bank and of its importance. He said nothing of the she-viper, but only that 'another animal' had given him the clue. It seemed that Whistler had no idea that the hole was there.

'I look downwards at the water, you see,' he told Adder, 'so I'd be looking the wrong way.'

'Yes,' said the snake. 'The hole faces the stream so, unless you could swim, you wouldn't discover it.'

'Well,' said Whistler, 'at last we've got something to get to work on. I'll tell Fox.'

Adder composed himself to wait, while the tall bird spread his wings. Fox received the information with grim satisfaction.

'Good,' he said. 'Now we'll gather as many together as we can and we'll have the resources to beard our friend in his own den.'

Once again Vixen was wary. 'I wish we could leave this to the humans,' she said. 'The Cat is sure to kill another deer sooner or later, and then they'll be combing the Park for it.'

'We can't trust to that,' Fox answered. 'It would almost certainly elude them again. Anyway, we know what they don't know. We've found its hidey-hole.'

'From what Adder told me, this lair seems to be used only periodically,' Whistler said.

'That's enough,' said Fox easily. 'We're bound to catch him at home some time.' Then he turned to Vixen again and said softly to her, with all his old affection, 'You've been a wonderful mate to me – no fox could have asked for a better one. I've always listened to your advice. But we've always looked after our own and our age doesn't alter our obligations. Husky's death makes it necessary for us to take some action now, when before we might have stood aloof. I have been thinking of Bold. Remember how he wore out his own life to ensure that Husky and his other offspring should be born here – in what he believed was a haven. I feel we owe his memory something.'

Vixen's eyes melted as she looked at him and, for a brief moment, she and Fox were lost in their own private world. Whistler stepped awkwardly away on his long thin legs. Neither of the foxes spoke any more but Vixen had given her answer.

It took some time for the animals to gather, for word of the discovery had to be taken around from creature to creature. By the evening, however, there was a large assemblage outside Fox's earth, while new arrivals swelled the numbers all the time. There were creatures of all sizes – foxes, badgers, stoats, hares, rabbits, squirrels, hedgehogs, weasels, even mice and frogs. In the nearby trees there were owls, rooks, magpies, crows, thrushes, jays, blackbirds, starlings and tree sparrows. The Farthing Wood animals and their kin kept in a group together. All of them had come, including the smallest – Toad and Mossy. Whilst none of these assembled

animals would have had the temerity to act of their own
accord, they felt safe in the heart of the gathering, and
even appeared to be enjoying themselves. Only the deer
herd had stayed apart. The deer were convinced that they
were the true quarry of the hunter, and therefore served
their own purpose best by staying together and trying to
protect each other.

During the night there were more arrivals. Fox was
content to wait until dawn. He knew the Beast was active
principally by night. So the most likely time to catch it
unawares was by day when it would probably be resting.
In the darkness many of the animals slept. At first light,
Fox was ready to move. With Vixen alongside, and with
all their relatives behind them, he set off for the stream.
After the foxes came Badger, Weasel and Leveret. The
rest of the creatures followed them, the largest at the
forefront. Overhead the birds flapped, with Whistler at
their head.

Adder's first realization that something was happening
was the sight of the heron accompanied by Tawny Owl,
with birds of all sizes strung out in their rear.

'It's begun,' was Whistler's announcement to the
snake. 'You never saw such a collection.'

Adder made no comment. He was waiting for Fox.
When he saw him approaching he slid forward. It was
still early morning.

'You've chosen a good time,' the snake remarked. 'A
short while ago I saw the Cat slaking its thirst down-
stream.'

'How far?' Fox asked at once.

'Oh, not far. About as far as the lair lies from here.'

'Then the game is on,' Fox murmured.

The animals moved on at their varying paces. The
most timid of them experienced a feeling of security in

the company of fiercer creatures that was quite unlike the normal pattern of their existence. For they all knew that there was but one aim in all their minds.

Adder guided the leaders as far as he dared. He indicated the mass of vegetation that clothed the entrance hole. It was indeed perfectly hidden from observation. Fox went down the bank and stepped gingerly into the water. Keeping near the shore he paddled out just far enough to see the lair for himself. Nothing could be detected inside. No sound issued from the den. He returned to the bank.

'Well, we must assume our friend is there,' he said. 'We have no proof.'

Many of the animals began to question him about his tactics. Would he go in? Would he wait for the Beast to come out? What were *they* to do in the meantime?

'There's nothing to do at present,' Fox told them. 'We have to be sure.' He looked thoughtful. What was needed was for one of the smallest creatures, and one who could swim well, to get as close as was necessary without being noticed. But how could he ask for a volunteer? As it turned out, he did not have to. Toad had come forward himself.

'I'll soon find out if he's in there,' he offered boldly.

'Are you sure, Toad?' Fox asked his friend dubiously. 'You see, it would mean going some way into the hole itself to be certain. I don't want to send you to – '

'Don't be concerned,' Toad interrupted. He had not bargained for doing any more than having a little swim, but he thought it would look cowardly now to withdraw. 'Is the Beast,' he continued, 'going to take any notice of a tiny inedible mouthful such as me?' He tried to sound humorous.

'Perhaps you're right,' Fox answered. 'But I'm still not very happy about it. Please, Toad, do use the utmost care!'

'Of course I will,' said Toad as he moved to the edge of the bank. Then, with a little kick from his hind legs, he jumped into the water. His small body hardly disturbed the surface. He swam in short spurts to the lair entrance and pulled himself out on to the muddy strand. Then, a few centimetres at a time, he crawled into the darkness.

Toad was probably the most suited of all the animals for the job. He was small and therefore light-footed, unexcitable, and naturally unhurried and quiet in his movements. Once he had left the stream he was hidden from view, and all the animals waited with bated breath in an unaccustomed stillness. Fox, above all, longed for Toad to reappear.

Time crept by. There was no sign of Toad. Fox began to fear the worst. Then, as if he had been engaged on nothing more serious than a pleasurable splash around, he was seen slowly swimming upstream, against the current, to where the others were assembled.

'Took rather longer – than I thought,' said Toad, arriving a bit short of breath. 'I had to – go in a long way. It's very dark; not much light gets in to see by. I could hear breathing – deep and steady, typical of a mammal when it's asleep. That gave me the confidence to go closer. The breathing got louder so I knew I was getting near. Then I saw a shape, curled up. I could make no more of it – too dark, you see. I wondered whether to leave then. But I thought – what's the good of that? I still don't know what's here.'

Toad paused for a rest. He was enjoying being the focus of attention and wanted to make the most of his story. Then he went on.

'I decided the only thing I could do was to go right up to the sleeper. So I did and I hopped all round, and it took me quite a while just to do that. I can tell you, the thing is enormous! It has silky fur, like a cat's – some of the hairs brushed me as I made my inspection. By then I was sure enough. No other creature of its size lives in *this* Park, except for the deer, and I know it wasn't one of them. So I left – slowly and cautiously. The breathing sounded the same. I heard nothing else. So I don't think I could have woken it. Now I don't know what you plan to do, Fox, but we should do something soon. The animal is there. We can seal off its exit and – we have it at bay!'

Toad's courageous deed was obscured by the urgency of taking action together. But it was not quite so simple, as Fox told him.

'We can't all stand or swim around in the water, Toad, waiting for it to come out. That's one escape route we can't deny it.'

'What about the strand?' Toad asked.

'How big is it?'

'Big enough for a few of the largest animals such as yourself to station yourselves there.'

'That's no use, then,' Fox commented. 'A few would just be tossed aside.'

'What shall we do then?'

'We must find out if there's another entrance to this lair. I think it unlikely the Cat would always get in from the water.'

Fox went off along the bank. He wanted to try and get in under the vegetation to see if there was an opening on the land side. The animals watched him go. They were keyed up, and some of the more highly-strung amongst them were no longer able to keep still. Rabbits and various groups of mice began to jump about nervously, wishing they had not come. It was quite apparent that the stranger would only have to show itself for them to turn tail and bolt.

Fox had set himself the most difficult of tasks. He did not want to rouse the sleeper. Yet it was quite impossible for him to avoid making a noise as he pushed himself into the clumps of growth. He thrust about with his muzzle, pausing tensely after each rustle and swish. Finally he managed to nose his way into the heart of the greenery. If there *was* another entrance he knew he might suddenly come face to face with the Beast, for every slight noise he made was magnified by his own fear. But he found nothing, though he made as thorough a search as he could.

As Fox was withdrawing from this screen he heard a noise break out; a noise of many voices. Animal and bird cries swelled in pitch and he knew something was astir. Above it all he could hear Vixen calling him and he hastily pulled himself clear. He imagined all sorts of horrors, but what he actually saw was so unexpected that it brought him to a halt. The collection of animals had pulled back, even the foxes. It seemed their confidence en masse had been a short-lived thing. Some of the rabbits had begun to run away, and were now paused at some distance, trying to gauge the situation. The smallest creatures – the mice and frogs – had already disappeared. And there, calmly seated by the waterside, was the Cat, watching them all with an expression of total disinterest. As Fox went by, the creature stretched each of its limbs luxuriously and then began to wash itself. It paid them less attention then if they had been a swarm of flies.

Fox joined Vixen at the head of the throng. He looked back at the stranger. It was a magnificent animal. Its body was clothed in glossy golden brown fur with darker blotches. It had long legs, a small compact head with rounded ears, and a long thick banded tail with a blunt end. It was easy to detect the power and grace of the creature even as it went through its cleaning performance. The muscles of the neck and shoulders rippled beneath its skin as it used its paws, feline fashion, to wipe its face; then it licked its coat, patch by patch, with loose, easy motions of the head. The animal's confidence in its own supremacy amounted to arrogance as it turned a disdainful glance on its audience. The motley collection of onlookers was, quite simply, overwhelmed. They had never seen such a beast before. They were overwhelmed by its size, by its majestic ease, and by a consciousness that it could scatter the whole pack of them if it should choose to do so. But they did not disperse. They were held by a fascination for the creature's beauty. To them it was perfection – a being from a strange world they did not know. They were lost in their admiration for it.

None of these lesser creatures could break the spell. That was left to the great Cat itself. When it was satisfied its coat was clean, it bent to take a few laps from the stream. Then, with a final glance in their direction that seemed to imply a sort of challenge, the Cat leapt into the water, dashing spray everywhere. In a few moments it had reached the opposite bank and, with a series of effortless bounds, it was away and lost from sight before the animals could draw breath.

But the spell was broken and all of the onlookers began to cry out to each other. Only then did they remember their purpose.

Whisper said to Fox, 'The Beast is huge – I think as big as a great mastiff dog that befriended Bold and myself. But this Cat is no friend. It's an enemy and an enemy we are powerless to stop.'

—12—
Thralldom

It was not long before the smaller and weaker animals disbanded. They did not even wait for their leader, Fox, to give them new directions. They had seen all they wanted to see. As far as they could tell, Fox was helpless, and they themselves were keen to get out of the unnaturally vulnerable position in which they were situated. Predators were on all sides.

The larger animals and the hunters among the group began to complain that they had come to do something and now the opportunity had been missed. They spoke from the safe knowledge that the Cat was no longer near.

The birds flew away. Their limited interest in the venture had soon been dissipated. Only Tawny Owl had the presence of mind to follow the Cat as far as he could.

Fox was silent. He knew his plan was a failure and he thought that probably it had been doomed from the outset. But he had felt a need to be doing *something* and so the expedition had been mounted. Now the Park's inhabitants would no longer believe he had any right to expect them to follow him. He had shown that he was as inadequate in dealing with the Cat as any of them.

Vixen watched him. She could guess much of what was in his heart. 'At least you tried,' she murmured to him.

'Tried!' he growled. 'The Beast showed its contempt for all of us. The entire Reserve is in thralldom.'

She tried to comfort him. 'We mustn't forget the skilfulness of Man,' she reminded him. 'There's always a chance the Warden will catch up with it.'

'Perhaps,' Fox said morosely. 'Anyway, that's our only hope now.'

The larger animals were gradually drifting away. Most of them were relieved that they had not actually had to prove themselves in a confrontation. As it was, they were not unduly pessimistic about the situation. They felt that, now the deer herd was in the open again, the rest of them would only be secondary targets. In the end only the Farthing Wood contingent remained.

'Did you find another entrance to the lair?' Toad asked Fox lamely.

'No. But there could be other bolt-holes all over the park, and what difference would it make?' Fox sounded bitter.

'We – we seemed to be hypnotized,' stammered Mossy. He was so purblind that he had not seen the Cat himself, but he understood the reaction.

'Exactly,' Badger corroborated. 'I found myself marvelling at the creature. I've lived a long time and seen all sorts of things, but never anything quite like that.'

The vixens were eager to get back to their dens and their cubs. It was only Fox the elder's call for solidarity that had induced them to leave them. So the numbers of animals dwindled bit by bit until only a handful were left, staring disconsolately across the water to where the Cat had vanished from sight.

'We don't seem to be achieving much by staying here,' Adder drawled, 'so I think I'll just slip away.'

None of the others attempted to stop him. Mossy was heartily glad to see the back of the snake. He was not sure that Adder was party to the conspiracy about 'Mole'. Toad alone called a farewell.

'I don't expect Tawny Owl will have achieved much either,' Weasel remarked. But his observation was not quite accurate.

There was a stretch of open land on the far side of the stream and Tawny Owl was able to keep the Cat in view quite well, though he could not match its pace. It moved very swiftly, with a bounding movement of its long legs. Owl realized it was heading directly for the Park's boundary but, surprisingly, on the side where it bordered a lane leading to human habitations. Eventually the Cat was lost among the first belt of trees. Tawny Owl flew on faithfully in its wake.

A ditch ran along the edge of the Park, just beyond the perimeter fence. Hazel bushes and young trees hung over it from the Park side. At one point under the fence animals had dug the soil away and there was a gap. The Cat knew about this, and it knew about the ditch. It had crossed a large chunk of the Reserve in broad daylight and now arrived at the boundary. It flattened its back and scrambled under the fence, then jumped down into the ditch. This channel was for drainage but it had not been cleared since the previous summer. Leaves and twigs had accumulated in it from the overhanging boughs, so much of it was reasonably dry. The Cat squatted in the bottom. Sunlight pierced the greenery irregularly, dappling the ground all about. The Cat's markings blended in perfectly with its surroundings. From the road it was hidden. No human stroller passing by would have noticed, nor suspected, the existence of a large beast skulking in the ditch. The Cat made sure its head was well out of sight. It had discovered that this spot was a good place to lie in wait for any prey that might wander in the trees. It had caught squirrels and rabbits here and once, in the evening, a deer had stepped almost close enough for a pounce. The Cat could see animals walking along the road too. It was not averse to the possibility of leaping out at an unaccompanied dog.

Tawny Owl reached this edge of the Reserve a minute or so after the Cat had hidden itself. He flew along the Park's perimeter, always searching for a sign of that tawny coat. He actually perched in a branch that overlooked the ditch, but the Cat's splendid camouflage fooled him for a while. Then the slightest of movements caught his roving eye. His head swivelled round and he stared long and hard. All was still. Was he imagining things? No, there it was again. Just a twitch of the back fur. A midge or spider had caused a moment's irritation. Now Owl could make out the long powerful body. What was it doing in the ditch? It certainly could not know it was being observed. Owl decided to move even closer.

He looked round and selected a stout sycamore sapling that grew right on the edge of the drainage channel. He fluttered over to it and alighted. It was not the best of landings. The sapling bent under his weight and he grappled for a firmer hold. The sycamore's leaves shook noticeably. The Cat turned sharply and looked directly at Tawny Owl. Its lips curled back in a soundless snarl, annoyed that it had been detected. This time Owl maintained his position, aware that he was out of reach, and stared back full in the Beast's face. The Cat's eyes did not waver and in the end it was Tawny Owl who looked away. But there was a magnetism about the Cat and it drew the bird's head round again. The Beast opened its mouth.

'I am of interest to you?' Its voice was strange, like a combination of a roar and a howl. It was a very strong voice and quite an alarming one. But although it spoke loudly and slowly, Tawny Owl had difficulty in understanding. This was partly due to his fright at the sound and partly due to the unexpectedness of it. He had never heard an animal cry of this kind before. He slipped a little on the sapling but quickly strengthened his grip.

'I – I'm afraid I didn't – er – follow that,' he fluted nervously.

In a grating sort of growl the Cat said, 'You have pursued me. You have much interest in me.'

Tawny Owl strained his ears and was able to catch the gist of the remarks.

'I'm certainly interested,' he replied. 'You're of interest to all of us.' He was very aware of his role as the mouthpiece of White Deer Park. 'Yes, I followed you. We need to know where you are.'

The Cat appeared to have no difficulty in understanding Owl and it snarled softly as he finished speaking. It did not like the idea of its movements being noted. 'You do not need to know,' it growled threateningly. 'Owls do not tempt my appetite. But you should not mistake. Trees are my playthings. I can stalk you.'

Tawny Owl marked the warning. Yet he realized the creature assumed he was speaking only for his own kind.

'The inhabitants of this Park,' he went on, 'are terrified of you. You arrived from we know not where with great suddenness – a frightening alien. Our humble little world has been rent apart. If we don't know where you are or when you might pounce, how can the animals guard their own safety?'

It was a foolish thing to say to a hunter and Tawny Owl soon perceived this when he saw a wicked feline grin spread slowly across the Cat's face.

'The secret of my success,' it acknowledged with a harsh sort of purr.

'No doubt,' remarked Tawny Owl. He had lost his unease and was beginning to enjoy himself. He anticipated what a celebrity he was to become – the first to hold a conversation with the great hunter! 'Your stealth,' he continued, 'is legendary amongst us. We respect your expertise and the way you even manage to evade the humans. But – '

The Cat interrupted him with a mocking roar. 'Humans!' it scoffed, growling. 'What do they know of my kind; our ancient lineage? They know nothing of our existence. We have roamed the land for longer than they. Never have they captured us, nor even seen enough to know what we are. We are survivors of the Old Animal Lore. How can they hope to comprehend? They think they are Masters. We know *no* Masters.'

Tawny Owl was rather taken aback by this mysterious speech, and did not himself understand much of it. In his familiar limited world Man was always evident. How could humans not know about the Cat and the rest of its kind? He was so puzzled he had to ask about it.

'Do you mean you have never been detected by Man at all?' he blurted out incredulously.

'Never,' roared the Cat with a sort of defiance. 'And so it will be. There are more creatures prowling their domains than *he* knows of.'

Tawny Owl was silent as he tried to digest the facts, which seemed to him almost unbelievable. He had to remind himself that none of the Park's animal population had ever seen such a Beast before. But humans were quite different – they were so clever, so wise, so all-knowing . . . . He tried to bring himself back to the subject in hand, but first he could not resist risking a gibe.

'I shouldn't roar quite so much,' he hooted with mock innocence, 'if you want to retain your history of secrecy.'

The Beast gave him such a withering look of contempt that Tawny Owl at once regretted the remark. He said hastily, 'Will you stay here long? Er – couldn't you perhaps hunt somewhere else?'

'Where I hunt is no concern of an owl,' the Cat rasped.

'But – but – you see,' Tawny Owl stuttered, 'we're all together in this. Er – I mean, we're all afraid and we feel while you remain in the Reserve we – er – we remain at risk. Er – all of us.'

The Cat flattened itself in the ditch bottom as a car approached along the road. When this had passed and its noise entirely disappeared, the animal said gruffly, 'I have told you. I do not prey on owls.' Then it added menacingly, 'Unless they try to meddle . . . .'

Tawny Owl knew it was hopeless. It was no use his endeavouring to explain that he was speaking for the whole community. The Cat would never understand they had a common interest in ridding their home of its threat. Nor could it ever appreciate how Owl and his closest friends were bound by the Farthing Wood Oath to help and act for each other. It belonged to a separate sort of existence altogether.

The Cat half pulled itself out of the ditch. Tawny Owl flew quickly to a higher point.

'You have been lucky,' the Cat told him. 'I made no special effort to avoid you. But I give you my word. You will go now and, after your departure, you will not see me again; not you nor any creature that ranges this area. *Though I shall still be here.* If I am wrong about this you shall have your wish. I shall leave for fresh terrain and never return, if any one of you, beast or bird, sets eyes on me and tells me so. Now go.'

With dumb obedience Tawny Owl took a last look at the strange beast and then flew away. He did not stop until he had arrived at one of his home perches. He pondered over the Cat's peculiar offer. Was it a challenge? Did it intend some amusement for itself, by giving such an exhibition of cunning and stealth to them all that it would exceed even that which had impressed them already? There was no telling what was in its mind. But Tawny Owl believed its word. To his way of thinking, they all had an incentive now. It only needed one sighting, by perhaps the lowliest of the Park's population, for the Cat's sway to end. So let the whole of White deer Park become like a thousand eyes looking inward, in a perpetual examination of every leaf, every twig, every blade of grass. Soon, surely, in this way the state of siege would be lifted.

—13—
The Pledge

Tawny Owl hastened to the side of the stream. When he had left it earlier, most of the population of the Reserve had been gathered there. Now it was deserted. Every bird, every beast, every reptile and amphibian had disappeared, just as if the assemblage had never existed. They had retreated like a defeated army. Tawny Owl saw it as the greatest demonstration of the Cat's power. It had won a complete victory without needing to deliver a blow.

Upstream a lone heron was fishing. Whistler had returned to his normal activities, almost as if he had never been interrupted. As Owl spotted him the tall bird bent his long neck and then stabbed down with his beak into the water. When he raised it again it contained a wriggling silver fish which was swallowed at a gulp. The entire sequence lasted but a few seconds.

'*He's* busy,' said Tawny Owl to himself. He was full of his conversation with the Cat and wanted to tell everyone. But he was also very weary and decided he would only do his tale full justice by relating it when he was more alert. He must get across to his friends the significance of the strange pledge the Cat had made. So he avoided the heron and returned to his roost. Daylight, he reflected, was definitely not the time when owls were at their best.

Dusk passed Tawny Owl by. The evening wore on and still he slept. So the warning that might have been carried sooner to the deer herd to be extra vigilant was too late to save another fawn. While Tawny Owl slumbered on, the Cat had ample time to select its victim, trail it and strike, first at the mother, then at her baby. Neither had an inkling that the predator was around. The hind was left where it had been killed. The young and tender fawn was carried off, limp and lifeless. The Cat was hidden again long before the deaths were discovered. But not in the ditch. That was abandoned. The owl would be the only creature to see the Beast there.

During the night Tawny Owl awoke. He rustled his wings sleepily without at first remembering any more than that the was in his own comfortable roost in the hollow tree. Then he remembered he was hungry. He was surprised to find he had left a couple of mice uneaten. He soon remedied that.

Whilst he was eating he thought he heard a voice calling him from somewhere in the tree. Owl was still dozy and could not at first make out where it was coming from. Then he saw Squirrel skipping down towards him from a high branch.

'We've all been wondering if you found out anything,' said the quicksilver creature, flicking his bushy tail restlessly.

Now Tawny Owl recalled his message and tried to hoot through the middle of a mouthful, nearly choking himself in the process. He swallowed elaborately.

'Yes, yes,' he spluttered. 'Most urgent. Glad you came, Squirrel. I've *spoken* to the Cat. It made a kind of bargain.'

Squirrel was showing his amazement by flicking his tail harder than ever. He sat on his hind legs one moment and then ran up a branch and back again the next moment, unable to keep still. 'The Beast *spoke*?' he chattered.

'More of a roar, really. A horrible sound,' Tawny Owl told him. 'But come with me, Squirrel. I must tell Fox and the rest.' He flew noiselessly away and Squirrel followed him, racing and leaping through the tree-tops.

It was some time before Tawny Owl managed to bring together Fox, Vixen, Weasel and Badger. He recounted his story with the exaggerations and embellishments that, by now, were expected of him. But his message was clear.

'We have a real chance this time,' he asserted. 'The whole Park was on watch before. But we must try harder this time. Our lives depend on it.'

'I'll talk to the Great Stag,' said Fox at once. 'The herd must be involved this time. They have to be especially wakeful. If the Beast wants a sort of contest of skills we'll give it one. Our eyes against his stealth.'

'That's what it will mean,' Tawny Owl averred.

'You did well to follow him,' Weasel congratulated the bird unexpectedly. 'Toad got close, but you alone have conversed with the Cat.'

Tawny Owl swelled visibly with pride. However there was no time for self-congratulation.

'We have a cause again,' Vixen remarked. 'Our future safety depends on us now – not just on our little band, but on every other one of the Park's inhabitants too. Even the smallest newt or fledgling has a stake in this, if it only needs one sighting for our home to return to its natural state.'

'Proof of a sighting,' Tawny Owl corrected her. 'And I'm afraid, as far as I understand, newts are dumb.'

'All right, Owl, I extended the list too far. But you told us – any creature, big or small, would serve the same purpose.'

'As far as I'm concerned,' said Fox, 'if I thought I could bring about our salvation I'd stay awake day and night till I found the brute.'

'And I too,' Badger wheezed. 'It would be one last useful achievement before I – '

'Now, Badger,' Weasel cut in. 'Don't start talking in that vein again. There's no question of it being a last anything, we hope. Think of Mo – er – Mole.'

'Oh yes. Poor Mole. How empty my tunnels would seem for him if I weren't around.'

'Well, then,' said Fox, 'shall we begin? We have to pass the word again. If we thought we searched and watched hard before, now we have a real test before us. I shall go straight to the deer herd.' He left and the group hurriedly broke up.

On his way across the Reserve towards the open area where the bulk of the white deer herd was usually found,

Fox fell in with Friendly. The younger animal confessed to his father that he had feelings of guilt about Husky's death.

'You weren't entirely to blame,' Fox told him. 'It was a rash adventure, but the reasons for which it was undertaken are commendable.'

'I feel I led him on – and the other youngsters,' Friendly went on. 'I shouldn't have pressed them into it.'

'I think none of us have really understood what we are up against,' Fox remarked generously. 'Now I think we're closer to it, after what we all saw by the stream. What were my empty words worth, about protecting and avenging our own? Dreams, Friendly, no more. We're out of our depth. I've felt myself to be weak and helpless as never before.'

Friendly looked at his father – the greying coat, the stiffer gait, the duller eye. Age was the great enemy, he thought. But Fox knew what was in his mind and denied it.

'Were I your age again,' he said, 'it would make no difference. I'd have no challenge to make to monsters.'

'Let's be thankful, then,' said Friendly, 'that we have some skills.'

'Yes,' conceded his father. 'At least we have our eyes.'

They went on together, feeling that they had helped to raise each other's spirits.

The Great White Stag saw them approaching, shoulder to shoulder, through the swift-growing grasses. He had the news of the killings ready for them.

'I am indeed sorry,' Fox responded afterwards. 'You have lost quite a few of this season's young?'

'Too many,' the Stag boomed in his deep voice. 'Fox, we appeal to you. You have been our friend since you came to our home. We deer have lived here, mostly at peace, for generations. But we cannot sustain these losses indefinitely. How do we fight back?'

'By the summer your antlers will have grown again,' Fox said. 'They are potent weapons. But it may not be necessary to wait for that. There is another weapon we all possess, Man and ourselves. Vision. And the hunter himself has told us how we can use it.' He went on to explain the Beast's pledge. 'Watchfulness,' he finished, 'from dawn to dusk and through the night. That's the only hope for any of us.'

'We have watched,' replied the leader of the herd. 'And when we were enclosed, the men watched for us. But still it was of no use.'

'We *must* have a chance,' Fox declared, 'and we must believe that we have it. The Cat is not invisible. We have to remember that.'

'We shall try,' the Stag said unhappily. 'What else can we do?' He began to walk away in his sedate manner. Then he turned back. 'Last time it killed my favourite hind,' he bemoaned. 'She had borne many young.' He looked away and murmured, 'It has such contempt for us all.'

His words were uncannily accurate. Even as they spoke, the Cat returned to drag away the hind's carcass. It meant to ensure that its larder was well stocked.

So word travelled round the Park again. Tawny Owl and Whistler spread it amongst the birds who were the best carriers of messages, and the beasts played their part too. Soon all were aware that they now had a real hope of banishing the threat from their lives by their own efforts.

Meanwhile the Warden was taking stock too. The morning after the kill he went to take count of the deer herd as he did every morning. He was paricularly concerned about the survival of the young, and he quickly noticed another was missing. He knew the hinds too; each one that had given birth that season. So he realized the mother had been taken as well.

The next day Vixen's words were borne out. A party of men began a systematic search of White Deer Park. Some were on horseback, some on foot. Many were armed. Others had brought apparatus for capturing the Beast. The search lasted throughout the day. The whole of the Reserve was combed. No trace of the hunter was found.

The other animals in the Park kept themselves out of sight, too, whilst the men roamed around. The more intelligent ones guessed what was going on, and hoped fervently that the Cat would be discovered and removed by human hand. But they heard no report of guns and the birds noted that the men went away empty-handed. Tawny Owl recalled the Cat's words and was not surprised. However, the men had not finished. They were about to use new tactics.

The day after the search they returned. Under the leadership of the Warden traps were laid at various points throughout the Reserve and baited with fresh raw meat. The Warden had taken the utmost care to ensure that these traps could only be sprung by a large and very powerful animal – the huge chunks of meat were set in such a way that no fox or smaller carnivore would have the strength to dislodge them. The men retired again and then the waiting began. The Warden reckoned that the hunter probably had sufficient food for itself for quite some time.

The days went by. The Cat went nowhere near any of the traps. Each day the Warden went to inspect them, sometimes by himself, and sometimes with a helper. The meat was renewed at intervals. At night many of the smaller animals had investigated these unusual food sources. The foxes had been suspicious and only sniffed at them. Some of the smaller meat-eaters had tried to pull the lumps away, failed, and then contended themselves with nibbling at them where they were.

After some time both the Warden and his charges began to think that the Beast had decided it had nothing to gain by staying around that part of the world any longer. For not only had the traps been avoided, but no further deer had been taken. Indeed no smaller prey had been attacked either.

'I'm beginning to wonder about this "pledge" of the Cat's,' Weasel commented one day to Fox. 'How do we know it isn't a final trick on us – you know, to put us all on our guard for nothing, while he himself is as far away as – as – '

'Farthing Wood?' suggested Fox wryly.

'Precisely!'

'Yes, I've thought of that too,' Fox admitted. 'But don't tell Owl. He'll think you're doubting his word.'

'I know, I know,' said Weasel. 'But what would that matter by comparison with the benefit to us all? To be sure that White Deer Park is ours again!'

' "To be sure",' Fox echoed. 'That's the crux of it, Weasel. How can we ever be sure again?'

Weasel looked crestfallen. 'I hadn't thought of it like that,' he muttered. 'I suppose it would be preferable for one of us to see the great hunter again.'

But nobody did. And, understandably, the animals' wariness began to slacken and their watchfulness to be relaxed. They no longer believed they were watching for any purpose. As for the Warden, he did not bother to replace the bait in his traps any more. Replenishing the meat was costly and it was all to no avail. Besides which, he had still a lingering doubt about the risks involved – perhaps one of the traps might catch an animal that actually had a perfect right to be in the Reserve. After a few more days and much cogitation, the Warden at last decided to remove the traps altogether. So the guard was down of animal and human alike. And that was exactly what the Cat had been waiting for.

It had eaten well at the beginning. The fawn and its mother provided plenty of meat. Eventually every scrap of the carcasses was gone, leaving only skeletons. The Cat even crunched some of the bones. It had managed to lap at the dew and take rainwater from the plentiful showers, so that thirst had been no problem for it. As time passed, hunger returned, but it knew it would not have long to wait, and it was content. It had found itself an underground home which served its need for secrecy and stealth perfectly. It waited with patience for its great cunning to work its effect.

Then one dusk the Beast knew that the time was right. It waited for the true darkness that came late at that period of the year. Then it crept forth from its den and embarked on a small orgy of slaughter, prompted by its long fast. It killed rabbits and hares and any small creatures it could find on the ground. Voles and frogs were snapped up at a gulp. Then it climbed into the trees and caught birds on their nests and squirrels in their dreys. Those creatures that were not eaten at once were carried back to the den for future use. But it did not approach the deer herd. It was too clever for that.

Leveret missed being taken by a whisker. The instinctive leap that took him to safety exposed his mate and she was taken instead. Leveret ran at full tilt through the grass. His electrifying pace could outdistance almost any creature. He did not stop to see if he was pursued. So he did not see the Cat. He kept right on running until he ran into Badger, nearly bowling him over.

'Leveret!' Badger gasped, badly winded. 'What's the alarm?'

The hare explained at once about the attack. Neither of them could be sure whether it was the Cat at work again, but they both jumped to conclusions.

'And we thought it had gone,' Badger murmured. 'It's been playing with us.'

'Well, it's not playing now,' Leveret said harshly.

Their suspicions were justified. Knowledge soon spread of the killings. There seemed to be a new savagery about these, as if the Cat had a lust to kill for the sake of it, to demonstrate its mastery over the rest of them.

No animal, no bird had seen it. But all of the Park soon knew the stranger was still around. There was only one clue that impressed itself on the more intelligent of the population. The slaughter had been confined to one corner of the Reserve. And that was the corner where the animals from Farthing Wood had established their homes.

'Can it be deliberate?' they asked each other.

'Is it hiding nearby?'

Squirrel was terrified and planned to move his home. Leveret discovered the loss of his mate and no longer cared if the hunter should return. Fox and Vixen racked their brains as to the whereabouts of the Beast. After such killings, how could it just vanish again? Tawny Owl perched in his tree and hoped no one would come near him. He had the awful feeling that in some way he was to blame for this: that the Cat meant to prove something to him. He was to be punished for his previous presumption, not personally perhaps, but through the deaths of his friends.

—14—

Hearts and Minds

The animal friends waited for the next strike with a fear that had become all-consuming. They scarcely dared to go about their necessary activities. The collection of food was now a hurried, furtive business – something to be done as quickly as possible before scurrying back to cower at home. Only the birds, Adder and Toad felt comparatively secure. Adder had not been seen for a while, but the others worried daily about the safety of their companions. Tawny Owl, in particular, was in a state of unending misery. He could not bring himself to talk to anyone. He had started to think that, if he did, that animal would be the next one singled out for the Cat's attention.

Friendly wanted to make one last attempt to go on the offensive. His mate, Russet, was terrified for her growing cubs, who had now reached the stage of wanting to explore farther than around their parent's earth. Other vixens, Charmer and Whisper, were in the same situation. Friendly thought they could not continue to live their lives under threat. He suggested to his father that the only way to break the dreadful monotony was to sniff out the blood trail once more, and follow it to the Cat's hideout.

'There would be no fighting,' he assured his father. 'It would just need one of us to go close enough to *see*.'

'I understand how you feel,' said Fox. 'But it's far too dangerous. Probably the Beast is waiting for just such a foolhardy creature as you to come along. What would another death achieve?'

'There will be deaths anyway,' said Friendly. 'Why skulk here where the hunter can pounce as it chooses? *I'm* willing to take the risk. I ask for no supporters.'

Fox admired his courage, not for the first time. 'Wait a while yet, Friendly,' he pleaded. 'I have a feeling the Cat might make a slip, and it only needs one.'

'What if it decides not to honour this wonderful pledge Owl talks about?' Friendly growled. 'There would be nothing any of us could do about it.'

'Then why do you wish to track it?' Fox asked at once.

Friendly had tripped himself up and knew it. He looked glum. 'All right,' he conceded. 'I'll do as you say. But I hope it won't result in suffering for my cubs.'

Since the gathering by the stream, Adder had had something else on his mind besides the Cat – something very private. It was a she-viper that occupied his mind, a female adder with a bold disposition and a coolness of temperament that matched his own. Whilst he wondered why she was in his thoughts, he constantly asked himself whether he was in hers. There was no doubt that, if Adder had been more familiar with such things, he would have realized that he wanted her company.

Of course, he would never have deliberately sought her out. But it was strange how he found himself, without intention, returning to the places where he had seen her before. She was not in any of them. It was hardly likely she would have been, he told himself. Why should she stay around there? So it must have been coincidence that prompted their next meeting.

Adder had caught and eaten two wood mice amongst the grasses. He was no longer hungry now, but his hunting instincts had not subsided and he was still very much alert. He caught the soft rustling of a creature moving through the stems close to the ground. He prepared himself to ambush another mouse. But, as the mouse came into view, with its nose quivering incessantly, another snake shot from hiding and seized it. Adder watched with feigned indifference as the plump little morsel went down another throat. The she-viper, in the ecstatic throes of a series of swallows, had not yet noticed him. However, when the last muscular ripple had passed along her body, she became aware of his presence.

'The solitude-lover,' she remarked, as if to herself. 'I'd better not stay here too long and risk complaint.'

'It's not necessary for you to move just yet,' Adder answered quickly. (He thought this sounded like someone else talking.) 'Er – have you caught many mice?'

'Very many,' she quipped. 'One gets through quite a lot in a season.'

'You know I didn't mean that,' he lisped with a mild sense of irritation. 'Are you always so clever?'

'Only when I have the opportunity,' she told him coolly. Her face was as expressionless as ever. 'Are you still looking for the Cat?' she asked next.

'I? *I'm* not looking,' Adder declared, as if the idea of his putting himself out was quite absurd.

'But I thought the plan was for every creature to keep its eyes open?'

'Oh, my eyes are open,' he responded, 'but I'm not – er – looking . . . .' (How silly that sounded.)

The she-viper refrained from comment but she stared at him. So Adder stared back. At last she said: 'You're looking fatter than when I saw you before.'

'Frogs, insects and mice,' he explained succinctly.

'I though the adder that came here from a distant place wasn't supposed to eat mammals?' she went on.

'I didn't know you knew who I was,' he answered.

'The shortness of your tail gives you away.'

'I see. Well, if you're referring to that ridiculous Oath I was made to swear before I was allowed to travel here with the others, it only forbade *certain* mice and voles from my diet. Those being, of course, the ones from my old home.'

'How do you tell them apart?'

'Oh, they're all dead now. They live lives of extraordinary brevity. Of course I left them alone while they did live. But they've produced so many generations since we arrived here that I can't tell the difference any more.'

'So what do you do?'

'Eat whenever I feel like it,' he declared. 'As far as I'm concerned that Oath doesn't stretch into infinity.'

'Very wise of you,' the she-viper remarked. 'The whole thing is difficult to understand – how you consort with mammals at all.'

Adder was in a quandary. He never liked to admit he

owed obligations to any creature. Yet there still remained a select few for whom, and with whom, he felt bound. Fox and Vixen, Badger, Toad and – yes, he supposed Tawny Owl and Weasel. All of them were bound irrevocably and for ever. But he was not going to tell the she-viper.

'I don't seek them out,' he said truthfully. 'But, you see, there is an old association.' That was as far as he would go.

The she-viper's next words startled him with their implication. 'How would you feel about a new association?'

How was he to take this? Was she suggesting . . . ?

'I'm not entirely sure . . . .' he began guardedly.

'Oh yes, Adder. You're quite sure,' she drawled with a certain amount of ironic humour. 'You're the lover of solitude.'

Now that he was being branded with this description, Adder was not completely happy to own it. There had been moments, he recalled, when he . . . . When he what? he asked himself. He did not know if he could bring himself to admit that he had hoped for company at times. And then again, *whose* company? Oh, he was in a rare old muddle.

'I do like solitude,' he hissed uncertainly. 'But I suppose how much I like it is governed by how much of it I get.' (What did that convey? he wondered. Had he given something away?)

'And that depends on how much of it you seek,' she returned. She was determined to put him on the spot and was relishing every moment.

'Well, yes, that would appear to be the case,' Adder said. (Wherever would all of this end? He was almost beginning to feel uncomfortable.)

'You can call me Sinuous,' she offered.

'Can I? Is that how you're known?'

'It's how I'd like to be known by you.'

Adder wanted to get away. He was not competent to deal with situations of this kind. But he could not put his body into motion.

'It's very warm,' said Sinuous. 'If you've eaten enough it would be a good time to bask.'

The invitation was obvious. Adder felt he was powerless to resist. He made no answer. Sinuous took this as a sign of agreement and began to slither away through the grass stalks. Adder followed her mechanically.

The she-viper led him to a small depression in the ground where the grass had been flattened by a larger animal. It felt dry and hot. Adder wondered fleetingly what creature had been lying there before.

'I like this spot,' commented Sinuous. 'It's well hidden.'

'It seems that another has found it favourable too,' Adder remarked.

'Yes, I saw him once or twice before I started using it,' she answered.

'Saw him? Whom?'

'The Cat.'

'The Cat! Does he still come here?' Adder hissed urgently.

'Oh no. He's disappeared, hasn't he?' Sinuous sounded uninterested. She was coiling herself up.

Adder was irritated. 'You're very secretive,' he told her. 'If we'd known this earlier, it might have saved – '

'It wouldn't have saved anything,' she interrupted. 'I know the terms of the Beast's so-called pledge and, since then, I've naturally kept a look-out here. But, of course, I don't expect to see anything now.'

'I see,' said Adder. 'No, it's not likely to return to any of its old haunts. It must know this whole Reserve better than any of us. Yet I still don't understand how it can remain in the Park and stay concealed.'

'Supposing it is not *in* the Park but under it?' Sinuous suggested nonchalantly. 'Perhaps that's the answer.' She seemed to want to finish with the subject and enjoy her sunbath. But the remark had the very opposite effect on Adder.

'Underground,' he hissed. 'Yesss.' All thought of repose left him. 'That's where it must be.'

Sinuous paid no attention. Adder could only think of those of his old companions who made their homes underground, and who might be able to make use of this theory. Fox and Vixen, Badger and Weasel sprang immediately to mind. It was a pity Mole, that champion tunneller, was no longer with them. But then Adder recalled something about one of Mole's kin who had come into the picture recently. The relationship escaped him.

'My basking will have to be postponed,' he informed Sinuous. 'This idea can't be kept to ourselves.'

'Ah – the old association,' Sinuous murmured. 'Well, you must go to your warm-blooded friends.'

'I must. But – er – well, I shall remember this place,' said Adder. He was unable to make more of a commitment than that. He slid away.

'Only the place?' Sinuous asked him. But Adder's hearing was not good.

He went first of all to Badger.

It was broad daylight and the old animal's snoring seemed to reverberate through his network of tunnels as Adder entered the set. The snake was glad of this, for the pitch darkness engulfed him almost at once, but he was able to guide himself to Badger's sleeping chamber by the sound. Badger was not easily woken. He slept deeply and Adder's lisping voice was not the most resonant.

The snake became more and more aggravated as his efforts to rouse the sleeper continued to fail. He considered whether he should risk a nip at the thickest part of Badger's coat, where his dangerous fangs would be very unlikely to penetrate the skin. Luckily such a gamble did not prove necessary. Badger stirred.

'At last!' Adder hissed. 'I've been here for an eternity.'

Badger quickly roused himself. 'Adder? Whatever are you – '

'No time for that,' the snake answered shortly. 'I need your advice. Listen.' He explained the theory of the she-viper without mentioning her.

'Oh no. That's not likely. I've already rejected the idea,' Badger informed him. 'There's no set or earth around here big enough to take that huge beast.'

'Who said anything about around here?' Adder queried impatiently. 'In the length and breadth of the Reserve there might be many holes it could hide itself in.'

'No,' Badger insisted. 'I would know about it. And if *I* didn't, it would be known by the foxes or the rabbits or the weasels or – or – the moles. Besides which, Adder, we know the Cat *is* in our neck of the woods.'

'Just because it hunted around here doesn't mean it hides around here,' Adder argued. 'Not all the time.'

'Well, Squirrel is convinced of it. He's taken his family and set up home in another quarter.'

'Squirrel is not the most knowledgeable of the community,' Adder drawled. 'I feel it would be worthwhile for all the foxes and animals like yourself, and maybe the rabbits, to be consulted. They may know of a likely den.'

'I'll ask Mole when I see him,' Badger said. 'He's the greatest digger of us all.'

'Don't be absurd, Badger,' Adder rasped. 'Your memory is playing you tricks again.'

'Oh no,' Badger contradicted him. 'You're mistaken. I often talk to him.'

Adder thought it was futile to continue this line of conversation, so he told Badger he was going to pay a visit on Fox and then leave everything to him. The cold and dark of Badger's set made him wish he had not left the warm sunny spot where Sinuous was now lying.

'Wait,' said Badger. 'I'll come with you.'

'No need,' the snake told him. Then he added unkindly, 'You'd better stay here in case Mole decides to make one of his miraculous returns.'

Fox responded in the same way to the underground theory. But he agreed to talk to all his relatives to see if they might know of a large hideout under the Park.

'It's more than possible,' Adder pointed out. 'You didn't know of the existence of the lair by the stream until I told you of it.'

'You're right, Adder,' Fox said. 'But where did *you* learn of it? You never did say definitely. Perhaps from the same source as this latest idea?'

Adder never had any difficulty in retaining his equanimity. His natural expression was one of immobility. His ceaselessly flickering tongue was the only sign of movement from his face.

'The source isn't important,' he replied enigmatically.

Fox knew he would not be permitted to pry any further. So he said, 'Have you spoken to Mossy?'

Adder searched his memory. 'Mossy?' he muttered.

Fox reminded him.

'A descendant of Mole? Well, it's likely that Badger will see him first then. Who knows – perhaps this Mossy will be in the company of his forefather!'

'I'm glad Badger's not around to hear that,' said Fox. 'Poor old creature, he's never been able to accept the loss of Mole. This game he plays is the only way he can come to terms with it.'

'I wish you'd explain, Fox. Badger was rambling on about Mole when I spoke to him just now. I think he must have been still half-asleep.'

'On no, it's quite deliberate. I thought you knew about it. The rest of us take part.' He told Adder about Mossy's role.

'Now I comprehend,' said the snake. 'But I certainly don't approve. I'm surprised at you all, making such fools of yourselves.'

'You sound just like Owl,' Fox remarked. 'Think of Badger. Haven't you any heart?'

'I shouldn't be talking to you now if I hadn't. But perhaps the reptilian variety hasn't the same capacity as a mammal's for spreading warmth.'

'Perhaps.'

'Don't worry, I shan't upset anything of your "game". And now I'll leave you to your subterranean explorations. I'm for a warmer place. Who knows' – and now Adder was talking to himself as much as to Fox – 'perhaps my heart will benefit from it.'

—15—

Mossy's Mission

Fox and Vixen discussed the underground theory with their kindred. Friendly and Russet, Charmer and Ranger, Whisper, Pace and Rusty had no knowledge that was of any use. Ranger volunteered to consult Trip and the other foxes in the Park. Meanwhile Weasel talked to his own kind whilst Leveret spoke to his cousins the rabbits. All of the inquiries drew a blank. Then the other badgers in the Reserve were brought in. All of them were of the opinion that none of the sets they knew about had entrances or tunnels wide enough to admit a creature the size of the Cat.

The Cat itself, since its last hunting spree, was lying low

in more than one sense. But it was about to replenish its stores of food. At the time when its hunger dictated, it emerged from its new lair. The night was dark. There was no moon, and clouds completely obscured the heavens. The Cat was well aware the animals expected another strike in the same neighbourhood. So it avoided that and slunk through the shadows on its noiseless way towards the stream. But not to where the stream ran past its old lair in the bank. Another lower reach of the water was its objective.

The Cat was a good swimmer and it decided now to explore the food potential not only of the banks, but of the water itself. It caught a couple of unsuspecting water-voles, hooked out some small fish, and completely obliterated a family of coots on their midstream nest. But it was not satisfied. It was disappointed in this aquatic hunt, and a few frogs made very little difference to its appetite. As the sky began to lighten, the Cat loped back towards its den, determined to snatch itself something more substantial on the way.

The Reserve seemed deserted. The animals were still spending most of their time out of sight. The Cat stopped dead, thinking of the taste of deer flesh. Its mouth watered. But it was too late now. The first signs of dawn were in the sky. It padded back, angry and frustrated, to its den. The next night it meant to eat deer again. At the entrace to its lair it roared its anger to the cowering inhabitants of the Park. The roar rose in pitch and finished in an unearthly scream that carried far beyond the boundaries of the Reserve. The Warden of White Deer Park woke in his bed, dressed hurriedly, snatched his gun and a torch and ran from the house. He stayed near the deer herd until broad day, but he saw nothing.

That night Mossy had decided to travel one of his tunnels that led into Badger's set. It was a passage that had been often trodden by his father. He began to call to Badger in between snacks of earthworms which he collected as he went along. Badger did not reply, so Mossy settled down for a proper feast. Eating was such an absorbing pastime for a mole that, by the time he dropped into the set, Mossy had no idea it was nearly daybreak.

Badger had returnd from a half-hearted foraging trip and was preparing himself for a snooze. But when Mossy appeared, he was delighted to postpone it.

'Mole! Just the fellow I've been thinking about,' was the greeting. 'Adder came to see me and – you won't guess! – he has the idea that the Cat is living underground like us.'

Mossy gave a cry of alarm but Badger soon reassured him.

'It's all nonsense,' he said. 'How could it do so? There's no hole big enough. I told Adder that, but you know Adder.'

Mossy did not. He had never associated with the snake in a personal way, nor did he want to. He did not like snakes at all and could not understand how Badger had made a friend of one. However, he was about to make a remark on the existence of a very large hole he had heard about, when there was a deafening roar. Both Mossy and Badger froze. Mossy's blood nearly curdled in his veins as the scream rent the outside air. The vibrations of the terrible sound seemed to echo through the maze of passages surrounding them. They turned to each other.

'The Beast!' they whispered together.

'That must be its h-hunting c-call,' Mossy stammered.

'I hope all our friends are safely at home,' said Badger. 'What a horrible cry.'

When Mossy had recovered himself he remembered what he had been going to say. 'The hole,' he said, and then had to stop again. He was still quivering.

'The hole?'

'Yes. My mother – ' Poor Mossy broke off again. He had started to explain that his mother Mirthful had told him of a great hole. Then he recalled that Mirthful could not be his mother, as far as Badger was concerned. Mirthful had been his father's mate. He hesitated. Now what could he say? It was *so* awkward.

'Your mother,' Badger prompted him. 'I've never known you to mention your mother before, Mole.'

'Er – no. What I mean is, the – er – female you called Mirthful – she – er – she told me that there *is* a great chamber underground in the Reserve. She came across it by accident once. She thought it was something the humans must have made.'

Badger drew his breath in sharply. 'Is this true?' he almost snapped at Mossy. All other considerations were forgotten now.

'Yes, quite true. I assure you, Badger.'

'Where? Where is this chamber?'

'I don't know. I've never been there. But – but – it can't be far from here. My – er – that is, Mirthful – she lived around here before she – er – mated.'

'Then we must find it,' said Badger. 'And when we've found it . . . ' he stopped and pondered, then he finished lamely, 'we'll know if the Cat uses it.'

'Oh dear. What if the Cat is there when we find it?' Mossy asked tremulously.

'We only have to *see* it,' Badger growled. 'I'll do the seeing. You only have to find the chamber.'

'But – but – '

'No "buts", Mole. This is our very last chance. You're the greatest tunneller of us all. If anybody can find it, you can. Then you can come back to me, tell me where it's situated and I'll go overland. I'll go by day. The Cat will be asleep perhaps. I make a noise' – Badger was enacting the scene in his mind – 'it wakes up. It sees me. I see the Cat. I tell it so – and the threat is removed. The Cat leaves White Deer Park.' He looked at Mossy triumphantly.

'You make it sound very simple,' said the little animal. 'Are you sure there's no more of a risk than that?'

'Only to me,' said Badger, 'and what does that matter? My days are numbered.'

'Oh, Badger,' Mossy pleaded, 'don't start on that again.'

'Very well. I'll say no more,' he answered. 'But I'm relying on you. You're the one now that the whole population of the Reserve depends on, whether they realize it or not.'

Mossy gulped. He did not know if he was equal to such a tremendous responsibility. 'I – I'll do my best,' he said, not very happily. 'I can't do more than that.'

'Of course you can't,' Badger assured him. 'But I know what "best" means for the most efficient of all tunnel travellers. Off with you now. There's no time to lose.'

Mossy scurried away. How was he to begin this impossible task?

He headed first of all for his own comfortable nest where, he was pretty sure, he had left some immobilized worms uneaten. He was glad to find that indeed this was the case. Whilst he was chewing on these, he tried very hard to think of all that Mirthful had told him about the great chamber. The network of underground passages used by his parents was all around him. Many of them he still used himself. In addition to these were some others that his mother had used before she had become mate to his father. Somewhere the two systems connected, because it had been at that point where his parents had first encountered each other. Mossy knew roughly in what direction this place would be, and so that must be the first stage of his exploration. Afterwards he would have to reconnoitre the old tunnels used by Mirthful, in the hope that one of them would bring him to the chamber he sought. He ate a last worm in a pensive sort of way and set off.

He found the connecting point without trouble and ran along the first passage. This led into another and that one into a further passage and it was remarkable, he thought, how free of debris they had remained in all this time. One passage came to a dead end and there, at the end of it, was the remains of an old nest. The materials – dry grass and leaves – had not yet disintegrated entirely. Mossy paused. A feeling of sweet but distant sadness stole over him. He had stumbled across one of his mother's old resting-places.

But there was no time for sentimentality. Underneath the nest was a bolt-hole. Mossy pulled himself into it and simply followed his nose. And it was his nose that was starting to cause problems. Along the passages the scent of earthworms pervaded the damp, close air. Their little burrows were everywhere and often they dropped unsuspectingly into a mole's tunnel. Mossy was having the utmost difficulty in ignoring the sensations picked up by his nose. Although he had eaten recently, he already felt hungry again. He tried to remember the importance of his mission, but the worms intruded more and more into his awareness and, eventually he was unable to resist any longer. He snapped at one and ate it hurriedly. Then he moved on, collecting one here, one there, and stopping each time to devour it. Without realizing it, his journey of exploration had become a worm hunt. He was so intent on satisfying his voracious appetite that he lost all idea of time, where he was going, and what he was meant to be doing. In the midst of grabbing a particularly plump worm from the earth walls, he suddenly seemed to lose his footing. The loose soil gave way beneath him and he found himself plunging down as if into a void. Then there was a bump as he landed abruptly at the bottom.

Luckily he had fallen on to more earth and he was more shaken by the surprise than the severity of the fall. Mossy pulled himself together. A dim light enabled him to see a little. He soon noticed a patch of daylight, like a round piece of whiteness against the mass of black. He knew it was from there that the feeble light filtered through, and he guessed it was a large entrance hole. Then, with a start, he realized where he was. He was in a sort of cavern. Out there, beyond the patch of daylight, lay the Park. Mossy had found the great chamber!

Now he was very frightened. The passage he had fallen from was high up the cavern wall and there was no way by which he could climb back up to it. The only way out was through the main entrance hole. But how could he get to it and out of it safely when the Cat might arrive at any moment? Then his heart turned over. The Cat might even now be inside the cavern, only a few steps away. He did not know – yet. Mossy held himself very still. His heart hammered wildly at the thought. He tried to test the dank air for animal scents, wrinkling his snout all around. There *was* a smell – a warm, sharp sort of smell, which was almost certainly given off by the animal's body. Mossy began to tremble uncontrollably. He could scarcely prevent his teeth from chattering with fright. How he wished someone else were there – Badger preferably – to suggest what he should do. Then he recalled that *he* had to report to Badger. He had to get out into the Park – somehow – so that he could describe the location of the chamber.

Mossy tried to calm himself. Even if an animal *was* present somewhere near him in that cavern, it might be something smaller and less ferocious than the Cat. So he argued to himself. But it was no use. He *knew*, without actually seeing it, that it was the Cat. Now he had two options. One was to try and creep to the exit without being noticed. He did not know if he had the courage to do that. The other was to wait, still and noiseless, until darkness fell again, and hope that the Beast would itself leave on a hunting trip. What an ordeal that would be. It was a good thing he had eaten well. But supposing he waited – how many more lives, perhaps of those whom he knew, would be lost if the Cat rampaged around again? If he could get out now he could prevent this happening.

There was no sound. Was the Cat sleeping or wakeful? At any rate, his – Mossy's – abrupt entry into the chamber did not seem to have been detected. So if his presence was not suspected already, a small animal like himself could have a fair chance of remaining unseen. Keeping close to the side of the chamber, Mossy moved a few centimetres. Then he froze, waiting for a reaction. There was none. He moved a little farther; then farther still in the direction of the disc of daylight. Oh, it seemed so far away. This cavern was really enormous.

Mossy reached a point along the wall where he got, as it were, behind the shaft of faint light that shone into the murky interior. Now he could see part of the chamber quite well where the light fell. And there he saw four huge tawny legs, belonging to a body the rest of which remained in shadow. It was obvious, from the position of the legs, that the body was lying on its side. Evidently the Cat slept. Mossy was encouraged. But he could not resist pausing to peer for a long time, through his weak eyes, at the impressive sight. He compared the huge paws with his own diminutive ones and this set him scuttling on his way again. The exit was closer now and the daylight seemed to be dimming. He could see foliage beyond – thick encompassing foliage that hid the entrance to the chamber from those abroad in the Park. Mossy moved on, nearer and nearer, still keeping as quiet and slow as he could. When he was about two metres from regaining the Park, he heard a stir behind him. The Cat had woken and was stretching its limbs where it lay. There was a muffled growl and Mossy thought he was discovered. He waited, almost dead with fright. But nothing happened. After a while, he started on again. He was nearly there. A breeze blew from ouside and wafted into the chamber, ruffling the Cat's fur. Some dust must have blown into its nostrils, too. Mossy heard a tremendous sneeze. Then the Cat was up and padding towards him. He tried to hurry but it was no use. The Cat, on its long legs, was there before him.

He was seen. The Cat growled softly. Mossy could think of only one thing to do. 'You're seen!' he cried. 'I see you!'

It might have been that the shrill squeaks of the little mole were more or less inaudible to the Cat, or it might have been that the great beast saw Mossy as a welcome extra morsel after the previous night's bad hunting. Either way it paid no attention to his feeble challenge, except to extend one vast paw to pull him close.

Somehow Mossy managed to circumvent the paw and he scurried out of the chamber and began to dig frantically at the soil outside. He was a lightning fast digger and, with three heaves, his head and front paws and half his body had disappeared to safety. He tore at the earth in fury, pulling his body after him, down, down and down into the familiar territory of darkness that enveloped him like a caress.

The Cat was not to be outdone, however. It saw where the tiny animal had gone and set about digging after him. It ripped up clods of the soft soil, scrabbling with both front paws in an angry fit of exasperaton. Mossy could hear the thunder above him and dug down deeper. But the Cat's paws were gaining.

A witness of the struggle flew desparately to help. The miserable and sleepless Tawny Owl was now brave Mossy's only hope.

Tawny Owl had been perched on a branch, away from his friends, unhappily contemplating the prospect of further deaths in the community. He had tried in vain to doze in the sunlight, although for a time he kept his eyes firmly shut. At last he gave up and when he opened his eyes he saw, at a distance, the Cat emerge from the midst of a thick bush and begin digging determinedly. Owl was too far away to have seen the small body of Mossy but he knew, better than any creature, that it was now time for the Cat to honour its pledge.

He launched himself into the air and flew swiftly to a nearby tree. Then, at the top of his voice, he cried, 'I CAN SEE YOU, CAT!'

The animal stopped its digging momentarily and looked around. When it spied Tawny Owl it snarled angrily. Owl quivered but held on. The respite allowed Mossy to tunnel deeper and get farther away.

Tawny Owl noted the Cat made no move. There was a look of fury on its face at being discovered. Owl said, 'You said I'd never see you again. You were wrong. I think you – er – must yield now.'

'YIELD?' the Cat roared terrifyingly. 'To an owl?'

'You gave your word,' Tawny Owl whispered, barely

able to speak. He guessed the pledge was worthless and that now there was no hope for any of them.

The Cat roared again, making the ground vibrate with the din. Badger had heard the first roar and had run to his set entrance in alarm. He had regretted sending the tiny molĕ on such a dangerous exploration and now he looked around for him in desperation. When the second roar rang out he could stand still no longer. He started to run towards the sound.

By the time he could see the Cat, the animal was digging again and Badger surmised immediately what it was digging for.

'Oh Mole,' he cried to himself in anguish and he increased his pace. Now he noticed Tawny Owl. 'Owl, Owl,' he called breathlessly. 'Do something!'

'It's no use,' the bird wailed. 'We're helpless. The Beast has broken its promise.'

Badger lumbered up, panting but filled with resolution.

'Leave that worthless morsel,' he gasped, putting himself in front of the Cat. 'What good is that mouthful to you? *I'm* more fitted to your appetite. Let me take his place.'

The Cat paused. It turned round and, with a malicious glare, stared at Badger in the fading daylight with undisguised contempt.

'Feeble, powerless weaklings,' it spat at him. 'I could slay *all* of you!'

Badger quailed, despite his determination. Tawny Owl watched in agony on his branch. What *could* he do?

The Cat's eyes blazed with the intensity of living fire. Suddenly a roar, like a distant echo of the Cat's, could be heard far away. The Beast's majestic head snapped round, its ears pricking up erect as sentinels. The sound was repeated on a higher note. In an instant the Cat forgot about Badger, Tawny Owl and the hidden Mossy and, in the failing light, lifted up its head and roared deafeningly. The call was answered, now not so distant. The Cat leapt up gracefully, clearing all the surrounding obstacles with ease, and bounded away through the trees.

Badger and Tawny Owl, the two old friends, looked at each other hesitantly. Was there *another* of the Beasts? As they held their silence, more roars could be heard, the one answering the other. Now more Park animals began to make themselves seen, asking each other what these awful sounds portended.

Badger said quietly to Tawny Owl, 'Let's go back and mix with the others. Mole will make his own way home.'

Now Tawny Owl understood about the digging. He made no comment on Badger's use of the name 'Mole'.

They found Fox and Vixen and Weasel in a cheerful mood that contrasted strangely with their own.

'Why such long faces?' Weasel chided them. 'This is cause for celebration.'

'Celebration?' Badger muttered. 'How can you – ' He broke off. A light seemed to penetrate his thoughts. 'Can it be?' he asked himself. And then he heard it. The cries of hundreds of birds, chirping and singing joyfully.

'Oh tell me, Weasel – Fox – someone – tell me what you think,' begged Badger.

'Those roars can mean only one thing,' said Weasel. 'The Cat has been called away. It's still spring. That could only be the call of a female crying for a mate!'

The roars were becoming fainter and, as they listened, dusk began to descend.

'Yes,' said Fox. 'It seems that what we've striven for so

hopelessly all along, has now been achieved by an outside influence.'

The birds were still singing. The animals thrilled at the sound. They were crying, 'It's left the Park! It's left the Park!'

Epilogue

During the last few days of spring the animals could not quite believe their Park had been returned to them. The Farthing Wood community had listened to Mossy's description of the cavern, and they had gone to the spot to look at the entrance behind the thick bushes that concealed it. Fox and Vixen had even scrambled inside to look. But the grisly remains of the Beast's last meals had soon prompted their return to fresher air. They told none of the others what they had seen.

Some of the birds who had so gladly broadcast the Cat's departure had not been satisfied with that alone. They had flown into open country to follow the route it took. They saw the other Cat that had called it away – a slightly smaller beast, but equally powerful in their eyes. And this one's power did not extend merely to strength. With some surprise, the birds watched the excited meeting of the two Cats. For the smaller animal appeared to dominate the great creature that had terrorized the Park. Wherever she led, the male followed. She called to him frequently as they went and, almost with a sort of meekness, he was content to do her bidding. He ambled in her wake quite happily, and such was their stride that they were soon a long way from the Reserve. It was apparent that the female's territory was in quite another area. Eventually the birds returned home with the news.

One of them remarked that 'it was as if the Beast had been tamed'.

So the roars and screams of the great Cat were heard no more in White Deer Park. The animals' lives resumed an ordinariness that at times seemed almost dull by its comparison with the frights and fears they had endured for so long.

'It almost seems now,' Friendly remarked to his father, 'that the danger we faced day after day added a sort of zest to our existence.'

Fox disagreed. 'When you reach my time of life,' he replied, 'what you call "zest" is something you only want to recall in your memories. And Vixen and I have plenty of those.'

Soon Squirrel came back to the fold and the group of old friends was more or less complete again.

The opinions of the older creatures – Badger, Tawny Owl, Weasel, Toad and Whistler – tallied with those of Fox. They looked forward to nothing more than a period of peace to enjoy for as long as they were able to gather together. But the opinion of one old friend was not known, and that was Adder's. He had not put in an appearance since the siege of the Nature Reserve had been lifted. Only Leveret had seen him since that time, and the snake's excuse had been, as usual, a cryptic one. His remark had puzzled Leveret who had passed it on to the others, hoping for some enlightenment. There was none offered. They were as mystified as he. For Adder had merely referred to the fact that he had recently become interested 'in a new association'.

The summer waxed and waned and the chill of autumn crackled with the clash of antlers of the stags in the white deer herd. The Great Stag had many rivals now and had more difficulty than ever before in holding his place. The fawns who had survived the ravages of the stranger's raids had grown too, and eventually the leadership would be passed on, perhaps many seasons hence, to one of these. Whatever happened, the herd that had given the Park its name would still be there, stepping gracefully through the woods and grassland of the Nature Reserve.

Another winter beckoned. Deep in his set, with a thick pile of bedding around him, Badger wondered if it would be his last. His old bones were beginning to ache with age and the cold, and he found himself thinking again about his ancient system of tunnels in Farthing Wood. In a soft, rather feeble but warm voice he said to Mossy, who was visiting, 'It was a wonderful set, Mole. Do you remember the Assembly, when the whole Wood gathered in my home to talk?'

'Oh yes,' said Mossy. 'I remember. I wonder what Farthing Wood is like now?'

Other great reads from **Red Fox**

Further Red Fox titles that you might enjoy reading are listed on the following pages. They are available in bookshops or they can be ordered directly from us.

If you would like to order books, please send this form and the money due to:

ARROW BOOKS, BOOKSERVICE BY POST, PO BOX 29, DOUGLAS, ISLE OF MAN, BRITISH ISLES. Please enclose a cheque or postal order made out to Arrow Books Ltd for the amount due, plus 75p per book for postage and packing to a maximum of £7.50, both for orders within the UK. For customers outside the UK, please allow £1.00 per book.

NAME_____

ADDRESS_____

_____

Please print clearly.

Whilst every effort is made to keep prices low, it is sometimes necessary to increase cover prices at short notice. If you are ordering books by post, to save delay it is advisable to phone to confirm the correct price. The number to ring is THE SALES DEPARTMENT 071 (if outside London) 973 9700.

Discover the great animal stories of Colin Dann

JUST NUFFIN

The Summer holidays loomed ahead with nothing to look forward to except one dreary week in a caravan with only Mum and Dad for company. Roger was sure he'd be bored.

But then Dad finds Nuffin: an abandoned puppy who's more a bundle of skin and bones than a dog. Roger's holiday is transformed and he and Nuffin are inseparable. But Dad is adamant that Nuffin must find a new home. Is there *any* way Roger can persuade him to change his mind?

ISBN 0 09 966900 5   £2.99

KING OF THE VAGABONDS

'You're very young,' Sammy's mother said, 'so heed my advice. Don't go into Quartermile Field.'

His mother and sister are happily domesticated but Sammy, the tabby cat, feels different. They are content with their lot, never wondering what lies beyond their immediate surroundings. But Sammy is burningly curious and his life seems full of mysteries. Who is his father? Where has he gone? And what is the mystery of Quartermile Field?

ISBN 0 09 957190 0   £2.99

Discover the hilarious world of Red Fox younger fiction!

ALIENS FOR BREAKFAST   Jonathan Etra and Stephanie Spinner

Richard's new cereal is *really* exciting – it contains Aric who has been beamed down from another planet to save the Earth from alien invasion.

ISBN 0 09 981550 8   £2.25

BILLY AND THE GHASTLY GHOST   Mick Gowar

Billy is convinced he has seen a ghost in the graveyard – but proving it to the rest of his class is difficult.

ISBN 0 09 981490 0   £2.99

BILLY AND THE MAN-EATING PLANT
Mick Gower

Billy has to come up with a prizewinning project for the class prize – but he never seems to have the time.

ISBN 0 09 981500 1   £2.50

THANKS FOR THE SARDINE   Laura Beaumont

Aggie decides that her boring Aunts need reforming so she arranges for them to have some training.

ISBN 0 09 997900 4   £2.99

MERVYN'S REVENGE   Leone Peguero

Mervyn the cat is outraged when his family go away without him, and he plots revenge with feline cunning.

ISBN 0 09 997520 3   £2.50

Have a chuckle with Red Fox Fiction!

FLOSSIE TEACAKE'S FUR COAT   Hunter Davies

Flossie just wants to be grown-up, like her big sister Bella – and when she tries on the mysterious fur coat she finds in Bella's bedroom, her wildest dreams come true . . .
ISBN 0 09 996710 3   £2.99

SNOTTY BUMSTEAD   Hunter Davies

Snotty's mum has gone away leaving him with lots of cash and the house to himself! Burgers for breakfast, football in the front room – and no homework! But can he keep the nosey grown-ups away?
ISBN 0 09 997710 9   £2.99

HENRY HOLLINS AND THE DINOSAUR
Willis Hall

Little did Henry think, when he found the fossilized egg at the seaside, that it was actually a fossilized DINOSAUR egg! He had even less idea that it would be no time at all before he would be travelling up the moorway on a dinosaur's back!
ISBN 0 09 911611 1   £2.99

THE LAST VAMPIRE   Willis Hall

The Hollins family are on holiday in Europe, and all goes well until they stay the night in a spooky castle, miles from nowhere. Even worse, they discover that they are in the castle belonging to Count Alucard.
ISBN 0 09 911541 7   £2.99

TRIV IN PURSUIT   Michael Coleman

One by one, the teachers at St Ethelred's School are vanishing, leaving cryptic notes behind. "Triv" Trevellyan smells something fishy going on and is determined to find out just what is happening!
ISBN 0 09 991660 6   £2.99

Other great reads from **Red Fox**

Action-Packed Drama with Red Fox Fiction!

SIMPLE SIMON. Yvonne Coppard

Simon isn't stupid – he's just not very good at practical things. So when Mum collapses, it's Cara, his younger sister who calls the ambulance and keeps a cool head. Simon plans to show what he can do too, in a crisis, but his plan goes frighteningly wrong . . .
ISBN 0 09 910531 4   £2.99

LOW TIDE   William Mayne

Winner of the Guardian Children's Fiction Award.

The low tide at Jade Bay leaves fish on dry land and a wreck high on a rock. Is this the treasure ship the divers have been looking for? Three friends vow to find out – and find themselves swept away into adventure.
ISBN 0 09 918311 0   £3.50

THE INTRUDER   John Rowe Townsend

It isn't often that you meet someone who claims to be you. But that's what happens to Arnold Haithwaite. The real Arnold has to confront the menacing intruder before he takes over his life completely.
ISBN 0 09 999260 4   £3.50

GUILTY   Ruth Thomas

Everyone in Kate's class says that the local burglaries have been done by Desmond Locke's dad, because he's just come out of prison. Kate and Desmond think otherwise and set out to prove who really is *guilty*.
ISBN 0 09 918591 1   £2.99

Other great reads ❮ *from* **Red Fox**

Enter the magical world of Dr Dolittle

Dr Dolittle is one of the great book characters – everyone knows the kindly doctor who can talk to the animals. With his household of animals – Too-Too the owl, Dab-Dab the duck, Gub-gub the pig and Jip the dog – and Tommy Stubbins, his assistant, he finds himself in and out of trouble, of money and of England in a series of adventures. These editions have been sensitively edited with the approval of Christopher Lofting, the author's son.

THE STORY OF DOCTOR DOLITTLE
ISBN 0 09 985470 8   £3.99

THE VOYAGES OF DOCTOR DOLITTLE
ISBN 0 09 985470 8   £4.99

DR DOLITTLE'S POST OFFICE
ISBN 0 09 988040 7   £4.99

DR DOLITTLE'S CIRCUS
ISBN 0 09 985440 6   £4.99

DR DOLITTLE'S ZOO
ISBN 0 09 988030 X   £4.99

DR DOLITTLE'S GARDEN
ISBN 0 09 988050 4   £4.99

DR DOLITTLE IN THE MOON
ISBN 0 09 988060 1   £4.99

DR DOLITTLE'S CARAVAN
ISBN 0 09 985450 3   £4.99

DR DOLITTLE AND THE GREEN CANARY
ISBN 0 09 988090 3   £4.99

Other great reads from **Red Fox**

Spinechilling stories to read at night

THE CONJUROR'S GAME Catherine Fisher

Alick has unwittingly set something unworldly afoot in Halcombe Great Wood.

ISBN 0 09 985960 2   £2.50

RAVENSGILL William Mayne

What is the dark secret that has held two families apart for so many years?

ISBN 0 09 975270 0   £2.99

EARTHFASTS William Mayne

The bizarre chain of events begins when David and Keith see someone march out of the ground . . .

ISBN 0 09 977600 6   £2.99

A LEGACY OF GHOSTS Colin Dann

Two boys go searching for old Mackie's hoard and find something else . . .

ISBN 0 09 986540 8   £2.99

TUNNEL TERROR

The Channel Tunnel is under threat and only Tom can save it . . .

ISBN 0 09 989030 5   £2.99

Discover the hilarious world of Red Fox younger fiction!

ALIENS FOR BREAKFAST   Jonathan Etra and
Stephanie Spinner

Richard's new cereal is *really* exciting – it contains Aric who
has been beamed down from another planet to save the Earth
from alien invasion.

ISBN 0 09 981550 8   £2.25

BILLY AND THE GHASTLY GHOST   Mick Gowar

Billy is convinced he has seen a ghost in the graveyard – but
proving it to the rest of his class is difficult.

ISBN 0 09 981490 0   £2.99

BILLY AND THE MAN-EATING PLANT
Mick Gower

Billy has to come up with a prizewinning project for the class
prize – but he never seems to have the time.

ISBN 0 09 981500 1   £2.50

THANKS FOR THE SARDINE   Laura Beaumont

Aggie decides that her boring Aunts need reforming so she
arranges for them to have some training.

ISBN 0 09 997900 4   £2.99

MERVYN'S REVENGE   Leone Peguero

Mervyn the cat is outraged when his family go away without
him, and he plots revenge with feline cunning.

ISBN 0 09 997520 3   £2.50

Other great reads ~~from~~ **Red Fox**

Have some supernatural fun with Jonathan's ghost

Dave is just an ordinary schoolboy – except he happens to be a ghost, and only his friend, Jonathan, can see him. With his love of mischief, Dave creates quite a bit of trouble for Jonathan to explain away – but he can also be an extremely useful friend to have when Jonathan's in a fix.

JONATHAN'S GHOST

Jonathan's starting at a new school – but who needs humans when you've got a ghost for a friend?

ISBN 0 09 968850 6   £2.50

SPITFIRE SUMMER

An old wartime ghost seems to be haunting Jonathan – and only Dave can help him.

ISBN 0 09 968850 6   £2.50

THE SCHOOL SPIRIT

A trip to an old mansion brings Jonathan into contact with a triangle of evil determined to find a new victim.

ISBN 0 09 974620 4   £2.50

JONATHAN AND THE SUPERSTAR

Everyone at Jonathan's school thinks Jason Smythe is wonderful – except Dave. Dave senses trouble afoot . . .

ISBN 0 09 995120 7   £2.50

Other great reads from **Red Fox**

Enjoy the Lenny and Jake stories of Hazel Townson

Lenny and Jake can't help getting into trouble – they were born that way. What with Lenny's hopeless magic tricks and Jake's endless curiosity, they always seem to be mixed up in some adventure.

THE GREAT ICE-CREAM CRIME
ISBN 0 09 948640 7   £2.25

THE SIEGE OF COBB STREET SCHOOL
ISBN 0 09 936650 9   £2.50

THE VANISHING GRAN
ISBN 0 09 935480 2   £2.50

HAUNTED IVY
ISBN 0 09 941320 5   £2.25

THE CRIMSON CRESCENT
ISBN 0 09 952110 5   £2.25

THE STAGGERING SNOWMAN
ISBN 0 09 956820 9   £2.25

FIREWORKS GALORE
ISBN 0 09 965540 3   £2.25

WALNUT WHIRL
ISBN 0 09 973380 3   £2.25

HOPPING MAD
ISBN 0 09 910291 9   £2.50

Other great reads *from* **Red Fox**

Giggle and groan with a Red Fox humour book!

Nutty, naughty and quite quite mad, the Red Fox humour list has a range of the silliest titles you're likely to see on a bookshelf! Check out some of our weird and wonderful books and we promise you'll have a ribticklingly good read!

MIAOW! THE CAT JOKE BOOK – Susan Abbott

Be a cool cat and paws here for the purrfect joke! Get your claws into this collection of howlers all about our furry friends that will have you feline like a grinning Cheshire Cat!

ISBN 0 09 998460 1   £1.99

THE SMELLY SOCKS JOKE BOOK – Susan Abbott

Hold your nose . . . here comes the funniest and foulest joke book you're likely to read for a while! Packed with pungent puns and reeking with revolting riddles, this one is guaranteed to leave you gasping for air!

ISBN 0 09 956270 7   £1.99

TUTANKHAMUN IS A BIT OF A MUMMY'S BOY – Michael Coleman

Have you ever dreaded taking home your school report or a letter from the Head? You're in good company! Did you know that Shakespeare was really "hopeless at English" and that Christopher Columbus had "absolutely no sense of direction"? There's fifty other previously unpublished school reports which reveal hilarious secrets about the famous which not many people know . . .

ISBN 0 09 988180 2   £2.99

THE FISH AND CHIPS JOKE BOOK – Ian Rylett

This book comes complete with a fish-and-chips scratch and sniff panel so you can sniff while you snigger at this delicious collection of piping-hot pottiness! Your tastebuds will be tickled no end with this mouth-watering concoction of tasty gags so tuck into a copy today! It's a feast of fun!

ISBN 0 09 995040 5   £2.99